HITLER'S ASHES

HITLER'S ASHES

How Hitler's Assassination Leads to the Development of Germany's Atomic Bomb

John T. Cox

iUniverse, Inc.
Bloomington

Hitler's Ashes
How Hitler's Assassination Leads to the Development of Germany's Atomic Bomb

iUniverse books may be ordered through booksellers or by contacting:

iUniverse
1663 Liberty Drive
Bloomington, IN 47403
www.iuniverse.com
1-800-Authors (1-800-288-4677)

ISBN: 978-1-4502-7714-3 (sc)
ISBN: 978-1-4502-7716-7 (hc)
ISBN: 978-1-4502-7715-0 (ebk)

Printed in the United States of America
iUniverse rev. date: 09/07/2011

Preface

Why didn't Germany produce an atomic bomb?

How could the nation that is generally credited with the discoveries that led to the era of modern physics *not* have done this? Consider that "Between 1901 [when the Nobel Prizes were first awarded] and 1932, [one year] before Hitler came to power, the Nobel Prizes in Physics went to ten citizens of Germany and one naturalized citizen of the United States. From 1901 to 1932, the Nobel Prize in Chemistry was awarded to fourteen citizens of Germany and to only two citizens of the United States." (Lev Navrozov, November 28, 2005) In addition, German chemists, Otto Hahn and Fritz Strassmann, first produced nuclear fission in late 1938 when they detected the element barium after bombarding uranium with neutrons.

Several factors contributed to this failure, the most important of which is that Adolf Hitler didn't grasp the potential of such a weapon. In *Inside the Third Reich*, Albert Speer states, "Hitler had sometimes spoken to me about the possibility of an atom bomb, but the idea quite obviously strained his intellectual capacity. He was also unable to grasp the revolutionary nature of nuclear physics." Therefore, it appears that Hitler was not interested in the bomb and was completely convinced that he could achieve victory with conventional weapons.

Hitler's control over all aspects of weapons development and production was complete—whatever he was interested in received top priority, and whatever he wasn't interested in received no priority.

Hitler was far more interested in the V-2 ballistic missile than the atomic bomb, which was diverting both financial and strategic resources, particularly chromium, away from the rocket program. This lack of priority by Hitler resulted in the abrogation of Germany's nuclear weapons program in the fall of 1942.

Another factor in Germany's failure to produce an atomic bomb was Hitler's pathological hatred of Jews. Hitler took power on January 30, 1933. On April 7, 1933, the Law for the Restoration of the Professional Civil Service was enacted, which, among other things, forbade Jews from teaching at the university level. The effects on German physics were devastating. Between 1932 and 1933, an estimated 1,100 university teachers in all fields were driven from their posts, about 14 percent of Germany's higher learning institutional and staff members. Out of twenty-six German nuclear physicists cited in literature before 1933, half emigrated. Ten physicists and four chemists who had won or would win the Nobel Prize emigrated from Germany shortly after Hitler came to power, most of them in 1933, including Albert Einstein.

Eight student assistants and colleagues of Max Born, the University of Göttingen's esteemed theoretical physicist, left Europe after Hitler came to power and eventually found work on the Manhattan Project. Among these were Enrico Fermi, who developed the first nuclear reactor, Robert Oppenheimer, who led the Manhattan Project, and Edward Teller, who became known as the father of the hydrogen bomb.

Associated with Hitler's anti-Jewish crusade was the growth of the movement against "Jewish physics," led by Philipp Lenard, who was convinced that he, not Wilhelm Röntgen, should have won world fame for the discovery of X-rays in 1895. At some point after 1920, according to Thomas Powell in his book *Heisenberg's War*, Lenard's resentment focused on the fact that Einstein was a Jew, and he began to attack the eminent physicist's work as "Jewish physics." The adherents of this movement believed, among other things, that the theory of relativity was unproven Jewish speculation. In the mid-1930s, Lenard published a four-volume collection of his lectures and gave it the title *German Physics*, arguing that just as surely as there is German literature, there is German physics. Of course, there were protests from many top-rank German physicists, but it was late in the day, as Hitler, with his anti-Jewish mentality, had come into power in 1933.

A lack of workers and other resources certainly played an important role in Germany's failure to produce an atomic bomb. The man in charge of the Manhattan Project, General Leslie Groves, had at his disposal the immense workforce needed to construct the huge facilities required for the production of the fissionable material that would go into the atomic bombs dropped on Hiroshima and Nagasaki. The estimated cost of the Manhattan Project was two billion dollars or about twenty-two billion dollars today (2010). It is quite possible that for even a nation as technologically advanced as Germany was at the beginning of World War II, the construction of the facilities needed for the successful completion of their atomic bomb project was simply beyond its capabilities.

It is also possible that the German scientists who led Germany's atomic bomb program deliberately slowed their research so Hitler would not be given the bomb. Thomas Powers concluded that Werner Heisenberg, the leading figure in the German atomic bomb effort, not only consciously obstructed Germany's development of the bomb, but also sought to dissuade the Allies from developing their own bomb. This attempt occurred in a famous meeting Heisenberg had with the eminent Danish physicist Niels Bohr in 1941.

Could the nuclear scientists left in Germany have produced an atomic bomb? While there is no definitive answer to this question, much can be deduced from events that transpired between early May 1945, just before the surrender of Germany and the dropping of the atomic bombs on Hiroshima and Nagasaki in August 1945.

The American and British-led Alsos mission was given the task of tracking down all information about the German development of an atomic bomb. In summary, they found that the German nuclear weapons program had not even produced a rudimentary working atomic pile, a feat achieved by nuclear physicists Enrico Fermi and Leó Szilárd on December 2, 1942.

Over the next few months, the Alsos team rounded up ten prominent German nuclear physicists, including Werner Heisenberg and Otto Hahn. These scientists were taken to a country house known as Farm Hall in the small town of Godmanchester in England, located about fifty-five miles north of London. They were held there by a wartime provision that allowed for the detention of individuals for up to six months. Known as "at His Majesty's pleasure," this very elastic legal concept allowed the Americans and British to hold the German scientists for about five months, after which they were allowed to return to Germany.

This was a very comfortable captivity. Each man had his own room, and they were free to walk in the rose gardens surrounding the house. There was a common room with a piano and library, and the food was excellent. They had little to do but talk among themselves, which was the entire idea, for unknown to the Germans, everything they said, whether in their private rooms or in the common areas, was recorded.

On August 6, 1945, when news of the atomic bomb's use on Hiroshima reached the German scientists at Farm Hill, they were incredulous and horrified that such a weapon had been used for destruction. Some were even thankful that Germany had *not* developed an atomic bomb.

On August 14, 1945, Heisenberg delivered a lecture on nuclear bomb physics to the scientists at Farm Hill, all of which was recorded by the secret microphones. With Heisenberg as tutor, the group of ten German scientists collectively invented a nuclear weapon with a fissionable core of U^{235} weighing fifteen or sixteen kilograms divided between two separate hemispheres, which was remarkably similar to the design of the bomb dropped on Hiroshima.

As stated by Powers, Heisenberg's analysis of the atomic bomb used by the Americans "... would seem to close the case on one point at least: if the Germans really thought two tons of U^{235} were required for a bomb, one need look no further for an explanation of their failure."

But this does not conclusively answer the question of whether Germany *could* have built an atomic bomb. It could be argued that Heisenberg did not understand the fundamentals of atomic bomb design until the war was over. It also could be argued, with equal conviction, that he knew all along how to design an atomic bomb, but had withheld this information so Hitler would not get the bomb. This could be deduced from the rapidity with which he developed his theory on atomic bomb design for his colleagues. This theory was presented to them on August 14, 1945, only eight days after the first bomb was used on Japan. Until his death in 1976, however, Heisenberg remained equivocal about his role in the failure of Germany to develop an atomic bomb.

This book reverses all the factors mentioned above for the purpose of the story. For example, Hitler is enthusiastic about the atomic bomb when it is first introduced to him. The atom was fictionally split in 1935, not 1938, as it really happened, and it was the Germans who discovered plutonium first, not the Americans Glenn Seaborg and Ed McMillan.

All the resources needed for the development of Germany's atomic bomb are made available to the scientists involved in this project. Although many of these scientists are lost to the Gestapo and their concentration camps, the project is driven to a successful conclusion, but only after Hitler and his associates are removed and the cleansing of Germany from its Nazi ideology has begun. A substantial amount of technological achievement in a very short period is described in the book, not the arduous one-slow-step-at-a-time approach that really took place in the development of atomic weapons during the Manhattan Project.

In addition, the Werner Heisenberg in this book clearly states that he and his associates knowingly slowed down their work on the bomb so Hitler would not have it, despite the very real danger of the Soviet's winning the war and imposing on Germany, and possibly the rest of Europe, their own kind of tyranny.

The Japanese bombed Pearl Harbor on December 7, 1941, bringing the United States into the war. It was not until December 11, 1941, four days later, that Hitler declared war on the United States. Yet, it was "Germany first," not the Japanese, that became the policy of the Allies in the prosecution of the war. This was driven by the fear of the German's getting the atomic bomb first, a fear largely removed by Hitler's lack of interest in the fall of 1942, less than one year after the United States entered the war.

Contents

PROLOGUE

Berlin
November 6, 1945 1:30 a.m.
The Keiser Wilhelm Institute for Physics

The man had been working on the bomb for just under an hour, and it was getting harder for him to concentrate. It was very cold and the work was tedious; one slip could result in an explosion that would accomplish his mission, but end his life. And he didn't want that to happen—not just yet. There was more to do after this.

The bomb was quite simple, really; just a few lengths of detonator cord and a detonator, an old car battery, a simple wind-up alarm clock which he had purchased at a local hardware store, and several sticks of dynamite that he had stolen over a period of several weeks from the local army base. It had been almost too easy.

He was working in almost total darkness to avoid detection. He had covered all the windows in the basement storage area, and allowed himself only a small flashlight for illumination. Even though he had practiced the assembly many times before, he felt the tension rising within him. This was the real thing now; once the clock was set, there would be no going back, no undoing what he had reluctantly set out to do.

Now for the most critical part—the timing mechanism which would allow him to arm the bomb and make an escape. He had tested this design using a half-stick of the dynamite in a still bombed-out part of the city where no one would notice. Even the small charge he used had completed the work that Allied bombs had started on the abandoned building he had chosen as his test subject. Since building collapses in this part of Germany's capital were still a common occurrence, no one noticed, just as he surmised.

The most difficult part had been making the decision to let his opposition take this form, and he hated himself for it. He abhorred violence in any form, but when he saw that there was no other way to delay or stop the mad rush to the project's completion, he decided that he must act, knowing full well that he would probably be caught, then tried, convicted, and jailed for the rest of his life. He rationalized that what he was about to do would be worth that price if only it would give him a public stage from which to shout to the world the true nature of the horror that was about to be unleashed.

There, he thought. *It's done.* The final connections were made, and the clock was set to 1:30. Thirty minutes to make his way back to his quarters. No one had seen him leave his apartment. He hadn't carried anything with him that would arouse suspicion. He had sequestered all the components for the bomb in the cluttered basement of the Institute over a period of weeks, and placed them right under the laboratory where the research was being done.

Outside now. No one in sight. God, it's cold! Much colder than anything I remember from New Mexico. Okay … now concentrate … be careful. Walk, don't run. Don't do anything that would arouse suspicion. Just be an old man who can't sleep taking a stroll through the city. Nothing unusual about that, he thought. He had even brought along a half-empty bottle of slivovitz, which he now drank to complete the deception. *Yes ... just an old man, who can't sleep, walking off a bit too much to drink ...*

He instinctively checked his watch. 1:53. Seven minutes to go. Then, without knowing why, he turned back to look at the building, just in time to see a light go on in the laboratory right above the bomb. *My God*, he thought. *Someone's in the lab, and he'll be blown to pieces in seven minutes! No, No, No! I can't let this happen. I'm not a murderer. Must warn him to get out!* He started to run back to the building, but his legs went out from under him. *Damn that slivovitz*, he cursed to himself. *What a time to be drunk!* He started to yell *"Get out! Get out!"* even though he knew it was futile.

His efforts to run back to the laboratory amounted to little more than staggering, and he fell several times. This probably saved his life, because as he was struggling to get up for the last time, the bomb exploded, and the shock wave knocked him down again and rendered him unconscious.

He was awakened by the unmistakable sounds of the police cars and emergency vehicles that had swarmed the site of the explosion. *Quite a different sound from the police cars in the states*, he thought in a haze.

He tried to stand up, and again he failed. As he dropped to all fours, he became aware of the flashlights moving toward him and the men who were carrying them. He looked for cover, but the closest buildings were too far away. *It's over*, he thought. *And for what? They'll just find someone else to work on the project. Someone else to ... Oh God ... replace the man I just killed.*

He tried to lie as flat as he could, as if to will himself into the ground, breathing as little as possible, hoping to become invisible. Then there were shouts of "I see something. Over here. There's someone over here." Then it was "You! Don't move! Stand up and put your hands over your head!" He tried to stand up, but again his body betrayed him, and he collapsed into a lifeless, useless heap. And the lights ... the lights blinding him, searing into his brain the magnitude of the terrible thing he had just done. He held his hands out and pleaded with them. "Please ... I didn't mean to kill anyone. No ... I just wanted to stop the research and tell everybody how wrong this is ... don't you understand? Just stop the re ... " And then everything went from blinding light to gray to black.

Chapter 1

The Prisoner

Berlin
July 8, 1946 10:30 p.m.
Café Kranzler

The two friends had known each other since they were children in Würzburg. Werner Heisenberg was a distinguished nuclear physicist who had led his nation's successful program for the development of the nuclear weapons that had forced the Americans and the British out of the war and were now bringing Germany closer to victory over its ancient foe, the Russians.

Johann Rinehart, a colonel in the German army, had accomplishments no less impressive than those of his friend. He had played several key roles in the change of government in 1943 that had removed Adolf Hitler from power, and he had collaborated with his friend Werner Heisenberg in the development of Germany's atomic bomb.

Café Kranzler was usually crowded, and this night was no exception. However, when the maître d´ heard that it was Professor

Heisenberg who was requesting a reservation, a table was immediately found in a quiet part of the restaurant.

Heisenberg had married a beautiful and vivacious woman in 1937, and his friend, the army officer, had served as his best man. He was completely devoted to his wife and his ever-growing family. Rinehart was also married, but for less than a year. His wife was a strikingly beautiful blond nurse from Sweden. He was almost seven years her senior, and they had met while he was recovering from a serious wound he had suffered in the line of duty. They were childless, having decided to postpone parenthood until after the war ended.

Their conversation centered mostly on their families and jobs, and it was Colonel Rinehart who had the most important news. His wife, Connie, had successfully interviewed for the position of assistant director of nursing at Charité Hospital, and upon being hired, she immediately became part of the team that was integrating the newest electronic patient monitoring equipment into the fabric of that venerable institution.

"So Connie is really enjoying her new job at Charité."

"Yes, Werner, she is. She says it's the most interesting work she's ever done. There's a different challenge every day, what with all the new medical equipment that's been developed since the war began."

"What exactly does she do, Johann?"

"Well, she's in charge of teaching the medical staff and the student doctors and nurses how to operate all the latest patient monitoring devices. She also works very closely with manufacturers' reps in assessing the effectiveness of these new devices so they can make improvements. It's evolving so fast that new models of the same device are coming out all the time.

"The way she's described it to me is that these monitors are based on oscilloscope technology. They have only one channel right now, so each of the monitors is highly specialized—one for blood pressure, one for the pulse, one for electrocardiographic measurements, and so on. Some of the companies are working on a display that will have two or three channels on the same screen, and this should be available in a few months.

"The main problem with these machines is their sensitivity to electrical interference. Also, these early models have no numeric readouts, and there are no alarms if the readings drop below certain levels. But Connie tells me that progress is being made on all of these issues, and she's very excited about the potential they have to save lives."

"It always seems to take something like a war to make this kind of progress, doesn't it, Johann?"

"Yes, it certainly does, Werner. Look at what's happened on the battlefield. We've recently introduced medical helicopter evacuation on a large scale, and it's already saved hundreds of lives. Seriously wounded soldiers who would have died under ordinary circumstances are now being saved because they can be picked up by a helicopter and flown to a surgical unit in the rear within fifteen or twenty minutes. Once they're stabilized, they can then be moved by medical train, or plane if necessary, to a place like Charité for further surgery and rehabilitation. This has had a tremendous impact on the morale of the troops, because they know that if they're wounded, they'll have a better chance of surviving than they did before.

"But now, Werner, enough about me. What's going on at your place that you can tell me without breaking the rules?"

"If you put it that way, my friend, there's nothing I can tell you. But since you were so involved with our first atomic weapon, I think I can bring you up to date without fear of compromising our nation's security.

"We've been able to make our uranium-based bombs and warheads quite a bit smaller and much more powerful, and several new models have been introduced with yields of over 100 kilotonnes. They can be carried by our latest medium bombers, as well as the heavy bomber that is being designed.

"Our biggest breakthrough has been in the development of a lightweight ballistic missile warhead based on plutonium. We finally got enough reactors going to produce plutonium in sufficient quantities to do our research and try out different designs. You know how unstable plutonium is, but we eventually came up with a workable design that will fit inside a warhead. It has a yield of over 500 kilotonnes."

"That's quite a lot of bang, Werner. But what about the super bomb? Is any work being done on that?"

"Not right now. Edward Teller always told us that he had it all figured out in his head. He said it was a 'neat' solution and just a matter of design and engineering. Well, he never got the chance to prove this, so we're back at square one on that project. I think it's going to be more politics than technical issues that determine whether or not we develop this weapon.

"But that's not the most exciting stuff we're working on, Johann. We've started to design a nuclear power plant for the generation of electricity. We think that we can build a plant that will provide enough electricity for a population five to ten times that of Berlin. They'll be tremendously expensive to build because of all the safeguards against radiation leakage that will have to be incorporated into the plant, but once it's up and running, the power it generates should be very inexpensive.

"Think of it, Johann. Even with all the oil we have now from the Arab countries, plus all that we will have once we conquer the Soviet Union, it's still a finite resource. This is the future, and we plan to offer this technology to the world as an alternative to fossil fuels."

"You're going to offer the world our nuclear technology? Isn't that a bit dangerous?"

"No. For weapons, a purity level of 90 percent or above is needed for the U^{235} to produce a nuclear explosion. With a nuclear power plant, you only have to produce enough heat to boil water to generate steam that turns a turbine, and this means that a substantially lower level of purity is sufficient. We think it will be something around 20 percent. Certainly nothing that could be used to make a bomb.

"But that's not the only use for nuclear power that we envision, and here I'm going to have to raise your security clearance to a higher level, Johann. We're going to take our nuclear power plant and make it small enough to fit in naval vessels. There's a new class of aircraft carrier being designed that will be powered by two nuclear power plants. Preliminary indications are that this ship will make thirty-five plus knots and be able to sail for twenty-five years without refueling. Imagine the possibilities, Johann: a navy that can sail anywhere without being tied to an endless, and very vulnerable, stream of refueling ships.

"And the nuclear power plant that we're designing for our submarines will make them truly invincible. They'll be able to cruise indefinitely at depths of three hundred meters and speeds of over forty knots, and they'll be quieter than anything we have in the water right now. In a few years, we'll mate these boats with a ballistic missile carrying our lightweight plutonium warhead, and this will provide Germany with a deterrent that no one will be able to counter."

Just then, Berthold, the maître d' of the café, came to their table. "Good evening, Professor, good evening, Colonel. Was everything prepared to your satisfaction?"

"Yes, Berthold, it was," replied Werner. "Please convey our compliments to your staff and the chef. And thank you again for finding a table for us on such short notice."

"It's always our pleasure to serve you, Professor. Oh, I almost forgot … several days ago, a gentlemen left a telephone message for you. I wrote down what he said. Now, where did I put that piece of … Ah, here it is."

"Thank you very much, Berthold." The maître d' bowed slightly to his guests and left. Heisenberg read the note and passed it to the colonel.

"Hmm … 'Imperative that you visit me as soon as possible.' What do you suppose he wants, Werner?"

"Probably the same thing he's wanted since he came to work for us: to know how we did it. I couldn't tell him anything because he didn't have the right security clearance."

"But now things are different, Werner."

"Yes, they are." He paused. "Maybe it wouldn't hurt to pay him a visit, even under these circumstances."

"I agree, and I think it would be most appropriate. If you let me come along, maybe I can fill in a few blanks. You also might need me to help you get in to see him."

"That's probably true. Are you free tomorrow afternoon?"

"That would be too late, Werner."

"Why?"

"If we're going to see him, we have to do it now. I found out earlier today that they've moved it up. He's scheduled to be hanged at five o'clock tomorrow morning."

Berlin
July 9, 1946 12:30 a.m.
Spandau Prison

J. Robert Oppenheimer was amazingly calm for a man who had just a few hours to live. His only real concern was dying without knowing how the Germans had beaten the United States to the bomb.

We almost won the race. The date for our test was set for July 16,

1945. But their test took place one month earlier, on June 15. Then they destroyed Norfolk, Scapa Flow, and the two Soviet cities on July 3, just thirteen days before our test. So close, but that doesn't count in this business.

How could it have happened? We had everything going for us: money, technology, even a slew of scientists who had left Germany after it became obvious what Hitler was doing to the Jews. Still, they had beaten us, and I have to know how.

Oppenheimer had readily admitted his guilt. He had only set out to sabotage the super bomb project, the "H-Bomb," as the press would later call it. He did not mean to kill his friend and colleague, but he had no way of knowing that he would be in the lab and working alone at two o'clock in the morning. When the blast occurred, it destroyed the lab at the Kaiser Wilhelm Institute of Physics where the main research on the hated H-bomb was being conducted, and it killed Dr. Edward Teller, its foremost proponent.

President Truman had brought the Manhattan Project scientists to Washington as part of the terms the Germans imposed on the United States following their capitulation. When they heard about the destruction of the naval bases at Norfolk and Scapa Flow, and the obliteration of Moscow and Stalingrad, they knew the Germans had beaten them to the bomb and that the first thing they would demand of the president would be an end to the American nuclear bomb project. Brigadier General Leslie Groves, the head of the Manhattan Project, had tried to organize a defense, but they were overwhelmed by troops operating directly under the orders of the president. The general, the men loyal to him, and some of his team of scientists had perished in the battle.

The survivors from Los Alamos, and other scientists from the Manhattan Project, including Leó Szilárd, Ken Bainbridge, George Kistiakowski, and John von Neumann, had been flown to Washington with only the clothes on their backs and without their families, and then turned over to the Germans. A few days later, after crossing the Atlantic on the ocean liner *Europa* and then traveling by rail from Wilhelmshaven to Berlin, they were at the institute where they were presented with a choice by its director, Walther Bothe: work for us on perfecting the plutonium bomb and the super bomb, or spend the rest of your lives in jail with no chance of ever seeing your families again.

An impossible choice, Oppenheimer thought. *But gradually, all of us came around, some more enthusiastically than others. Teller had leaped at the chance to continue work on the super bomb. "This is the world we live in, Robert. The Germans beat us to the atomic bomb, and with the H-bomb, they will be able to ensure the peace we all want." I tried to reason with Teller, pointing out that this had been the promise of every advance in weaponry since the beginning of recorded history, and that all these promises had been broken by even more terrible wars. The way he dismissed my argument really hurt.*

Just thinking about those events and the betrayal of so many of his friends was making him depressed. He didn't hear the footsteps approaching his cell and wasn't aware of the men looking at him until one called his name.

"Robert," said Werner Heisenberg, "we came to see you. May we come in?"

"Oh, God, I thought you'd get here too late. I managed to call the café just before they put me down here. That's when they told me they were moving up the time, and that no one on the outside would know. Yes, of course, please do come in and sit down," he said with exaggerated politeness.

The guards opened the door to Oppenheimer's cell, let the two men in, and then moved to the other side of the corridor so they could be within earshot.

"You are dismissed!" The command from Colonel Johann Rinehart was unmistakable and not to be disobeyed, regardless of the strict rules on the supervision of visits to prisoners on death row.

The guards clicked their heels, made a smart left face, and marched out of the cellblock, leaving the three men alone.

Even though they had worked closely together for some time, the pleasantries among them were awkward.

Finally, Oppenheimer said, "You know what I want. How did you do it?"

Werner and Johann looked at each other for a long time before answering.

"Well," Werner said, "we started off a little bit behind you, but we caught up very quickly and then ran away from you."

"How did you do this?"

"We had a lot of help from the very top at an early date."

"You mean—"

"Yes. Adolf Hitler himself. It started like this …"

Chapter 2

The Pact with the Devil

Berlin
November 5, 1934 9:00 a.m.
The Old Reich Chancellery

"The führer will see you now. You have fifteen minutes. Heil Hitler!"

The two men returned the now-obligatory Nazi salute with their own "Heil Hitler!"

They had argued about this the day before. Werner Heisenberg had paced back and forth in a high state of agitation. "They're nothing but a gang of pompous asses strutting around in those ridiculous uniforms, and I'm not going to give them a damn Nazi salute!"

"Calm yourself and sit down, Werner. Now listen." Johann Rinehart put his hand on his friend's shoulder and spoke to him quietly. "Yes, they are a gang of pompous asses. We both agree on that. But right now, these pompous asses are in charge, so it would be best not to antagonize them, even if this means an occasional 'Heil

Hitler.' It's just play-acting, but it's important. Look, old friend, the way I see it is this: Anyone who has read *Mein Kampf* can see that sooner or later we will be at war with the Russians. No one has ever defeated them in a conventional war, so the Nazis need what we have to offer. But we have to play their games and use their tactics to get what we want. So, when we go in to see him, follow my lead. You'll know what to say, but remember this: keep it simple, and flatter his ego by telling him how big it will be. He likes things that are big, okay?"

"Yes, okay. I'm sorry, Johann, but they are so opposed to everything that you and I were brought up with. Well … you know what I mean. I still have a lot of problems about giving this man the atomic bomb. I have nightmares thinking about what he might do with it."

"I understand, Werner, and I feel the same way. But let's do this thing tomorrow in the interests of the Germany we once knew and loved, and perhaps someday things will change for the better. First things first, and that is to ensure our survival when we go to war with Russia. If we don't deal with this issue, Germany will be lost, you'll end up either working for them or spending the rest of your life in one of Stalin's gulags, and I'll be shot. Agreed?"

"Yes, agreed. I'll be okay, Johann."

Now they gave the Nazi salute to the man who would decide their future and the fate of Germany.

"Heil Hitler!" they said in unison.

Hitler returned their salute with a perfunctory wave and indicated they were to sit.

There were no preliminaries.

"So! I have a letter of introduction here from Erwin Rommel. I've never met him, but he seems to be an interesting man with an excellent war record."

Hitler sat down and opened a folder lying on his desk. "How long have you been attached to his staff, Lieutenant?"

"Since he came to the Dresden Infantry School in 1929, Führer. I was a student there, and upon receiving my commission, he invited me to join his staff."

"Hmm. I see. How well did you do at the school?"

"I'm proud to say that I finished at the top of my class, Führer."

"Yes, yes. Most excellent. You are a credit to our country, Lieutenant."

"Thank you, sir!"

"And you, Professor Heisenberg, so many accomplishments for such a young man." He opened another folder. "Let's see … lecturer in theoretical physics at the University of Copenhagen under Niels Bohr at the age of twenty-five, and then professor of theoretical physics at the University of Leipzig the very next year. Very impressive, very impressive, indeed."

Hitler closed the folders and returned them to the bottom drawer of his desk. He turned his steel-blue eyes on his two guests for a minute.

"Now. What do you have for me? Rommel says in his letter, 'these gentlemen, who are both known to me, have a proposal for you which, if acted upon in an expeditious manner, could revolutionize warfare by bringing to bear weapons of unimaginable power, so that a smaller nation, but one with superior science and technology, could overcome any force they might encounter, no matter how great.' Tell me exactly what is meant by this, Lieutenant."

Johann Rinehart took a deep breath and began. "Führer, in *Mein Kampf,* you wrote of the right of the German people to expand, and that the only direction in which this expansion could take place was to the east. This obviously means Russia, and they will not give up their land without a ferocious struggle. We know how the Russians wage war. They put their Slavic people in the front lines to absorb bullets and wear the enemy down. Then they retreat, sucking the enemy into the Russian wilderness and stretching his supply lines until they break. Add a few months of General Winter, and then the Russians strike back with overwhelming force, completely annihilating the enemy. This is the way the Russians have always fought, and there is no reason to think they will do otherwise in the coming conflict."

"Yes, yes, we know all that." Hitler waved his hand dismissively. "Go on."

"Sir," Johann continued, "by the time our forces are up to strength, the Russians could have as many as sixty to eighty million men and women under arms, not counting the Slavs. This would give them an army larger than the population of our country! Stalin has had over nine years to read your book. He's no fool, so he knows we're coming, and he'll be ready for us."

He paused. "We will be hard-pressed to win a conventionally fought war, Führer, so Professor Heisenberg and I have a proposal that would not only ensure our victory in the coming conflict, but would make us invincible for a thousand years!"

A thousand years! These men have indeed done their homework, Hitler mused. He nodded his approval, and the professor of nuclear physics continued the conversation.

"Führer, we propose that Germany immediately initiate a program to develop nuclear weapons, which are revolutionary in concept and infinitely more powerful and destructive than any conventional weapon ever produced. These weapons would be based on nuclear fission, which we believe will work like this: when two masses of fissionable material, such as highly enriched uranium, are brought together under controlled conditions, there is a tremendous release of energy, an explosion of unimaginable power."

"Just how big of an explosion are we talking about, Professor? Please be precise."

"We believe," Professor Heisenberg replied, "that it is possible to construct a weapon with a yield of ten to fifteen thousand metric tonnes of high explosive. It would be so powerful that one plane carrying just one bomb could destroy a large city.

"Or an entire army," Lieutenant Rinehart added.

Hitler jumped up from his chair and, in a state of agitation, began to pace. "Can this really be achieved?"

Professor Heisenberg seized the opportunity to drive home his point. "Führer, the next war will be fought not just by massive armies with their tanks and planes, but with science and technology. I can say to you without any fear of contradiction that whoever gets the atomic bomb first will win this war. Whoever comes in second will lose!"

"How much of this fissionable material is required for such a bomb? How big would it be?"

"We're not certain of this yet, Führer, and we won't know until we do more research."

Heisenberg hoped Hitler had been convinced because he knew this statement to be a lie. He was almost certain that a nuclear explosion could be realized with only a few kilograms of fissionable material. But he wanted to keep the option open of being able to tell the Nazis that it would take as much as two tons of fissionable material to make a bomb, just in case Hitler turned out to be a monster who shouldn't have this weapon at his disposal. "This is an impossible task," he would then tell them, "both for us and for the Allies."

Hitler paced up and down his office several times before he sat on the edge of his desk. He folded his arms and stared at Professor Heisenberg for a long time. The professor shivered. *It's true what people say about Hitler's eyes,* he thought.

"Who else knows about this?" Hitler asked. *Is Heisenberg Jewish,* he wondered. *I'll have Himmler look into this.*

"The existence of uranium is no secret among technologically advanced nations. Its potential use in making fissionable material, however, is a relatively recent development. Our greatest adversaries would be the United States and England because of their depth of science and technology. The United States is of particular concern because of its vast manufacturing capabilities. They have many eminent scientists in the field of nuclear physics, as do the British. Should the British combine their efforts with the Americans, this would constitute a real threat to us. And then there are the Russians—"

"The Russians!" Hitler exploded. "Those Slavs ... they're subhuman, no better than animals. What can they possibly know about such things?"

It took all of Professor Heisenberg's courage, but after a pause, he quietly replied, "Führer, what you say may be true of the vast majority of the Russian population. But there is an educated class who are quite capable in several fields, one of which is theoretical mathematics. Nuclear physics, at its foundation, is all theoretical mathematics, and the Russians are the best theoretical mathematicians in the world."

"This cannot be true! They're barely out of the Stone Age!"

Werner Heisenberg was terrified now, but he continued. "Führer, in twenty or thirty years, when we begin our exploration of space, we will plot the course of our rockets based on tables created by Konstantin Tsiolkovsky, a Russian schoolteacher."

Hitler glared at the nuclear physicist and saw him flinch. This is not what he wanted to hear about the Russians.

Barely able to control his rage, he returned to his desk and sat down. *Could this be possible? No! We'll still be able to defeat the Russians in a few years, with or without nuclear weapons. And yet, something this big and powerful would allow Germany to dominate the world for a long time. Yes! Perhaps nuclear weapons are the key to making my dream of a thousand-year Reich a reality. Nations would not only respect us, they would fear us, and that's the key to dominance—fear of total destruction! And this power would be mine!*

"All right! What do you need?"

Heisenberg was ready for this question, but he was so excited that he stammered when he replied. "We need m-money, Führer, l-lots of it … f-f-for b-b-basic research." He caught his breath and then continued with confidence. "This means equipment, special materials, and qualified people. We will need every professor and every graduate in theoretical mathematics, chemistry, and nuclear physics working for us."

"Done! I'll get you all the money you need. And every graduate in theoretical mathematics and nuclear physics, or any other field you require, will be assigned to you. Anything else?"

"Yes. We need a source of uranium ore to make the fissionable material. There isn't any in Germany."

"None?"

"We think there may be large uranium ore deposits near Crossen and Seelingstädt, but it would take years to bring these mines into operation, even if we started today. There is, however, a very large deposit of uranium ore that has been actively mined for years just across the border in Jáchymov, Czechoslovakia."

He pulled a map from his briefcase and showed Hitler the location. "We'd have to increase production substantially and build a large processing plant." He paused, and then added, "You may be interested to know that Marie Curie did her studies leading to the discovery of radium on pitchblende ore from this mine."

Hitler looked at him, nodded, and then studied the map for some moments. "This is part of the Sudetenland," he declared.

"Exactly," said Johann. "So, when you begin the reunification of all German peoples, as you promised in *Mein Kampf,* you might want to start with the Sudetenland. We'd get the uranium mines we need as an extra bonus."

"No. We will start with Austria, because it is the place of my birth. But Czechoslovakia, with its German population and uranium mines, will be next. I promise you that. Anything else?"

"Yes, one more thing," said the professor. "We believe that for now anyway, this should be a civilian program run out of the Kaiser Wilhelm Institute of Physics. We have the resources and the administrative staff to do this. Besides, working for our institute might be much more attractive to new recruits if it was not associated with the military."

Hitler thought about this for a long time. "You're probably right. The military isn't capable of administering anything like this … yet. There may come a time when this is not only possible, but necessary as well. Yes, for now, everything will go through Kaiser Wilhelm. My only concern is security. We don't want to arouse any suspicions among our potential adversaries. You'll have to keep this quiet in all respects. No papers published on your discoveries, no lectures, or anything like that … understood?"

"Yes, Führer. Completely understood."

"You may want to publish a few innocuous books and papers and give some low-level lectures as a way of diverting attention from what you're really doing, but nothing more."

Professor Heisenberg couldn't help but laugh. "We do that anyway, Führer. At our level, it's either publish or perish."

Now all three men were laughing.

"Very well," Hitler said. "Now, we all have work to do, so I will bid you a good morning, gentlemen."

Johann and Werner rose and gave the Nazi salute. This time, a very pleased Adolf Hitler returned the gesture with enthusiasm. The two men marched in lockstep toward the door and left the room.

Hitler sat at his desk, opened another folder, and began to prepare a list of the major industrial firms in Germany and their directors. He brought the list to his secretary, who immediately jumped out of his chair with a stiff-armed salute and a cry of "Heil Hitler!"

This man is such a fool, Hitler thought. *Very efficient, very competent, but still a fool to be dealt with later.* "Schmidt, I want you to schedule appointments for these men to be in my office beginning at nine o'clock on Friday. Today is Monday, so they will have a few days to cancel their other obligations before they come to Berlin. Assign them one hour each, and tell them to bring their treasurers with them. But first, get me Dr. Wehrner von Braun on the phone. He's our rocket expert. I'm not sure exactly where he is, but find him. Also, I want to see Himmler as soon as possible."

"Immediately, sir! Heil Hitler!"

Maybe sooner rather than later, Hitler thought, shaking his head.

Chapter 3

The Unlikely Chancellor

Berlin
July 9, 1946 1:30 a.m.
Spandau Prison

"So your nuclear program got started in 1934. We never suspected anything like that."

"That was the whole idea, Oppy. We didn't want anyone in Washington, London, or Moscow to be alarmed by what we were doing. We got our *Uranverein*, our nuclear club, going much earlier than you did. We brought together all the key people from Berlin, Hamburg, Heidelberg, Leipzig, and many other centers of research. At first, we were all competing for money, materials, and military exemptions for promising students. But as our research progressed and began to show results, we became much closer and more cooperative."

"Well, it certainly worked, Professor. Our Uranium Committee wasn't organized until after Pearl Harbor, and the Manhattan Project didn't get started until August 1942. So what happened next? Did you get everything that Hitler had promised you?"

"Adolf Hitler supplied us with enough money for everything we wanted to do," Johann replied. "The other day, I happened to run into Willi Schmidt, Hitler's first secretary. He was transferred to the army, and then to a guard unit at Auschwitz. He didn't want to talk about that part of his life, but after a few drinks, he had plenty to say about Hitler. I asked him about the meetings with the industrialists, and he said they were all there that first Friday—Krupp, Flick, Rheinmettal, IG Faben, and Siemens—and that after meeting with Hitler, most of them had been reduced to tired and frightened old men. He remembered that Alfred Krupp had a heart attack after his meeting with Hitler and had to be taken to the hospital. Hitler literally terrified them out of billions of reichsmarks. Schmidt said that these meetings went on for many days, and that more than once he had to clean up the mess in *der Führer's* office left by these men. Anyway, yes, Dr. Oppenheimer, we got everything we wanted: the money, the workers, the special materials, and eventually, all the U^{235} we needed."

Werner then took up the story. "We knew we were behind schedule. Ed Lawrence had invented the cyclotron in 1929. We didn't have anything like that, but we pushed ahead and within a few years, we had a six-meter unit on line. Among other things, we confirmed the existence of plutonium, which we had only theorized about prior to its discovery. We actually got there a few months before Glenn Seaborg and Ed McMillan, but of course, we didn't tell anybody. We called it '239' at first, but after we found out that your side had stopped calling it 'seventy-four' and started calling it 'plutonium,' we adopted that name.

"After researching plutonium for a few months, we found it was even more powerful than uranium, and this set off a debate. Should we explore the use of plutonium as well as uranium for use in our weapons, or should we concentrate solely on uranium? It was my call, so I decided to put all our limited resources into the development of uranium weapons. I based this on the fact that it appeared plutonium was much more unstable than uranium, and this could lead to problems of preignition between the two fissionable masses. It looked like going from U^{238} to plutonium would be easier, but because of the greater instability of plutonium, we decided to go with U^{235}.

"The breakthrough came when Paul Harteck of the Technische Hochschule at Hamburg remembered the work done by Jesse Beams at the University of Virginia in 1934 when he developed the process of separating isotopes by using a vacuum ultracentrifuge. Otto Hahn and his team of chemists discovered that dissolving uranium oxide in nitric acid results in a solution of uranyl nitrate. Hahn purified this solution and treated it with ammonia to get ammonium diuranate. He then reduced this with hydrogen and converted it with hydrofluoric acid into uranium tetraflouride. He oxidized this with fluorine to get uranium hexafluoride.

"Harteck worked with Will Groth, who was director of a centrifuge project at Göttingen, and they came up with the idea of pumping this gas into a centrifuge and spinning it up to get U^{235} in sufficient purity to make our weapons. They worked with some geniuses at Siemens to develop centrifuges with air bearings that spun at 100,000 rpm and arranged them in cascades to produce progressively higher concentrations of U^{235}. We then treated the gas with calcium to get the U^{235} in a form we could use to make our weapons. We got more than 90 percent purity using this method, which reduced the amount of fissionable material we had to use for an explosion. It ended up being about the size of a pineapple, Oppy.

"Once we had this all figured out, we placed an order with Siemens for 20,000 of these centrifuges and located them in tunnels in the Harz Mountains near Niedersachswerfen, which isn't too far from our test site in Ohrdruf. They set up five production lines, each of which produced twenty centrifuges a day. One hundred days of production got us 10,000 centrifuges. Eventually, we had 50,000 centrifuges spinning at Niedersachswerfen."

"So you skipped the gaseous diffusion and electromagnetic separation steps and were able to move right into centrifuges?"

"Yes, Oppy, we were able to do that."

"And to think that we had it first in 1934, but we didn't believe it would work."

"Right again, Oppy."

"My God, you saved so much time and expense. But what about controlling the nuclear reaction? Fermi and Szilárd did that in late 1942 in Chicago."

"We did it in early 1937, Oppy. We just didn't tell anybody about it. But before that, we produced nuclear fission in 1935 when Otto Hahn and Fritz Strassmann detected the element barium after bombarding uranium with neutrons. We didn't tell anybody about that, either."

"Nineteen thirty-five! No wonder you were so far ahead. But the design of the weapon itself ... when did you start on that?"

"That was delayed. One of the main problems was that the Gestapo kept removing our Jewish scientists. The Law for the Restoration of the Professional Civil Service passed by the Nazis in 1933 completely politicized the education system in Germany, Oppy. We lost more than a dozen nuclear physicists who were critical to our program, and a lot of them ended up leaving Germany to work for you. This really slowed us down. Himmler almost got me in 1938, and if my mother hadn't met with Himmler's mother and resolved the issue, I might have gone up the chimney with everyone else. Max Planck, who was president of the Kaiser Wilhelm Society and probably our most eminent scientist, met with Hitler in 1933, and even he got nowhere. He told Hitler that forcing Jewish scientists to emigrate would seriously hurt Germany and that the benefits of their work would go to foreign countries. Hitler responded with one of his typical rants against Jews, and all Planck could do was sit there and take it, and then leave. The Nazis didn't change their policy until July 1942, a little over a year before Hitler was assassinated.

"But despite all these problems, we were getting to the point in mid-1939 that we thought we knew enough to begin designing a weapon. Then the war started, and when it became obvious in 1940 that the British were going to be a problem, our team was broken up and assigned to other projects. I went directly to Hitler to protest, and he told me very bluntly that 'Germany can win the war without your little firecracker, Professor Heisenberg. But right now we need you and your men for more important things, do you understand?' Well, from his tone of voice, I understood very clearly—either produce results, or my family and I would be transported to the east, if you know what I mean. So I answered, 'Yes, Führer, of course. I will be honored to work wherever I am sent.' So off we went to our different assignments. But by some miraculous oversight, the technicians in charge of the production of U^{235} were untouched, and so the centrifuges kept spinning. That's how we accumulated our very substantial stockpile of fissionable material by the time our team was reassembled."

"How much did you have?"

"Enough to make the bombs and missile warheads we used to get the United States and the British out of the war and to seriously hurt the Russians."

Johann picked up the story. "Things went pretty well for us during the first part of the war. After Dunkirk and the French surrender, we felt we were pretty much in the driver's seat and that things would be over quickly. Then Hitler started planning for the invasion of Russia, even before we had finished with England. Nothing anyone said could dissuade him. Even reminding him of what he had written in *Mein Kampf* about the danger of fighting a war on two fronts had no effect except to make him very angry, and by this time, we all knew better than to do that. We all felt very uneasy when Operation Barbarossa was launched in June of 1941, but we hid our feelings and managed to radiate enthusiasm whenever we were in his presence. Things did go well at first, Oppy. But after the setbacks at Moscow, and then Stalingrad and Kursk, there was a growing feeling in certain circles of the army that something had to be done about Hitler, or we would lose the war and Germany would be torn apart. There were also rumors about what was really happening to the Jews, but only in military circles."

"Is that when the plot to kill Hitler and the others began to take shape?"

"Actually, there had been some very quiet talk about this earlier, but things didn't get serious until after Kursk, which was August of 1943. At first, only a few of us dared to speak openly about killing Hitler and his inner circle. These were all very important and well-guarded men. It would be difficult enough to get them all together at the same place at the same time, much less penetrate their security and kill them, and then take over the government. Control of Berlin and the army was critical to our success. But we planned very carefully and selected only the most important people to be involved. There were almost two hundred of us involved in this plot, mostly military, but with a few key civilians. We each knew what had to be done when the time came."

"So, how was it actually done? Do you know?"

"Yes, Dr. Oppenheimer, I know how it was done. I was there. I'm the one who killed Heinrich Himmler and Martin Bormann."

Werner's eyes widened in amazement. "Johann! You never told me this before."

"Didn't I? Forgive the oversight, old friend, and let me make it up to you now. It was good planning, to be sure, but it was also a lot of luck. Forget everything you've read in the newspapers. This is how it really happened ..."

Berlin
November 9, 1943 10:30 a.m.
Outside the Old Reich Chancellery

"You're sure about this, General?"

"Yes. I got it from Bormann himself. They will all be there, Colonel. This may be our last opportunity for a long time. Hitler says that after this, we will meet more often at Wolfsschanze so we can be closer to the fighting. We have to kill them now."

This is it, Stauffenberg thought. *No more talk. From now on, it would be decisive action. If it goes wrong, it will cost me and many others their lives. So much depends on the decisions I make in the next few minutes.*

Claus Schenk Graf von Stauffenberg had been born into one of the oldest and most distinguished aristocratic Catholic families in Germany. He had been taught the ideals of service and loyalty to country from early childhood. After joining the army, he had vacillated between his strong personal dislike of Hitler's policies and a respect for what he perceived to be his political and military acumen. After all, he had taken Austria and parts of Czechoslovakia without firing a shot. Anyone could have stopped Hitler at this point, but no one had lifted a finger. He had torn up the Treaty of Versailles and rearmed Germany, and the world had turned a blind eye. But now, with the reversals on the Russian front and the growing revelations about what was happening to the Jews, Stauffenberg had come to the inescapable conclusion that Hitler had to be replaced if Germany was going to win the war and regain its respect among the nations of the world.

"All right, General, we go. Make your phone calls."

"Yes, Colonel," replied General Ludwig Beck. He was one of the highest-ranking officers involved in the plot, and it was agreed that he would become führer after Hitler's death.

Now Stauffenberg had work to do. Returning to his quarters, he made four phone calls to other members of the conspiracy. In his conversation, he was cheerful and casual, but in all cases, he included the phrase, "Yes, Nina, the children and I will be together this weekend. It might be the last time we see one another for quite a while." That, plus "Will you be at the meeting Hitler has called on the morning of the eighteenth?" This gave them the information they needed: the assassination of Adolf Hitler, Hermann Göering, Heinrich Himmler, Joseph Goebbels, and Martin Bormann would take place on Wednesday, November 18, right after the meeting of top-level officials that the führer had called for 0900 to discuss the progress of the war. Stauffenberg himself was to present a report on work force reserves.

The men he had spoken with had worked out their own codes with the people they subsequently called. Stauffenberg had insisted on this, because, he reasoned, if the same code words were repeated someone might get suspicious. "You never know who might be listening," Stauffenberg had told them. Before the end of the day, everyone involved in the plot would be informed.

Stauffenberg then realized that November 18 was three days after his birthday. He would turn thirty-six. *Will I live to see thirty-seven?* he wondered.

Berlin
November 18, 1943 9:00 a.m.
The Old Reich Chancellery

The meeting Hitler had called proceeded as an old, familiar stage production; the major players knew their lines and delivered them on cue and with enthusiasm. Reich Marshal Göering discounted the bombing campaign of the British and the Americans, saying the problem would be taken care of by Germany's improved air defenses. No one mentioned that he had once promised Hitler that no American or British plane would ever drop bombs on German soil.

Admiral Karl Dönitz reported that although the Americans were growing in strength, he still believed his submarines held the upper hand and that it would be just a matter of time before the convoys sailing between the United States, England, and the Soviet Union would be halted, and that American and British warships would be chased out of the Atlantic. Supreme Commander Wilhelm Keitel said that while the setbacks at Moscow, Stalingrad, and Kursk had been serious, he felt that with fresh armies and new equipment coming on line, the initiative on the ground would be regained by an offensive being planned for the coming spring.

And so it went all morning and into the afternoon. Even Stauffenberg's report was glowing and optimistic. He said that there were large numbers of reserves available to replace those who had been killed or wounded. At 3:30, the meeting ended. There had been no tirades by Hitler, and everyone had kept their jobs—and their heads. This was no small accomplishment.

When the meeting ended, Hitler, Göering, Goebbels, Himmler, and Bormann left first, followed by admirals Raeder and Dönitz, and generals Jodl and Keitel. Two guards carrying submachine guns flanked them. Not expecting an attack from the rear, they kept their eyes focused forward. The last rank consisted of the assassins: Colonel Stauffenberg, Lieutenant Rinehart, Major General Henning von Tresckow, and General Ludwig Beck.

Back in the meeting room, the other officers were beginning to leave. But General Helmuth Stieff and Captain Friedrich Klausing, who had produced Lugers, met them at the doors and motioned for them to stay inside the room.

"Please remain here, gentlemen." said General Stieff. "Take your seats, remain silent, and keep your hands on the table where we can see them. This should all be over in a few minutes, and then you will each have to decide whose side you are on."

One of the colonels stood and said, "What is the mean—" His question was cut short by a shot from General Stieff's Luger, which was accompanied by a very stern warning, "Sit down, Colonel. We don't want to hurt anybody, but if you try to stand again, I will kill you."

The shot from the meeting room startled everyone in the hallway. Except for the assassins, everyone stopped and began to turn toward the sound of the gunshot. The assassins, who had already drawn their weapons, pushed aside the four surprised senior officers and opened fire. Lieutenant Rinehart and General Beck directed their fire at the guards. Rinehart's bullets struck home, and the guard crumpled forward in a heap on the floor. General Beck's shots were equally accurate, but his guard fell backward, and with a reflexive action, he pulled the trigger on his submachine gun, sending a spray of bullets from floor to ceiling. Several bullets struck General Beck, killing him instantly.

Stauffenberg and Tresckow had also produced weapons from their briefcases. Stauffenberg had lost his left eye, his right hand, and two fingers from his left hand during an attack by RAF fighters in Tunisia, but he had taught himself to shoot with this handicap. He cradled his open briefcase with his right arm and produced a Mauser machine pistol with his left hand. Stauffenberg pointed it at Adolf Hitler, who had started to turn to the left in response to the sound of the shot fired by General Stieff, and emptied it into his face. Hitler fell to the floor without making a sound.

He's dead. If we fail, at least Hitler will be gone, thought Stauffenberg.

With a well-practiced motion, he threw down his first weapon, produced another machine pistol from his briefcase, and emptied it into the body of Hermann Göering, who was still fumbling with his own sidearm. Göering let out a scream and fell heavily to the floor.

Mausers fired by Tresckow and Rinehart dispatched Goebbels and Himmler. Bormann, only slightly wounded in the initial assault, started to crawl away. Rinehart grabbed the submachine gun from the body of the guard he had just killed and sprayed him.

The assassins looked around in amazement, stunned at their success and the reality that they were still alive. *Too bad about Beck,* thought Stauffenberg. *We'll have to come up with someone else to be our new führer.*

Raeder, Dönitz, Jodl, and Keitel, shocked to be alive and uninjured, found themselves covered with pistols in the hands of General Tresckow and Colonel Stauffenberg. The men instinctively raised their hands in surrender. Stauffenberg told them they could lower their hands, and they complied.

"You have a choice to make, gentlemen." Stauffenberg began. "You can either join us in making a new Germany that is free from fear and governed by high moral principles, or you can join them." He pointed his pistol at the dead men on the floor.

Keitel, ever the opportunist, spoke first. "I have never been a Nazi at heart, Colonel. I only did what I was ordered to do with the hope that someday things would change for the better. Now that day has come, and I gladly join your cause!"

"And what about the rest of you? Your assistance would be most welcome." The three other survivors looked at one another, considered the alternative, and nodded their heads in agreement.

Stauffenberg knew he had to move quickly to secure Berlin, inform the other members of the plot that Hitler and his inner circle were dead, and dispose of the bodies of the men they had just killed.

"Rinehart, you stay here," Stauffenberg said. "The rest of us will return to the conference room. I want you to dispose of these bodies. I don't care how you do it, but there must be no trace left of what has happened here. I'll send you some help. You're in charge."

Stauffenberg and the other assassins, together with admirals

Raeder and Dönitz, and generals Keitel and Jodl, quick-stepped their way back to the conference room where they found that General Stieff and Captain Klausing had everything under control.

Sensing what was about to happen, Keitel whispered to Stauffenberg, "Let me handle this, Colonel. I'll bring them over."

"The stage is yours, General."

When the men walked into the room, they were bombarded with questions. What were all those shots all about? Why were we detained? In God's name, tell us what has happened?

Keitel raised his field marshal's baton and the room immediately fell silent. "Officers of the Fatherland! Our national nightmare is over! A new day has dawned! Adolf Hitler, Hermann Göering, Heinrich Himmler, Joseph Goebbels, and Martin Bormann are dead! Germany is now free from the terror it has been living under for the last ten years. This revolution, led by this brave man," he pointed to Stauffenberg, "has restored our honor and cleansed our national soul!"

Stauffenberg began to feel more than a little uneasy. He saw what was coming.

Keitel continued. "We have been liberated from the tyranny imposed upon our brave men at arms by this demonic clique of rank amateurs. Now we will be able to show the world how Germans can fight!"

A voice spoke up from the back of the room. "Are you then to be our new führer, General?"

"No, no, not me. There can be no one else as our new leader but the one who led the revolution that has secured our freedom. Gentlemen, I give you our new führer, Claus Schenk Graf von Stauffenberg!"

Stauffenberg felt the breath leave his body as fifty pairs of heels clicked together and fifty arms raised in salute. The room shook with "Heil Stauffenberg! Heil Führer Stauffenberg!"

Stauffenberg appeared paralyzed for what seemed an eternity. The men in the room were still at attention, their arms raised in salute. Stauffenberg returned their gesture of fealty, not with the

Nazi salute, but with the more traditional salute he had learned while serving in his family's cavalry regiment. Gathering himself, he addressed the men.

"Gentlemen, officers of Germany. Thank you for your confidence. It is a confidence that I shall never betray. I wish it to be known that starting now, I shall not be addressed as the führer. Let that title die with Adolf Hitler. Let the Nazi salute die with him as well. I will be known as chancellor, and we will salute one another as I have just saluted you. Now, there is much work to do, and it must be done very quickly. You are to return to your quarters and await further orders, which will be coming soon. First, I want all lieutenants, and you, Captain Gehre, to go down the hall and assist Lieutenant Rinehart with the disposal of the bodies. I've placed him in charge, so follow his orders. That is all."

He saluted the men, and they returned his salute with differing degrees of correctness. "Old habits die hard," he said to no one in particular, "but they'll learn."

The new chancellor had to move fast to consolidate power and keep order. His first priority was to put Operation Valkyrie into effect. This was an emergency operations plan for the Territorial Reserve Army of Germany to execute in the event of a general breakdown in civil order. Hitler had approved it, and Stauffenberg appreciated the irony of this; Hitler's plan would now assure the establishment of the government that would replace him. Apart from Hitler, only General Friedrich Fromm, commander of the army reserve, could put Operation Valkyrie into effect, so he had to be either won over to the conspiracy or in some way neutralized.

Stauffenberg acted. "General Stieff, take a couple of the lieutenants from the party I just sent down the hall and find General Fromm. He's at Bendlerstrasse headquarters. He's the only one who can activate Operation Valkyrie, so bring him here—at gunpoint, if necessary. Show him Adolf Hitler's body and give him a choice. Either join us and activate Operation Valkyrie, or join Hitler on the floor. Fromm's been sitting on the fence long enough, and seeing Hitler dead might help him to make up his mind."

Back at the site of the assassinations, Lieutenant Rinehart looked at the eight dead men on the floor. "No trace left of what happened here," were Stauffenberg's orders. *But how?* Just then, Captain Gehre and a number of lieutenants came running down the hall. They stopped and stared in shocked horror at the scene before them. Most of them had seen battle before, but nothing prepared them for the sight of the men who had been the gods of Germany now lying dead on the floor.

Rinehart knew he had to take charge of the situation immediately. "All right, listen up. We have to remove all traces of this. Captain, take one man with you, go to the motor pool, find a staff car and an enclosed van. Bring them to the side entrance. Make sure you put an extra can of petrol in the trunk of the car. You four … find some buckets and mops and clean up the mess after we've put the bodies in the van. Not one spot of blood is to be left, understand? Now, does anyone know—"

He was interrupted by the arrival of General Stieff, who saluted and said, "I have been assigned by Chancellor Stauffenberg to find General Fromm and bring him here. I need two of these men." Lieutenant Rinehart returned the general's salute as best he could and nodded his assent.

Chancellor Stauffenberg? He had not expected this, but since he had heard it from a general on their side, he immediately felt at ease.

"Now, does anyone know the location of a funeral home with a crematorium?" Rinehart asked.

"I do, sir." It was Lieutenant Müeller who spoke up, "My uncle runs such a place at the corner of Unter den Linden and Friedrichstrasse."

"That's where we'll take the bodies then. Get your uncle on the phone, Lieutenant. Tell him we're coming over right now and that our work takes priority over anything else he's doing. Tell him we'll need eight caskets suitable for cremation, seven regular size and one extra large." He was thinking of Reich Marshal Göering, who had become quite corpulent in recent years.

"Sir, my uncle will want to know who is to be cremated. What shall I tell him?"

"Tell him it is in his best interest that he does *not* know. Tell him to leave the rear entrance open so we can bring the bodies in without being seen. After that, he is to leave us alone. We'll put the bodies into the coffins ourselves and nail the lids down. He and his staff can then perform the cremations. Understood?"

"Yes, sir. I'll make the call right now." Müeller disappeared to find a telephone.

Captain Gehre and the lieutenant returned and reported. "Lieutenant, we have two vehicles from the motor pool. We think you will find them to be most satisfactory," said Gehre.

"Any problems, Captain?"

"None at all, Lieutenant."

With the first shots fired by the assassins, all of the offices in the Chancellery had emptied, their occupants fleeing for safer ground. Lieutenant Rinehart went into the closest office, sat down at the desk, and found the pen and paper he was looking for. After he finished writing, he summoned one of the lieutenants. "Lieutenant, take this note to the chancellor. It is for his eyes only. Wait to see if there is a reply and then return here. We will wait for you." The lieutenant saluted, did a smart about-face, and quick-stepped out of the office.

General Stieff, the two lieutenants, and a much shaken General Fromm came through the door. Fromm looked at the bloody scene before him, then at General Stieff. Without a word, he nodded in acceptance, and they marched to the chancellor's office. Operation Valkyrie was about to be put into effect.

"Okay," Rinehart said. "Now go into the offices and gather up as many chairs as you can that have wheels. We'll put the bodies in the chairs and transport them to the van. Find some towels to lay over the chairs so they won't get bloody."

And so the strange procession down the hallway to the side entrance began. When they got there, Lieutenant Rinehart saw that Captain Gehre had indeed done very well, for there was a gleaming, six-wheeled Mercedes-Benz staff car, the one Hitler used when he paraded through the streets of Berlin or any other city he had conquered. Backed up to the entrance was an enclosed van with its rear doors open and ready to receive its grisly cargo.

"The can of petrol is in the trunk of the Mercedes as you ordered, Lieutenant." Rinehart nodded his approval.

One by one, the bodies of the dead Nazis were loaded into the van and the doors were closed. Lieutenant Rinehart got behind the wheel of the staff car and invited Lieutenant Müeller to sit next to him. Captain Gehre sat in the back. The funeral home was not far. From the Old Reich Chancellery, it was only a few blocks to Wilhelmstrasse, then right on Unter den Linden, and then right on Friedrichstrasse to the side entrance to the funeral home.

On the drive to the funeral home, Lieutenant Rinehart asked Müeller if he knew anything about cremation.

"Yes, sir, I do. I'm supposed to take over the business when I leave the army."

Rinehart nodded. "Go on."

"Well, a crematorium is basically a furnace heated up to almost one thousand degrees centigrade using coke. It takes a couple of hours to cremate an average male body, but in the case of the Reich Marshal, it will probably take three hours. What you get in the end is about three kilos of ashes, bone fragments, really. The ashes can be placed in an urn or a cardboard box."

Two to three hours for each body! I'll be here until the next afternoon. But there's no other way to dispose of the bodies without leaving a trace as the chancellor had ordered. And I have plans for the disposal of the ashes.

Berlin
November 18, 1943 6:00 p.m.
Müeller Funeral Home and Crematorium

Hans Dieter Müeller had served his country with honor in the First World War. As a captain, he had led his men with skill and courage and always from the front. The war had taken them through Belgium and into France with very few casualties compared with other units. Captain Dieter, as the men had called him, had always been very careful with their lives, and they loved him for it.

As they moved closer to Paris, French resistance had stiffened. It was at a farmhouse about one hundred kilometers from the French capital when it happened. His unit was pinned down and taking heavy casualties. The orders from that imbecile of a colonel had left his men with very little cover. But they were holding their own, and relief was sure to come.

But it didn't come soon enough. The French had managed to get some of their artillery into position, and Müeller's men were being slaughtered. Suddenly, a shell penetrated the thin wooden wall in front of Müeller and exploded not far from him, filling the right side of his body with shrapnel and splinters. He knew he was badly wounded, perhaps mortally.

For the next few months, Müeller was in and out of consciousness, alternating between what seemed like hours of excruciating pain and merciful sleep. When the fog finally lifted, a nurse informed him that he was in a Catholic hospital in Berlin, and that the nuns regarded his recovery as a "miracle of God." At the time, he had accepted that explanation, but later, he attributed it to his own iron will.

Müeller was bitterly disappointed when the doctors told him that not only this war, but all future wars, were finished for him. His wounds, although mostly healed, had left him a physical and mental shell of his former self, and as hard as that unwelcomed news was to bear, he knew it to be the truth.

So what was he to do? He had seen the human wreckage of disabled soldiers prowling the streets of Berlin seeking handouts, with some resorting to stealing and even murder just to feed themselves and their families. He had made up his mind to avoid this at all costs. His one hope was his elderly uncle who ran a funeral home. He had no children of his own to pass the business to, so Müeller thought that perhaps he would be receptive to his offer.

That was exactly what happened. His uncle was quite pleased to take on a younger assistant, especially a member of the family. Hans Dieter Müeller showed a real aptitude for the work, and after a few years of what was really an apprenticeship, he was made a partner. When the old man died in 1926, Müeller inherited the business, and with the introduction of modern techniques of administration, the small company prospered and became an institution. Its location at the corner of Unter den Linden and Friedrichstrasse placed it in the most fashionable business district of a renewed Berlin, and his business thrived. Even in this line of work, he often mused, location is everything.

Müeller knew Germany was changing, and he sensed it was not necessarily for the better. Like many others, he was uneasy about Adolf Hitler and the Nazis, but as long as they left him alone, he was content with the way things were going, even with the growing abuses of the Jews.

But they were the ones who had stabbed Germany in the back at the end of the war, he reasoned. *Now they were just getting what they deserved. Hitler had revived the economy and made everyone proud to be German again. And nobody cared when we marched into Austria and Czechoslovakia. We are so strong now that no one would dare to oppose us! And besides, business is growing, money is coming in, and my employees are happy. Yes, I did have to let a couple of them go because they were Jewish, but if that's the price of living in Germany these days, it's a small one.*

In late 1942, he decided to expand the services offered by his company by adding a crematorium. He contacted the furnace makers Topf and Sons of Erfurt. To his surprise, he was told it would be at least two years before they could fill his order because all of their production was committed to other projects funded by the Nazis. Müeller was about to give up when he noticed that one of the directors at Topf was an old comrade of his from the war. He thought perhaps he could intercede and make his order a reality. A quick trip to Erfurt, a quiet dinner at a local French restaurant with brandy and cigars afterward, and the deal was struck. His new crematorium was delivered and installed in February 1943.

Now this call from his nephew Georg was most upsetting.

"Prepare your crematorium for eight bodies," Georg had said. "No, it is best you *not* know who is to be cremated." He paused. "Yes, Uncle, right now. This is official government business, and it must be kept very quiet, do you understand?" Then, "Sorry, but all your other clients will have to wait until this job is done." And, "No, there won't be any paperwork. Just put the eight wooden coffins and the lids in the receiving area with some nails and hammers. We'll take care of the rest. I almost forgot; one of the coffins has to be very large." Then, "Do you have enough coke on hand for eight bodies? Good. Also, we'll need seven cardboard boxes and one urn for the ashes. Yes, make it a good one, Uncle. Yes, you will be well paid for this, I assure you. We'll see you in a little while. Yes, open the door for us after you put everything in the receiving area and then leave. Better start stoking the furnace right now, Uncle. Good-bye."

Müeller had a very bad feeling about the conversation. *Cremation of eight bodies, to be kept very quiet, and with no papers. I don't like this at all. But my nephew is an aide to a very important staff general, so there must be a good reason for this.*

Müeller had initially approved of his nephew's choice to join the army, but with the rise of the Nazis to power, he had begun to express to him his concerns about what was happening to the military. But when he heard about the oath that every German soldier was now required to take, his concern turned into outrage.

I swear by God this sacred oath that I shall render unconditional obedience to Adolf Hitler, the führer of the German Reich, supreme commander of the armed forces, and that I shall at all times be prepared, as a brave soldier, to give my life for this oath.

Swearing this oath to a man? Such an oath is reserved for Germany; not a man, even our leader, he thought. *Was our new* führer *identifying himself with Germany so strongly that he was placing himself above his country? Best to keep a wary eye on this Hitler.*

But then came the good times and with them the revival of German pride, improved economic conditions, the rearmament, and then Austria and Czechoslovakia. Müeller's misgivings about Hitler were largely pushed aside. But not now.

Director Müeller called his secretary into his office. "Traudl, please tell everyone to drop what they're doing and come in here. This is most urgent."

With his staff assembled, Director Müeller explained the situation, placing emphasis on the urgency and secrecy of the work they were about to do. He told the crew operating the furnace that they would be engaged for at least seventeen hours and that they would be paid double. After this, he personally supervised the preparation of the receiving area and made sure there were eight wooden coffins, one extra large, together with their lids and enough nails and hammers to do the job. He then opened the large door fronting Friedrichstrasse and returned to his office to await the arrival of his mysterious and unwelcome guests and their eight unnamed bodies.

He didn't have long to wait.

"The director is expecting you." Traudl moved to open the door to the director's office, but she was rudely brushed aside.

"I will announce myself," snapped Lieutenant Rinehart. He had a role to play now: that of an arrogant German officer who was used to giving orders and having them obeyed instantly and without question.

He strode purposefully into the director's office. "Herr Director Müeller, I am Lieutenant Rinehart of the general staff. Is everything in order?"

"Yes, Herr Lieutenant, everything has been done as you instructed." Müeller felt that under these circumstances it would be best to adopt a subordinate demeanor. He knew better than to cross a German officer in high dudgeon. He had seen the consequences of such behavior all too often during the First World War.

"Then show me to your receiving area."

"This way, Herr Lieutenant." He led Lieutenant Rinehart to the back of the building and opened the door to the receiving area. Everything was laid out in proper order—the eight wooden coffins with lids, and nails and hammers to do the job. The door to the street was open and the van, with its rear doors still closed, was backed up to the entrance of the receiving area.

"Excellent! How long will it be until your crematorium is ready to receive the first body?"

"About one hour, Herr Lieutenant."

"Very well, Herr Director. Return to us when your crematorium is ready. We will have the coffins prepared for you by that time. Knock on the door before you come in."

"Very good, Herr Lieutenant." He closed the door behind him and returned to supervise the preparation of his oven.

Lieutenant Rinehart breathed a sigh of relief. "All right, gentlemen. Let's begin. Adolf Hitler first."

The doors to the van were opened and the horribly defaced body of Adolf Hitler was removed and placed in the nearest open coffin. The lid was placed on top of the coffin and nailed shut. Rinehart made sure that everyone hammered a nail into the coffin. They were now members of a very exclusive club: the last ones to see Adolf Hitler. Rinehart marked coffin with the number 1.

"Next is Göering. Move that large coffin next to Hitler's and put his body in it." Even with the larger coffin, the Reich Marshal was still a tight fit, and the coffin lid required a lot more nails than Hitler's. Rinehart marked this one with the number 2.

And so it went. Himmler was number 3; Goebbels, number 4; Bormann, number 5; the two anonymous bodyguards, numbers 6 and 7; and General Beck, number 8. Shortly after they finished nailing the lid on General Beck's coffin, there was a soft knock on the door. It was Director Müeller. "We're ready for the first body, Herr Lieutenant."

"Very well, Herr Director," Rinehart stepped back into the role he had played before. "Take them in the order in which they are numbered. After each body has been consumed by the fire, collect the ashes and place them in cardboard boxes with the same number on each box as was on the coffin. Do this for the first seven bodies. For the last body, place the ashes in an urn of the finest quality. Bring all the boxes of ashes and the urn to me as they become ready. Do you understand, Herr Director?"

"It shall be done as you order, Herr Lieutenant. Is there anything else you require?"

Rinehart thought about this for a few seconds before he replied. "Yes. This is going to be a long night. I shall require some dinner and a large thermos of black coffee. Have someone on your staff get this for me at a nearby restaurant." He reached into his wallet and produced two one hundred reichsmark notes. "I think this should cover it."

"Yes, Lieutenant, as you request." The director exited the

preparation room. Four men then entered, picked up the coffin containing the body of Adolf Hitler, and removed it from the room. It had finally started.

Rinehart saw that the men under his command were drained physically and emotionally, but he had one last duty to perform for them. The arrogant German officer who had presented himself to Director Müeller was gone, and in his place was a comrade, a friend addressing the men he had served with on the front lines.

"Gentlemen, we have performed an extraordinary service for our country today. Under other circumstances, we should be proud to tell our friends and families about this. But these are not ordinary times. I would urge you, in the strongest possible terms, to remain silent about everything that has happened today. Even when you are old and gray and your grandchild asks you, 'What did you do in the war, Opa?' You should say, 'I served my country with honor as a member of the general staff,' and let it go at that.

"So return to the Old Reich Chancellery with the van, wash it out thoroughly so there's no trace left of today's activities and make sure all the wastewater goes down the drain. Do this before you return it to the motor pool. Then go to your quarters, change your clothes, and get cleaned up. You're all a bloody mess, and this could raise some questions."

"Lieutenant, I have an idea," Captain Gehre offered. "I have a brother who works at the Rummelsburg power station. He actually tends the fire. Suppose I collect all of these uniforms and the towels, put them into a couple of laundry bags, and take them down there. I could get a motorcycle with a side car from the motor pool without any trouble."

"Captain, you're a genius. What would it take to persuade your brother to take a long break so you could stuff the laundry bags into the fire?"

"Well, my brother likes the Turkish cigarettes he buys on the black market."

"Do you think this would keep your brother supplied with Turkish cigarettes for a while, Captain?" Rinehart produced several one hundred reichsmark notes from his wallet.

"I think so, Lieutenant."

"Then make it so, Captain."

Georg Müeller spoke up. "Lieutenant, what do you intend to do with the ashes?"

Lieutenant Rinehart became very serious at this point. "Gentlemen, I have a plan for the disposal of the ashes, but it must remain known to me alone. I do this not out of a lack of respect for you. Indeed, we have become brothers in arms like very few before us. I do this because I want to protect you in the event that things go wrong and our plans fail. If this happens, you will be questioned most severely as to what became of Hitler's remains, as well as those of the other Nazi leaders. You will have to be able to say truthfully, even under the most extreme pressure, that you do not know because I made the decision not to tell you. I will take the location of these ashes with me to my grave, whether that occurs tomorrow or years from now. Do you understand why I have made this decision?"

To a man, the response was, "Yes, Lieutenant, and thank you."

"Then it's time for us to part company. Gentlemen, I salute you and hope we meet again soon in a better Germany." His salute, the new one ordered by Chancellor Stauffenberg, was returned smartly and with genuine affection.

Lieutenant Rinehart turned and walked back into the preparation room, doing his best to hold back the tears he felt welling up in his eyes. These men, under his command, had put their lives on the line for their nation, and he had just told them that they could never divulge this secret. As he sat down to await the arrival of Adolf Hitler's ashes, Traudl, the director's secretary, arrived with a meal of sausage and sauerkraut and a large thermos of black coffee. He devoured it hungrily, knowing that it might be his last meal for a long time. He wondered if it would be his last meal—ever.

Berlin
November 18, 1943 7:00 p.m.
The Old Reich Chancellery

Chancellor Stauffenberg had spent the hours after the assassination of Adolf Hitler and other top Nazis making phone calls to other members of the conspiracy to inform them of its success. General Fromm had done his part, probably not so much out of loyalty, but out of fear, and Operation Valkyrie was being put into effect. Key civilian and military installations, including the concentration camps, were being taken over by forces loyal to the new government, and all armed forces, including the Waffen-SS, the Gestapo and the Leibstandarte—Hitler's personal bodyguard regiment—were being placed under the control of its officers. The influence of Generals Keitel and Jodl was most helpful in bringing the army under this control, and Admirals Raeder and Dönitz assisted with the navy. General Adolf Galland was flown in to replace Reich Marshal Göering. The respect the men of the Luftwaffe had for Galland made their acceptance of the new government a foregone conclusion. Albert Speer, who had been appointed Reich Minister in charge of armaments production by Adolf Hitler in January 1941, was also present. Stauffenberg asked him to stay on in that position, and he readily accepted.

With the initiation of Valkyrie, the tension in the room eased. The new chancellor summoned his senior staff, including Albert Speer and Erwin Rommel, to a small conference room and closed the door.

"Gentlemen," said the new chancellor, "I think we have the situation under control. Valkyrie is being put into effect thanks in no small measure to your assistance. I have therefore decided that it would be in the best interests of our country that you four senior officers, General Keitel, General Jodl, Admiral Raeder, and Admiral Dönitz, remain at your posts.

"There will be a major difference in the way things are done. You will have more responsibility for the conduct of the war. Unlike Hitler, I will not attempt to make tactical decisions. In addition, the overall strategy of the war will be a joint effort involving all of us, not just me.

"Now I want an honest appraisal of how we are doing, what our major problems are, and suggestions for measures to overcome these problems."

The response was quite sobering. Keitel and Jodl reported the facts about the losses at Moscow, Stalingrad, and Kursk. More important than the actual numbers lost, they said, was that the momentum of the war had definitively shifted to the Soviets and that in their opinion, they could not be stopped, regardless of how many men, planes, and tanks the Germans threw at them. They said that even though Soviet troops were being killed at a ridiculous rate, there always seemed to be more of them, and they just kept coming.

Admirals Raeder and Dönitz reported that while German submarines were still sinking large numbers of Allied ships, they had not managed to completely stop the convoys sailing from the United States to ports in England and Russia, and that control of the Atlantic Ocean was still being contested. They reported that while only thirty-five of their submarines had been lost in 1941, more than twice that had been lost in 1942, and that so far in 1943, more than two hundred boats had been sunk. They said further that they were concerned about the growing number of American destroyers of advanced design in the Atlantic, and that the

Americans seemed to be able to produce them faster than Germany could replace the submarines it was losing. They said that British, and now American, bombing raids on their submarine pens had caused some serious damage and that more raids were expected as the Americans increased their strength in the air.

General Galland delivered the most damaging report. He said that up until 1941, most of the bombing raids had been made by the British, but now that the Americans had entered the war, this was expected to change. What he said next really got their attention: production of the major German fighter aircraft, the Messerschmitt Me 109, Focke-Wulf 190, Messerschmitt 110, and Messerschmitt 210, was expected to be approximately 8,900 units in 1943. American light, medium, and heavy bombers, according to intelligence sources, would total more than 12,500! The Americans by themselves were producing more bombers than the Germans were producing the fighters being used to shoot them down. Furthermore, he added, they can attack and destroy our fighter factories, but we cannot attack and destroy their bomber factories.

Speer reported that the bombing had caused some serious problems with industrial production, and that he expected more damage in the coming months as more American planes became available. He said that the use of foreign slave labor was increasing as more and more Germans were inducted into the army, and this was problematic because of the possibility of sabotage, loss of quality control, and unrest. The men sat in stunned silence for several minutes. No one had known that things were so bad—Hitler had not allowed it.

Finally, Stauffenberg broke the awkward stillness. "Gentlemen, it seems that we have two choices. The first is to sue for peace. This means throwing ourselves on the mercy of the Allies, and given the situation, it is doubtful that they would show us any. The Soviets will accept nothing short of the complete destruction of our country. The

British are very angry with us for bombing their country, and both the Americans and the British are outraged over our treatment of the Jews. Are we all in agreement with these conclusions?"

The men in the room didn't know what to say at first. Hitler had never asked their opinion on such matters, This was something completely alien to them, but then, this chancellor, as they were finding out, had a new way of looking at things. It took some time for them to find their voices, but the facts as outlined by the chancellor were irrefutable, and so they reluctantly, but firmly, agreed.

"The other alternative," Stauffenberg continued, "is to fight on and pray that the Gods of War will favor us. Now, what do we have that can help our cause? We know that we cannot hope to defeat our enemies with the weapons we have now. Is there anything in development that can improve our situation, and what do we have to do to bring it on line as soon as possible?"

"Chancellor," Keitel began, "there is very little hope for us on the ground. We have a new tank under development to replace both the Tiger and the Panther, but it will be at least two years before it is ready. In addition, we have started to use the Focke-Wulf 190 in a ground attack role, but we don't have enough of them to make a difference yet. We need time to train the pilots and develop a new doctrine of ground support before this weapon can be effective."

Admiral Dönitz spoke. "Chancellor, we have two experimental projects underway that, if successful, could stop the American convoys and give us supremacy in the Atlantic. One is the Type 21 submarine, which is a true submersible as opposed to our present class of U-boats, which must surface every day or two to recharge the batteries. We are also developing a wire-guided torpedo, and if this proves successful, we will marry it to the Type 21 submarine. With enough of these, we should be able to defeat any number of American ships thrown against us. The development of these weapons, however, has been slowed by the constant American and

British bombing. If this bombing were stopped, we could have our Type 21s and their wire-guided torpedoes available in quantity within six to eight months."

Adolf Galland then added to this optimistic note. "There is a good chance we can stop the American air offensive before it gets any worse. We have a jet-powered fighter, the Messerschmitt 262, which is 160 kilometers per hour faster than anything the Americans or British have. The reason it has not been deployed as an interceptor until now is that Hitler insisted that all planes have an offensive dive-bombing capability. We have not been able to deploy this plane as an interceptor because of this limitation. We also have the Arado 234, which needs more development, but has the promise of becoming a medium bomber that flies too fast and too high for any Allied aircraft to catch. The problem with both of these planes is the engines. They operate at very high temperatures, and as a result, they last less than twenty-five hours before they have to be replaced.

"We are developing a guided bomb that shows some promise of improving the accuracy of our attacks. It's wire-guided, so it can't be jammed. We've started to experiment with putting a television camera in the nose of the bomb and a TV screen in the airplane. As long as the operator keeps the target in the middle of the screen, a hit is guaranteed. We will use this against high-value targets such as ships, bridges, and industrial buildings to ensure their destruction with one or two hits.

"So we need several things: First, the release of the Messerschmitt 262 for use as an interceptor. Second, we need to bring the Arado 234 on line as quickly as possible as both a high-speed bomber and as an interceptor. Third, we need to increase the production of our existing jet engines. Fourth, we need to research new materials for the development of jet engines with substantially longer life and increased power, and fifth, we need to end the production of obsolete aircraft such as the Messerschmitt 109. I firmly believe that the only fighters we should be producing at this time are the Messerschmitt 262 and the Focke-Wulf 190. Everything else is either obsolete or close to it, and their production should be ended so our resources can be put into the production of more effective planes."

"So, the way I see it is this:" Stauffenberg summarized, "the most important thing we have to do right now is stop the bombing before the Americans get into high gear. Use the new planes as you think best to accomplish this. I don't need to be involved in every operational decision like my predecessor. The new weapons we have discussed, and the strategies for their use, are to be developed and integrated into our forces as soon as possible, and the production of obsolete weapons, as determined by you and your staffs, is to be discontinued. Coordinate your plans and requirements with Reich Minister Speer."

Erwin Rommel had remained silent during this discussion, but now he spoke with the authority of a man who had led troops in both victory and defeat. "Gentlemen, all these wonderful weapons you have described are but pinpricks against the military and industrial might of the United States and the Soviets. Yes, we may score a few impressive victories with these new toys, but in the end, we will be overwhelmed by sheer numbers. We need a war-winner that will so terrify the Americans and the Soviets that they will be helpless against it. The development of such a weapon was started back in 1934 and was actually approved by Adolf Hitler."

"What is this weapon, General?" asked the chancellor.

"It's a nuclear bomb. This weapon is so powerful that one plane, dropping one bomb, can destroy a large city, or an entire army.

"Hitler funded this weapon in late 1934, about eighteen months after he became führer. He was initially excited by its possibilities and lavished significant resources on the project. Great technical progress was made, but once the war started, he lost interest because we were winning without it, and it was never mentioned again. He even assigned the project's top scientists to other work. Enough fissionable material was accumulated to make quite a few bombs, but the scientific team was broken up before they could design the weapon."

"How do you know all of this?" asked Keitel.

"One of my aides, Lieutenant Johann Rinehart, is a close friend of the project's top scientist, Professor Werner Heisenberg. They were the ones who presented the proposal to Hitler in 1934 through a letter of introduction from me. Rinehart has kept me up to date on this project ever since."

"What is the status of the project right now?" asked Stauffenberg.

"I don't know, Chancellor, but I suspect it's largely dormant. I believe it's imperative that we locate Heisenberg and have him report to us on where things are and how soon he thinks an operational weapon can be produced.

"Rinehart once told me that the nation that gets the atomic bomb first wins the war. The nation that comes in second loses. I share this belief, gentlemen. We know that the Americans, with help from the British, are working on such a weapon. Their project is called The Manhattan Project. They have been unusually secretive about what they're doing, but we do know that many of the scientists working on it were driven out of our country by Hitler's anti-Jewish policies."

"All right," said Stauffenberg. "Find this Professor Heisenberg and have him assess the situation and then report to us. I'll get you an order permitting you to extract Heisenberg and anyone else he may need from whatever work they are doing now. Do you need anything else, Rommel?"

"No, sir, I think that will be quite sufficient." *Back in the driver's seat again,* he thought.

"Now, before we leave, I have some new assignments to make. General Jodl, in addition to your duties as Chief of Staff, you are assigned the task of integrating the SS, particularly the Waffen-SS, into existing army units. I want the SS as a separate entity to disappear gradually, and the same for the Gestapo. Their reign of terror has lasted far too long. I'm placing the Gestapo under your command, General Rommel, and I want you to form them into army fighting units to be sent to the Russian front where they are to be given the most dangerous assignments, if you understand what I have in mind for them.

"And one more thing, gentlemen. I want us all to be on our best behavior tomorrow. We are taking a trip to Auschwitz."

The shock of this announcement was quite pronounced. Finally, Keitel spoke. "What are we doing this for, Chancellor?"

"General, we are going to tour this death camp and then start the process of very publicly closing it down. I've invited all the news organizations to come along with their cameras, so this will be on the front page of every newspaper in Germany the day after tomorrow and the film of our visit will be in every movie house within a few days. We have a long way to go to reverse the damage done by Hitler and his gang over the last decade, and we're going to start tomorrow.

"General Jodl, you and your staff will be responsible for dismantling this apparatus of murder. Close all the camps, return all those whom you can to their families and homes, and restore all their property to them. This will mean the removal of many powerful families from the houses they expropriated when their original Jewish owners were transported east. That's the way it has to be and there can be no exceptions. Care for those who are ill but can be restored to health, and deal mercifully with those who are too sick to leave the camps. We leave from here at 0430 tomorrow, gentlemen. Get plenty of sleep and be on time. We have a long drive and an important day ahead of us, and then a long drive back. I will address the nation the following morning. For now, you are dismissed."

The men, some of them ardent Nazis just a few hours ago, rose to their feet, saluted their new chancellor, and left in silence. They were all apparently thinking the same thing: *My God, this man has courage. If he can pull all this off, we might have a chance; if not, at least we will have given it our best effort and gone down fighting with our national honor restored. And I'll follow him to hell and back, no matter what, if that's what he wants from me.*

Berlin
November 19, 1943 1:00 p.m.
Müeller Funeral Home and Crematorium

"Here are the ashes from the last body, Herr Lieutenant. In a decorative urn, just as you ordered."

The director had been up all night with his staff personally tending to every aspect of the cremation of the eight bodies brought to him yesterday. He was tired, but maintained his military bearing as he brought this last parcel to the lieutenant.

"Thank you, Herr Director. You and your staff have done very well." He started to hand the director several one thousand reichsmark notes.

"That will not be necessary, Herr Lieutenant."

"Take it anyway, Herr Director. I insist. If not in payment for your services, then for the discretion of your staff. I'm sure you understand what I mean," said Lieutenant Rinehart, stuffing the reichsmarks into the director's handkerchief pocket.

"Thank you, Herr Lieutenant; I understand completely."

"Then I bid you a good afternoon, sir." Lieutenant Rinehart bowed slightly at the waist, turned, and exited the funeral home. He placed the urn containing the ashes of General Ludwig Beck alongside the seven boxes of ashes in the back seat of the Mercedes-Benz staff car.

About thirty minutes later, he reached his destination, a little used road just north and west of Tegel Airport on the banks of Tegel Lake. There had been an air raid the previous night, and when the sirens began to wail, Major Rinehart and the funeral home employees had dutifully gone to the shelter, which was just a few blocks away. They were about one hour into the cremation of Hermann Göering, so the timing was perfect. After the "all clear" had sounded, they returned to the funeral home and found him still cooking with about thirty minutes to go.

The big staff car had been an asset in getting through the streets of Berlin, which were now being tightly patrolled in the aftermath of the air raid. He had been waved through all the checkpoints with no questions asked.

If the guards had only known what was in the back seat, he thought. *It was Adolf Hitler taking one last ride through Berlin in his favorite car with the top down. All those people shouting "Heil Hitler!" and going crazy when he would look at them. This time, he was not riding as a conquering hero, but as dust about to be dumped into a lake.*

Johann Rinehart looked for a place to pull over. Now the staff car was a liability. If anyone saw him out here, he would have a lot of explaining to do.

He found a place to park near the water and carried the boxes of ashes to the lake one at a time. Once all the boxes were all there, he began to empty them into the water: Hitler first, then Göering, Himmler, Goebbels, Bormann, and finally the two guards. The water was clear and quiet but turned progressively grayer as the ashes were dumped.

How ignominious an end to Hitler's thousand-year Reich, he thought. *These five men had set the world on fire, a fire that might eventually consume Germany itself. Now they had been reduced to ashes by fire, and their final resting place would be known to me alone.*

The seven empty cardboard boxes that contained the ashes then had to be disposed of. Rinehart removed the can of petrol from the trunk of the Mercedes, splashed it on the boxes, and lit them off. It was all over in a few minutes, and mercifully, no one had noticed. As he scattered the ashes from the cardboard boxes, it began to rain. The same clouds which had saved Berlin from any serious damage the previous evening by obscuring the vision of the four Mosquito target-marking planes and 440 Lancaster heavy bombers, would now provide rain to cover Rinehart's return to the city. It was the cold, biting rain that Berlin gets in mid-November, the kind that drives everyone inside homes, or to coffee houses and chocolate bars.

Rinehart put the top up and drove back to the motor pool. The rain had cleared most people and traffic off the streets, and he was not stopped. After he got out of the car at the motor pool, he cleaned out the few ashes that had accumulated on the backseat; *it would never do for officials of the new government to dirty their pants with the ashes of their Nazi predecessors*, he thought.

He made his way back to his quarters without challenge, cradling the urn containing General Beck's ashes. Rinehart now realized how tired he was. It had been a long day and night. Hitler had been dead for about twenty-four hours, turning Germany and perhaps the world upside down. But right now, he didn't care. He placed the urn with General Beck's ashes in the corner of his wardrobe, covered it with dirty clothes, and was barely able to remove his uniform. He was asleep before his head hit the pillow.

Berlin
November 20, 1943 10:00 a.m.
Army bachelor officers' quarters

The next morning his friends were beating on his door. "Johann! Get up! Where have you been? Come and listen. The new chancellor is about to speak."

Johann Rinehart rubbed the sleep from his eyes and tried to clear his head. How long had he been asleep? Now he was being hustled out of bed by his comrades in the bachelor officers' quarters and dragged to the radio in the common area. This was the first time Chancellor Stauffenberg had addressed the nation. In measured tones, the radio announcer said, "This is an important message from our new Chancellor, Claus von Stauffenberg."

"People of Germany, I want to report to you on the many changes that have taken place recently in Germany and the challenges that lie before us. Two days ago, on November 18, Adolf Hitler was removed from power. He is now dead. Hermann Göering, Joseph Goebbels, Heinrich Himmler, and Martin Bormann are also dead. Their bodies have been cremated and their ashes scattered in an undisclosed location. I have replaced Hitler, not as führer, but as chancellor. The title of führer is too closely associated with him. It has now died with him, along with the Nazi salute.

"Here in Berlin, and throughout Germany, Nazi leaders have been arrested and imprisoned. This process will continue until the cancer of Nazism that has infected our beloved country is eradicated. For too long we have lived under the fear of the false ideas promulgated by this cult of evil men. Just yesterday, we saw firsthand the horrors that they have brought on Germany. We visited the Auschwitz death camp located outside of Kraków, Poland. This is but one of many such places where millions of people, mostly Germans, but including people from other countries as well, have been brought by the Nazis to be murdered.

"Who are these people? For the most part Jews, but also gypsies, mental patients, homosexuals, and anyone else the Nazis didn't like, found to be inconvenient, or not meeting their standards for so-called racial purity. They all had one thing in common: they were human beings, most of them our fellow citizens. They were all gassed to death under horrific conditions, and their bodies were cremated in ovens. Pictures of what we saw will be printed in every newspaper, and a film of our visit will be shown in movie theaters all over our country. I urge each of you to see these pictures and films so that you can understand the evils with which the Nazis have infected our nation.

"This unspeakable horror will be brought to a halt. I have asked General Jodl to supervise the closing of all the Nazi death camps, and the return of the prisoners to their families and homes. This will be a long and difficult process, but it must be done if justice and dignity are to return to Germany. As a nation, we have a lot to be accountable for, and we will start right now, no matter how painful it may be.

"Now, we are fighting a desperate war against very powerful enemies. I am very sorry to have to tell you this, but you have not been given the truth about this war. We have suffered severe setbacks in the Soviet Union at the cities of Moscow, Stalingrad, and Kursk. More than one million of our finest soldiers have been either killed or wounded, and over one hundred thousand have been taken captive.

"The Soviets are now moving relentlessly to the west. In addition, we are facing the growing strength of the British and Americans in the air and on the seas. We believe that it is still possible to achieve victory in this struggle. We are developing new and very powerful weapons that we are confident will help to turn the tide in our favor.

"The days ahead will be filled with hardship and sacrifice for all of us. I am certain if we all do our part and give our best, we will emerge victorious. Let us move forward with confidence in our vision of a new Germany, a Germany where all of us are included in the promise of justice, freedom, and peace!

God bless you, and may God bless our sacred Germany!"

Berlin
November 20, 1943 10:15 a.m.
Müeller Funeral Home and Crematorium

Hans Dieter Müeller was having a cup of coffee as he listened to the
new chancellor on the radio. After he heard him speak about the
disposition of the bodies of Adolf Hitler and the other top Nazis, he
put his coffee cup down, donned his heavy coat, and left his office.

"I won't be back for the rest of the day, Traudl."

"Yes, Herr Director." She noticed he was a little pale. "Are you
feeling well, sir?"

"I'm fine, Traudl. Just tired."

"Of course, Herr Director. The last few days have been very
difficult for all of us, but most especially for you. Go home and get
some rest. We'll take care of everything here."

"Thank you, Traudl." He paused, looked at her, and said,
"Traudl, I don't think I've ever told you how much I have valued
having you here."

"Why thank, you, Herr Director."

He turned and left before she could say anything else. *Strange,*
she thought, *after all these years. But why now?*

Müeller lived in a modest apartment off Unter den Linden,
a short distance from the funeral home. He felt very tired as he
climbed the flight of stairs. He opened the door, hung his coat in the
closet, and went into the bathroom. Although he had shaved earlier
in the morning, he shaved again to assure a close cut. He brushed
his hair with great care and splashed on a touch of cologne.

He had kept his boots and uniform from the First World War.
Now, he took his boots out of the closet and put a glossy shine on
them, just as though he and his unit were going to be inspected by
a general. He went to the large cedar chest at the foot of his bed
and removed his captain's uniform. He took pride that the uniform

still fit perfectly. His officers' sword gleamed as he attached it to his belt.

Hans Dieter Müeller was ready. He walked to the night table next to his bed, opened the drawer, and removed the Luger that he had defended himself with in the First World War. He lay down on the bed, propped himself up on the backboard with a pillow, put the barrel of the Luger in his mouth, and being very careful to aim it slightly upward, pulled the trigger.

Berlin
November 23, 1943 10:00 p.m.
Astor Cinema on Kurfürstendamm

The photographs that appeared in the special edition of *Der Spiegel* had shocked and horrified the nation. This would prove to be the beginning of the end for the Nazis.

Lieutenant Rinehart and his friends were in an apprehensive mood when they arrived at the Astor Cinema, having had a late meal at Café Kranzler with plenty to drink. They and the rest of the audience, mostly the sophisticated gentry of Berlin, had no idea what was in store for them.

The people of Berlin now got their first good look at the Auschwitz death camp. The still photos in *Der Spiegel* had been horrible enough, but viewing these same scenes in a motion picture was unbearable. The skeletal figures, more dead than alive, but still alive, leapt from the screen and seared themselves into the minds of people who just months ago had screamed, "Good-bye, Jews! Good-bye, Jews!" hoping they would be gone, but not knowing that this was the place they had sent them to with their good-byes.

Then there were the gas chambers, and finally the crematoriums where the remains of the Jews had been consigned. When these images appeared on the screen, many people in the audience started to gag and retch. There were a few who openly clapped and cheered, but they were hushed into silence by the outraged and stunned witnesses to the horror.

There were audible cheers as Camp Commandant Rudolf Höss was led away in handcuffs and silent approval as the most senior warriors of the German people stood around an open fire in a barrel tearing up their Nazi membership cards, and appropriately enough, letting them be consumed by the flames. This scene would be repeated tens of thousands of times throughout Germany over the coming months as the nation, both publicly and privately, moved as one to dissociate itself from these horrors and the Nazis who had perpetrated them.

Berlin
November 25, 1943 9:00 a.m.
The Old Reich Chancellery

"Most succinct, Professor Heisenberg. That gives us a very clear picture of where our nuclear weapons research is at the present time." Chancellor Stauffenberg leaned forward in his chair and looked intently at the professor.

"Now the crucial question, Professor. Can your team of scientists build us a deliverable bomb before the Americans build theirs?"

"Chancellor, to be able to answer that question with any degree of certainty, we would have to know where the Americans are in their work. They have been very secretive about their program, so I cannot answer your question. I do believe, however, that with the scientists we have left, we can build a weapon that is both deliverable and producible in quantity."

"You say with the scientists we have left, Professor. Just what do you mean by that?" inquired General Keitel.

"General, we started our program in 1934 with a handicap, which was Hitler's anti-Jewish policies. This cost us quite a few very brilliant people, many of whom are now working for the Americans on *their* program. Since the pause in our program in 1940, more have been lost to the gas chambers. We can finish our work with the scientists who are left, and if we have enough time and a lot of luck, we may finish first."

"Oh, come now, Professor. It can't be all that bad."

"General, let me illustrate the problem we have with a true story. David Hilbert is one of the greatest mathematicians of this century. He retired from Göttingen in 1930, but kept in touch with the university. He was very distressed by the laws passed in 1933 that forbade Jews from teaching at German universities. He was at a banquet and was seated next to the Nazi's newly appointed Minister of Education, Bernhard Rust, who asked him, 'And how is mathematics in Göttingen now that it has been freed of the Jewish influence?' 'Mathematics in Göttingen?' Hilbert replied. 'There is really none anymore.' Does that answer your question, General Keitel?"

Silence greeted Professor Heisenberg's answer. "I think we all understand, Professor," said Stauffenberg. "Now that you have had an opportunity to assess the present state of our atomic weapons program, what do you need to bring it home?"

"Chancellor, I've prepared a report on our requirements. It's quite extensive, but I believe it is doable. The main thing we need to do now is relocate all of our operations to our facility at Ohrdruf in Thuringia. It's a very lightly populated area, and it's close to the Harz Mountains where we are processing our U^{235}. We will do our research, assembly, and testing at this facility."

"Now, Professor," said Stauffenberg, "this is very important. The research and development of the bomb is to be matched step-by-step with design and manufacturing. I want the device that you test to be as close to an operational weapon as you can make it, so that five minutes after your successful test, the weapon can begin serial production. The reason is this, Professor: as isolated as your test site is, an explosion this big will be noticed. Someone on the other side will figure out that we have detonated an atomic device. I don't want them to think there is a lot of time left to perfect their own weapon and use it on us before we use ours on them. They might try something that we don't expect and are not prepared for.

"And one more thing. I'm assigning Lieutenant Rinehart to be liaison between your staff and Speer. I'm going to promote him to staff captain so he will have the authority necessary to get his work done. Anything you need, you will get."

"I understand Chancellor, and thank you. Now, if you will excuse me, I have a lot of work to do. But … one last thing. I would suggest that we relocate all the people around our test site for about fifty kilometers in all directions. The fewer prying eyes, the better."

"Thank you, Professor. We'll get right on that."

Stauffenberg turned to his generals and admirals. "Gentlemen, we have another problem before us that we must start to work on right away, and that is how to deliver our atomic weapon to the United States in such a way that it will scare them out of the war. We have to get across the Atlantic Ocean undetected and with enough deliverable force to make it clear to them that unless they accept our terms, we will destroy their East Coast military bases and population centers.

"Air Marshal Galland, I want you and Admiral Raeder to assign your very best people to this mission. Take a close look at what we have now and what we realistically might have in the immediate future. Work quickly and thoroughly and get back to us in a couple of months, if not sooner. I think that's all, gentlemen."

He had been putting this next business off too long. "Heidi," he said into the intercom, "find Lieutenant Rinehart and have him report to me. Thank you."

Ten minutes later, Lieutenant Johann Rinehart reported to the chancellor. He didn't even have a chance to make the snappy salute he had been practicing before Stauffenberg put him at ease.

"Lieutenant, I am stealing you from Field Marshal Rommel and promoting you to staff captain, effective immediately. You have earned the rank, and you will need the authority that goes with it for your next assignment. You will be our liaison with Professor Heisenberg and his scientists. They are moving their base of operations to Ohrdruf in Thuringia. This is where they will do their research and assembly of atomic weapons, and I want you there to keep us informed of their progress and to make sure that they have everything they need.

"Johann, this atomic project is the only chance we have to stop the Soviets. If it fails, we're doomed, so it's got to work. They are to have top priority for everything—equipment, special metals, laborers—whatever they need. Work with Speer on this, and if you run into any resistance, move them out of the way by any means possible. Understand?"

"I understand, Chancellor. Your meaning is perfectly clear. But there may be some problems with shifting priorities that you need to know about.

"What kind of problems?"

"Hitler was very impressed with the V-2 rocket program, sir, and he gave it top priority, particularly in the allocation of strategic materials such as chromium. Von Braun and Dornberger are going to be more than a little upset when you tell them that their supplies will be diverted to the atomic weapons program."

"I see," said the Chancellor, "and thanks for the warning. I'll call General Dornberger myself and give him the bad news that I'm cutting off his access to strategic materials and transferring whatever he may have stockpiled to Heisenberg at Ohrdruf. From what I've heard about him, he's a good soldier, so he'll understand that it's Heisenberg's atomic bomb that will win the war, not his rocket.

Now there's one other thing I want to talk with you about." The Chancellor moved his chair closer to Rinehart and then spoke to him in a very quiet voice.

"Johann, that day you disposed of the bodies, you had them cremated and then you scattered their ashes in a place known only to yourself. That was an extraordinary thing you did, and the others and I will never forget your act of bravery in assuming this burden. But tell me this, what happened to the ashes of General Beck? Did you dispose of them as well?"

"No, Chancellor, I still have them. They are in an urn hidden in my closet. I was hoping that at some future date there might be a more appropriate resolution of his particular situation."

"I see. I'm glad you kept them, Captain. The problem is that Beck had no family, so there's no one to give the ashes to. Any ideas?"

"Chancellor, someday this war will come to an end, and if we are on the winning side, we will be the ones who will build the memorials. Of course, there will be the big memorials to the soldiers, sailors, and pilots who died, but I was thinking that there should also be a memorial to those who died on November 18. This might be a fitting place for General Beck's ashes."

"Excellent idea, Captain. It's not widely known, but we had quite a few casualties that day, in addition to Beck. A number of Waffen-SS units in the larger cities resisted the change, and we paid heavily for this. Altogether, out of the two hundred or so of us, we lost forty-five. Pretty high casualty rate, and they all deserve to be honored."

"My God! I had no idea so many of us perished!"

Both men remained silent for a moment.

"What should I do with General Beck's ashes, sir?"

"Bring them to my office, Captain. I want them as a reminder to myself and to those who visit me that this was the price paid for what we have done for our nation. And I like your idea about a memorial for them. I'll ask Speer to look into this when he has some spare time."

"I think we'll all be a little short on that for the foreseeable future, Chancellor. I'll bring the general's ashes over sometime when I'm sure you're in your office so I can put the urn into your hands. But … I'd like to ask you something personal, if I may."

"What's that, Johann?"

"What was it like for you at Auschwitz?"

Stauffenberg got up and closed the door to his office. When he returned to his desk, he leaned back in his chair and considered his answer before responding. He had been troubled since the visit to the death camp. *Now is as good a time as any to begin to talk about this. Rinehart is a friend whom I can trust to be discreet.*

"Johann, it was the most overwhelming experience I have ever had. We know how horrible combat is, but this was worse, much worse, and on so many different levels."

"How's that, sir?"

"It was a total assault on all of my senses, Johann. We've both seen and smelled death on the battlefield. At Auschwitz, there was the same smell, but it was more intense because these people were still alive! In combat, men are mostly killed by the random bullet or artillery shell; at Auschwitz, death was calculated and deliberate. And that made it so much worse to experience than on a battlefield.

"I shall never forget the woman who put her arms around me and thanked me. She said that although she knew she would not leave this camp alive, she would now die free. Johann, I could feel her bones, and I could smell the death that came from her. But she was still alive, if you could call it that. And there were thousands like her at Auschwitz."

"The Nazis have a lot to answer for, sir."

"Not just the Nazis, Johann; all of us. We are all responsible. No one can hide from this atrocity, and no one can say he or she didn't know what was happening to these people. We should have made it our business to find out, Johann, but we didn't. We didn't want to know because they were Jews.

"Even if we win this war, we won't be able to call ourselves truly victorious until we examine ourselves and discover what there is about us that permitted this horror to happen. Is it something about the German character, or is it a more general human condition? I don't know, but we will have to find out.

"The Nazis certainly have a lot to answer for, and they will be held accountable. Those who deserve to be punished will be, but a much deeper inquiry is called for. This is one that I hope will lead to reconciliation with those whom we have harmed, and if possible, their forgiveness. This might not happen within our lifetime, Johann, but we have to start. I don't know how we will go about this, or when we can begin, but I know it has to be done if we are to regain our self-respect, regardless of how the war turns out.

"For now, I want what I have said to stay with you. I may need your services in the future to turn this into a reality, but for the present, keep this to yourself."

"I understand, Chancellor."

Rinehart stood, saluted his commander-in-chief, and exited the room, filled with awe and respect for the man who now held the fate of Germany in his hands.

Berlin
February 8, 1944 9:00 a.m.
The Old Reich Chancellery

Admiral Raeder and Air Marshal Galland smartly saluted Chancellor Stauffenberg and sat down at the conference table. General Jodl and Albert Speer were also present.

"So, what do you have for us, gentlemen?" asked Chancellor Stauffenberg.

Admiral Raeder began. "Chancellor, we made a thorough examination of the problem you gave us in reaching the East Coast of the United States with nuclear weapons. Our options are limited. We do not have a long-range bomber of sufficient performance to reach the intended targets, and Hitler was never interested in aircraft carriers."

He unfolded a large drawing on the table. "So, this is what we came up with. This is a Type 14 submarine supply boat; we call it the 'milk cow.' We propose modifying it to carry six V-l flying bombs that can be launched against targets on the American East Coast. Each missile will carry a payload of slightly over one metric tonne. We believe that two missiles could be launched within the space of thirty minutes to one hour. Furthermore, we believe that this approach is preferable to using long-range bombers because of the time it would take for a force of bombers to make a second strike."

"Very interesting, Admiral, and I concur in your evaluation of the effectiveness of a submarine-launched missile versus a bomber attack. The submarine could remain on station with several missiles and these could be launched very quickly if required. This would have a devastating impact on the Americans. But what about accuracy? Can the boat make it to a predetermined launching point and then have the missile fly to its destination and detonate close enough to destroy the target?"

"Yes, Chancellor, we are confident that this can be done. We have made significant progress in the development of accelerometers and gyros, and we believe that we will be able to put the missile on the target with a 50 percent chance of a hit within three kilometers. The missile will fly to the target and then intersect a beam that will shut off its fuel, causing it to pitch over and dive to its target. This beam will be generated by another submarine."

"Very well, the plan for the use of the submarine-launched

missile is approved. Two more things, gentlemen. First, do you think the Allies are reading our communications?"

The chancellor's remark came as a complete surprise to the men.

"Well, I suppose it's possible, sir," said the admiral. "We've always assumed that our Enigma system was safe, and—"

Stauffenberg interrupted. "Forgive me, Admiral, but that's the problem: underestimating the enemy. A classic mistake. We should never assume we are dealing with people who are not just as intelligent as we are. I want you to work with General Jodl and Admiral Canaris on two things. The first is a short-range fix for the problem. Something like adding two more wheels to the Enigma machine and scrambling things on the inside a bit more to make it harder for the other side to decipher what we send. The assumption I am making is that they have broken our codes and are reading our communications as quickly as we are.

"Improving the Enigma system is only a temporary fix, because if they understand the basic principles of its operation, they will eventually get through the two new wheels we add to the machine. This is the reason for the second order, which is to come up with an entirely new system of sending and receiving coded messages, perhaps one that is not so dependent on a mechanical system like Enigma. Is everything clear?"

Both men stood and saluted. Air Marshal Galland then asked, "Sir, if I may; what progress is being made on the atomic weapons program?"

"As of now, Air Marshal, Professor Heisenberg is moving the entire operation to Ohrdruf. This is where the research and development of these weapons will take place from now on. Assembly will take place in the Harz Mountains where the U^{235} is being produced. When this will be completed, however, I cannot say."

"Thank you, sir," replied the air marshal.

"I assure you," said the chancellor, "that you will be the first to know."

Chapter 4

Atomic Cheese at Ohrdruf

Berlin
July 19, 1946 2:30 a.m.
Spandau Prison

"We didn't get anything like that in our newspapers; just the basic story that Hitler and his gang had been killed and replaced by Stauffenberg. But everyone believed he was just another ruthless Nazi who decided to take over Germany by killing Hitler."

"That's about right, Dr. Oppenheimer," replied Rinehart. "We were all painted with the same brush. Anyone in charge of Germany was automatically a Nazi, and so was everyone else in Germany. Those pictures of Hitler driving through the streets of Berlin with the swastikas flying and the crowds screaming 'Heil Hitler' were burned into everyone's minds.

"But things did begin to change. After Stauffenberg and his staff visited Auschwitz, arrested the camp's commandant, and denounced what the Nazis had done, just about everybody tore up their Nazi party membership cards and started burning Nazi flags. Sure, there were some fanatical holdouts, but in the end, they couldn't resist the great mass of people who were so ashamed of what they had seen. Support for the Nazis among the general population evaporated with the death of Hitler and the others. We were quite surprised at how quickly it happened.

"And things were beginning to turn around for us in the air and at sea, Dr. Oppenheimer. We were able to stop the bombing by the Americans and British by mid-1944 through superior weaponry and tactics. When we introduced our interceptor version of the Arado in strength, it had an immediate impact. In March 1944, both the Eighth Air Force and Bomber Command attacked Wilhelmshaven, and we were ready for them. Over the next few days, we shot down over 65 percent of their bombers. We knew they would get better at defending themselves, and they did, but we still maintained a kill rate of between 35 and 40 percent per raid, which meant that the life expectancy of a bomber crew was less than two weeks. The Eighth Air Force and Bomber Command tried to cover this up, but the *Manchester Guardian* broke the story, and the public outcry was so great in both England and the United States that the bombing campaign had to be 'temporarily halted for a review of operational tactics,' or something like that. Anyway, the final result was an end of the heavy bombing campaign.

"This didn't end the bombing completely. The Brits had one weapon that we never completely defeated, and this was the de Havilland Mosquito. This was a very fast fighter-bomber made almost completely out of wood, which made it largely invisible to radar. We tried everything short of burning down all the forests in England, and nothing worked. We bombed their Merlin engine plants at Derby, Crewe and Glasgow, only to find out that they were using engines cannibalized from Spitfires and Lancasters. And because they were made out of wood, every carpenter and cabinet maker in England was involved in making parts for the plane. These parts would be picked up at night and taken to camouflaged assembly points, put together and mated with their engines, and they'd be flying against us the next day. We destroyed all of England's petrol reserves and refineries, and sank all the tankers coming from the United States, and still the Brits got it up in the air. This plane continued to harass us until the day Churchill capitulated.

"With the end of the heavy bombing, we were able to get our Type 21 submarines out to sea. Raeder and Dönitz came up with a plan to deploy thirty of these boats into the Atlantic all at once, while keeping another thirty in reserve, so when the first group used up all their torpedoes, the second group would be ready to take their place. This had an immediate effect, and by mid-1944, the lifelines from the United States to England and the Soviet Union had been almost completely severed, and the Royal Navy and the United States Navy had been chased back to Scapa Flow and Norfolk. We then …

Oppenheimer interrupted. "Forgive me if I appear to be impatient, Colonel, but I'm a little short on time. Professor, Can you please tell me about the bomb?"

"Well, Dr. Oppenheimer, no one has heard this before, but it went this way …"

Near Ohrdruf, Thuringia
October 14, 1944 2:00 p.m.
German Nuclear Research Center

Discussion on the design of the nuclear bomb had been going on for several weeks and still no progress had been made. Professor Heisenberg was beginning to feel that he and his team, now greatly diminished by Hitler's death machine, would soon reach the limit of their abilities. This was most upsetting to him.

So close, he thought. *Someone once told me that nuclear physics was like any other complicated endeavor: the first 90 percent of the work takes 90 percent of the time, and the remaining 10 percent of the work takes 90 percent of the time. Now I understand the truth in this.*

"Excuse me, Professor Heisenberg." It was his friend Rinehart, now recently promoted to major, who had asked to be allowed to sit in on the discussion.

"Yes, Major. What is it?" Heisenberg immediately felt ashamed of the exasperated tone he had used on his friend of so many years.

"Professor, from what I have heard, it seems to me that the assumption is being made that the two pieces of fissionable material that are brought together to create a reaction have to be of the same size and shape. Is this true?"

"Yes, Major. We have always made that assumption." He was beginning to take more interest now. *My friend might have a strictly military background, but he was no fool.*

"But what if two masses of fissionable material of different size and shape could be brought together to create a reaction? Has this been investigated?"

"No, Major. We've always assumed that it had to be two masses of equal size and shape."

"I see. Professor, is it *possible* that two masses of *dissimilar* size and shape could produce a reaction?" He was pressing his friend hard now, and he knew it.

Professor Heisenberg hesitated. He clearly didn't know the answer to this question, but he was afraid to admit it. He knew what had happened to scientists, or anyone else for that matter, who didn't have the right answer.

Major Rinehart put him at ease. "Professor, it's all right to say you don't know. Under the previous regime, this might have been fatal, but not now. We all understand that this is a new and emerging field of study, and that there are a lot of things that have yet to be discovered."

The silence was so heavy everyone could feel it. A new threshold in German science was about to be crossed—or not.

"All right, Major, we don't know." Heisenberg looked at his friend, saw him nod in understanding, and immediately perceived that his answer had been accepted for what it was—a frank and honest admission that this was an unknown and no one would lose their head because of it.

"Thank you, Professor. Now if you will excuse me, I have other business to attend to."

"Of course, Major."

It had been a long and frustrating day, and Heisenberg was tired. Major Rinehart had departed very purposefully as though something was up. Heisenberg wondered what it was.

He didn't think too much about it, because he was looking forward to the evening's entertainment. A tradition had been created at the camp that Saturday night was a time to put everything concerned with nuclear physics aside and raise hell. Heisenberg was all for this. Everyone would gather at the dining facility and somehow a large keg of excellent beer and mounds of sausage would make an appearance. There would be a lot of singing, especially the dirty songs that the men had learned from their university days.

Then there would be the not-so-serious entertainment. Short skits on various subjects, usually made up on the spot, were performed to thunderous applause, especially when lines were forgotten or bungled due to severe drunkenness.

Heisenberg, to his own surprise, had joined in, performing a very fine impression of Adolf Hitler; one he had gained from personal experience. He would slick down his hair, put on a fake mustache, and strut around the stage screaming at no one in particular and Nazi-saluting anyone who would Nazi-salute him back in the most exaggerated manner possible. Heisenberg always broke up when this happened, and the entire room would collapse in laughter. The last couple of Saturdays, Major Rinehart had joined him on stage doing the most hysterical and accurate impression of Himmler he had ever seen. To see an officer of the general staff doing this never ceased to amaze him. Heisenberg wondered if Rinehart would be there tonight. He had left the meeting under such mysterious circumstances.

Heisenberg was more than a little irked when a courier brought him a message from Reinhart to visit him in his quarters.

"Most urgent. You will not be disappointed," the message read. *Very well. But what could be "most urgent" on a Saturday night?* Heisenberg made the short trip to the major's quarters with mixed feelings. His knock on the door was immediately answered by a smiling Major Rinehart.

"Come in, Werner, this won't take long, and then we can go to the Saturday night festivities. Please, sit down. I found an excellent Gewürztraminer and some specially aged Edam cheese at Ohrdruf. Had to spend a lot of money on this, and I didn't buy it at a regular store, either."

"You invited me here for wine and cheese, Johann?" That slightly exasperated tone he had used on his old friend earlier in the day emerged again, and again he instantly regretted it.

Rinehart ignored this and continued. "Yes, Werner, but this is a special kind of cheese." He carried a tray of wine and cheese from the kitchen. The tray held the bottle of wine, two glasses, and two items covered with towels.

Very curious, thought Heisenberg.

"This," Rinehart said with mock seriousness, "is atomic cheese."

"Atomic cheese?"

"Yes, atomic cheese." Rinehart removed the two towels. Heisenberg saw that one of the pieces of cheese was a large, round ball of Edam from which a cone-shaped piece had been cut. The other piece of cheese was cone shaped.

"And now, Professor," continued Rinehart, "please give me your very best nuclear physicist opinion. What would happen if this piece of atomic cheese," he held up the cone-shaped piece, "was rammed into this piece of atomic cheese," he slammed the cone-shaped piece of cheese into the space left in the ball of Edam, "with great force?"

Heisenberg understood immediately. He was amazed that the solution was so simple. He was also slightly humiliated, not only because he and the rest of his highly educated team had not come up with this idea, but because an army officer, with no background in nuclear physics, had.

"I think," Heisenberg said, pausing for dramatic effect. "I think there would be a very, very big explosion."

"You think so, Werner?"

"Yes, Johann, I think so. Goddamn right, I think so." He was surprised at his use of profanity, because he had rarely sworn in his life. But now it seemed quite appropriate.

Heisenberg took a deep breath and let it out audibly. "Johann, I think I will have that glass of Gewürztraminer you offered me earlier."

"My pleasure, Werner." Rinehart poured them each a glass. "What shall we drink to, Werner?"

"I'm not sure, old friend. We both know what this means."

"Yes. Having the nuclear bomb might very well win the war for us, but at a terrible cost. Suppose we drink to 'uncertainty' and leave it at that."

"To 'uncertainty,' then. Now, I think we should go to our Saturday night festivities. We're going to start work on this tomorrow morning, and I want everyone to be reasonably sober."

The party was in full swing when the professor and the major arrived. Great applause greeted the two men. The crowd anticipated another fine evening with character actors Adolf Hitler and Heinrich Himmler to entertain them, but instead, a very serious Professor Heisenberg addressed his men.

"Gentlemen, I'm afraid that this evening has to come to an end."

The expected groans accompanied the occasional, "Now what?" and "Oh shit."

"Believe me, I wouldn't be doing this unless something extraordinary has happened, but this is exactly the case; something extraordinary *has* happened."

Now he was dead serious. "Go home, gentlemen, and get plenty of sleep. It's the last you're likely to get for quite awhile. Be at the lab at seven o'clock sharp tomorrow morning, reasonably sober and prepared to work like hell until we finish. We have a new direction, it's quite exciting, and the major and I will show it to you tomorrow. Now, good night!"

There was no grumbling among the men now. They had all sensed their leader's enthusiasm. Something was up, and now at last, they would have a chance of pushing this across the finish line.

Near Ohrdruf, Thuringia
October 15, 1944 7:00 a.m.
German Nuclear Research Center

Professor Heisenberg and Major Rinehart were waiting for the men as they came into the lab. Everyone was on time; there were no stragglers. Some looked better than others, but they were all alert and full of anticipation.

"Gentlemen, behold atomic cheese." Heisenberg told the astonished group the story of the previous evening and concluded with his strong belief that this was the direction in which they must go to achieve success.

Then he added, "Major Rinehart and I have known each other since we were children in Würzburg. Our careers obviously took different paths, but we have always stayed in touch, and our friendship has never ceased.

"I was greatly pleased when he was assigned to be our liaison with the general staff, but I was also suspicious, because I knew from experience what this usually means: lots of meddling and too much political infighting. I should have known better. Major Rinehart has always managed to get us what we need, he has never interfered with our work, and for this, we can all be extremely grateful. Now we have this breakthrough, which was entirely his idea. We can claim no credit for it, even though history will probably never know about atomic cheese, or believe anyone who would come up with such a fantastic story."

Laughter and applause greeted the professor's comments, along with lots of handshakes and backslapping. Major Rinehart appeared thoroughly embarrassed, but he took the congratulations in stride.

"Now, gentlemen," the professor continued, "you see the work that is before us. We have to turn these two pieces of cheese into a workable *and* mass-producible weapon. This weapon will be in two forms. The first is a free-falling gravity bomb to be dropped from our newest high-speed jet bomber. We know the capabilities of this plane and the size of its bomb bay, so our weapon must be configured accordingly. And it must be made so safe that it can be handled like an ordinary bomb and survive the vibrations of a rough ride in an airplane.

"This is going to be difficult, but it is nothing compared to the second weapon, which is a missile that will be launched from the deck of a submarine. Our nuclear weapon will have to be able to fit inside the missile, weigh no more than one metric tonne, and be able to survive in several most inhospitable environments. Like the gravity bomb, it will first be transported by rail, not to an airport, but rather to a seaport, where it will be loaded on board a submarine.

"At the time of its launch, it will be moved to a hydraulic lift, where it will be raised to the deck of the submarine, and pushed onto a launching ramp. From there, it will be accelerated to flight speed using rocket boosters to move it down the launching ramp and into the air. Then it must survive the flight to its target, where the missile will pitch over and discard its wings. The missile will dive vertically toward the target, and at a height of approximately 600 meters an altimeter will detonate the warhead. In both cases, the design will have to be rugged enough to survive some rough handling by both men and equipment. It must be absolutely safe so it doesn't explode while it is being handled, and it must be reliable so that it does explode when we want it to."

The professor continued, now addressing the machinists. "Up until now, your role has been one of waiting and watching. Your wait is over. You are now equal partners in our joint venture. We have been instructed by our high command to produce a weapon that can be started in production as soon as, and I'm quoting here from Chancellor Stauffenberg himself, 'five minutes after the first successful test.' This means you are to work very closely with our scientists in the design of the weapon. We don't want to test merely an atomic *device*; we want to test an atomic *weapon*."

Then the professor addressed the entire group. "You all know what your areas of concentration are; we've been over them plenty of times. We know that only a few kilos of U^{235} will be needed to produce an explosion of about 13.6 metric kilotonnes of explosive power, so size your fissionable components accordingly. It is probable that most of the weight of your device will be consumed by lead shielding, but there has to be sufficient capacity left for detonation components. Get busy with your calculations based on the rough outline of two dissimilar masses of fissionable material—one a globe with a cone-shaped piece missing, and the other the cone-shaped piece. We have to figure out the best way to accelerate the cone-shaped piece into the sphere, and direct this acceleration so the cone-shaped piece lands precisely in the center of the globe. We know from our experiments that two masses of U^{235} don't start to react with each other until they are about 2.5 millimeters apart. However, there's no margin for error here. The slightest deviation would result in an atomic fizzle instead of an atomic explosion, and we don't want that. Now, let's get to work on this.

"We are so indebted to you, Johann," said the professor. "So is all of Germany, if I may say so. But now I'm embarrassing you, so let me stop there."

"Thank you, my friend," returned the major. "I really appreciate everything you have said and for knowing when to stop. Now I have some work to do. I'm going to get you a couple of Arado 234C-2s, one of the new models with four engines. This will be the plane that will drop the bombs. I'll also get you a V-1 warhead to play with. We have to make sure that everything fits and that it all works. There's plenty of work to do inside the Arado. We may have to squeeze in another crewmember to handle the bomb. He'll have to remove the safeties, so remember to include them in the design so no one blows himself and everything around him to hell. And be sure to give us a foolproof firing mechanism that we can test without setting off the bomb. That's very important. So good-bye for now, good luck, and be damn careful, Werner."

"Thank you for your concern, old friend. Let me assure you that I have no intention of making my wife a widow and my children orphans. Besides, this is too damn exciting. I want to be around to see what happens next!"

Near Ohrdruf, Thuringia
January 14, 1945 9:00 a.m.
German Nuclear Research Center

"Sorry it took so long, Werner. The Luftwaffe was reluctant to part with two of its newest jet planes, and work on the V-1 was just wrapping up. But here they are, along with the crews needed to ensure the proper fit."

"Very good, Johann. Your timing is perfect. Now, I have something to show you."

They went to the lab where Heisenberg unfolded a set of drawings. "Your atomic cheese scheme was very elegant, but unfortunately, it didn't work. We made mock-ups of your sphere and cone with steel as a substitute for uranium, surrounded them with lead shielding, and then connected them with a tube, also made of lead shielding. For a detonator, we used C-4, which is quite powerful. The problems started when we put this assembly on a vibration machine. It disintegrated when we cranked it up to what we could expect from a ride in a bomber and from a submarine launch. It just fell apart. The cone didn't enter the sphere evenly, and this would cause a fizzle instead of an explosion. Also, our manufacturing people told us that this design would be very difficult to mass-produce.

"In the new design, we still use the gun barrel method, with a tube separating the two fissionable elements, but there the similarity with your design ends. The moving portion, which we call the bullet, is in the form of a cylinder of U^{235}. It's moved down the tube by a charge of C-4 to a mass of U^{235} in the shape of a larger cylinder with a hole in its base that's the exact shape and size of the bullet. We call this larger mass the tamper. When the bullet enters the tamper, the reaction occurs, and *bang*. Much more rugged and much more producible than the sphere and cone idea you had. Our manufacturing people tell us that with this new design, each of our four assembly lines working around the clock should be able to produce four devices per day. That's sixteen nuclear weapons a day, Johann. They've been making trial runs with steel using this design for several days now, so when it comes time for them to work with U^{235}, they'll be ready to go, and within five minutes, as the chancellor instructed."

Professor Heisenberg put his hand on his friend's shoulder. "Sorry about your atomic cheese design, Johann; it just didn't work out. But it was your breakthrough with dissimilar sizes that gave us the basic idea for the design that we're using now."

Near Ohrdruf, Thuringia
June 15, 1945 2:00 a.m.
German Nuclear Research Center

Professor Heisenberg had finally chosen a name for the test site: Loki, for the Norse God of Fire. Someone said that Loki is also the God of Trickery, and the professor had said, "Yes, and if this doesn't work, we will be the ones who get tricked."

The professor was at Loki now, hooking the bomb up to the controls that would be operated from the bunker from which he and the scientists would set it off and watch the results. There would be other important people at the site as well; the chancellor had arrived the previous evening, along with Generals Keitel, Jodl, and Rommel; Admirals Dönitz and Raeder; Air Marshal Galland and Albert Speer. Rinehart had called the chancellor right after the date and time of the test had been determined.

"The goose is ready to lay its egg, Chancellor," said Major Rinehart. This was the code name they had agreed to use when talking about the bomb.

"When will this happen?"

"Next Thursday at 0500. Will you be here?"

"Yes, Major, I will be there. I'm going to bring along the usual crew."

"Very good, sir. We'll look forward to seeing you."

And that was it. Everything came down to what would happen just a few hours from now. The last five months had been a whirlwind of activity leading to this moment. Fifty dummy bombs had been produced in four days, giving the production crew much needed experience in handing the equipment that would be used to make the real thing. Half of the dummy bombs had gone to Peenemünde where they were installed in the V-1 missiles and launched off an exact replica of the deck of the submarine that would be used in the attacks on the United States.

All of the missile tests had been successful. The new submarines from which the missiles would be launched had completed their sea trials with only a few problems, all of which were easily corrected. They were now at Wilhelmshaven awaiting their deadly cargo.

From the outside, the missile launching-submarine maintained the ungainly appearance of the Type 14 supply boat on which it was based. The major changes that transformed this submersible truck into a deadly instrument of war were on the inside. The cargo hold directly under the deck was reconfigured into a storage area for six V-1 missiles with their atomic warheads. Each missile was mounted on a wheeled launching sled which made it easy to move from the storage area to the elevator which took it to the launching ramp. All the remaining space in the boat not required for the crew, the command and control center, the diesel engine and its fuel, and the space required for buoyancy, was crammed with the same powerful motor and batteries used in the Type 21 submarine. This increased the boat's submerged speed from a sluggish six knots to a more respectable fifteen knots. This was done at the insistence of the missile sub captains who wanted a fighting chance against the American air-dropped acoustic torpedo, which had already claimed a number of Type 21s.

This new menace, as advanced as it was, had two major weak points: a top speed of only twelve knots, and range of less than four kilometers. A missile sub with a three-knot speed advantage could avoid destruction if it remained in front of this torpedo for only ten minutes, after which it would run out of fuel.

Maintaining the threat of instant annihilation was an important part of the high command's overall strategy. Accordingly, they gave these submarines every survival capability available so they could remain on station even in the most hostile environment.

The Arado 234C-2s that Major Rinehart had requisitioned from the Luftwaffe had also been quite busy. The dummy warheads had been fitted inside standard bomb casings that were compatible with the plane's bomb bay. The addition of three safety releases in the cockpit had been no problem at all, and it was concluded that it was not necessary to place a third crewmember in the already crowded cockpit.

After a number of trials, it was calculated that the optimum bombing height would be 9,855 meters. This would give the bomb forty-three seconds to reach an altitude of 580 meters, where it would be detonated. The Arado would have plenty of time to execute a 180-degree turn and escape the shock wave from the blast. Three squadrons of the new planes were being formed for making the atomic bomb attacks.

The test range had been thoroughly instrumented so that the effects of the bomb could be accurately recorded. Remotely controlled, high-speed cameras were installed at distances ranging from two hundred meters to thirty kilometers away from ground zero. All kinds of structures and electronic equipment, ranging from ordinary radio and television sets to the most sophisticated radars and radar-jammers were placed at various distances around the test site. Every conceivable piece of military hardware, including planes, tanks, and armored personnel carriers, was scattered around the site. Then there were the animals. Their lives would be sacrificed so that the effects of the blast and radiation could be measured and then translated into what would happen to human beings.

The time was getting close, about one hour to go. Heisenberg and his crew had finished installing the bomb in its one hundred meter tower at Loki and connecting it to the control cables that would remove the safeties and detonate the device. In a few minutes, the order to clear the test range would be given, and everyone responsible for the equipment and the animals around Loki would have to seek shelter in one of the reinforced-concrete bunkers located in the control area.

The nuclear bomb assembly teams in the Harz Mountains were also put on alert, because right after the test, they would be instructed to begin mass production of the atomic weapons, a process that had already started. Professor Heisenberg was so confident that the test would be successful that he had ordered the assembly crews to have the first weapons almost completed, so that upon hearing the announcement of the test's success, it would be a just a matter of tightening the last screws, so to speak, to finish the first batch of atomic weapons.

The chancellor and his party had arrived. Thirty minutes to go.

"Good morning, gentlemen," said Professor Heisenberg. "Please be seated. Before we begin this morning's events, you will need to know a few things for your own protection. When the bomb is detonated, there will be a very bright light. Anyone who looks directly at this light will be permanently blinded. For this reason, you have been given a dark glass shield to hold in front of your eyes. When the instruction 'shields up' is given, please place this shield in front of your eyes and leave it there until the bright light has passed. You may then lower your shield to witness the rest of the test. The next phase—"

"Professor Heisenberg, please excuse this interruption." It was the chancellor. "I am very disappointed with the way I have been treated this morning."

"H-H-How's that, s-s-sir," Heisenberg asked, quite surprised and visibly shaken.

The chancellor was turning his shield over and over in his hands. "I have been issued this very large and cumbersome shield, when I only need something half this size. Could you not have been more considerate of my ... shall we say ... special needs?"

Everyone understood the huge, self-deprecating joke the chancellor was making, but there was very little laughter.

"Well, sir," Heisenberg recovered, "the next time you attend a test, we will make sure your shield is cut to proper size."

"Thank you, Professor," replied the chancellor with exaggerated seriousness. "Carry on."

"Thank you, sir."

The tension had been broken and Professor Heisenberg continued. "The next phase of the explosion will be a large cloud of gas and dust rising from the test site followed by a shock wave that will probably be felt here. It would be best if we all remain in this shelter until the shock wave has passed."

It was close now. Horns and sirens sounded to warn everyone to get to a shelter. The scientists and VIPS got to their feet and assumed their positions at the viewing ports. No one left his eye shield behind.

"Five minutes. Remove the first safety." The television cameras monitoring the bomb showed the first safety, which would stop the bullet from reaching the tamper in case of an accidental detonation, being removed. The equipment on the test range was powered up.

"Four minutes. Remove the second safety." The second safety was a backup in case an accidental detonation shot the bullet past the first safety. The second safety was removed.

"Three minutes. Remove the third safety." The third safety kept the detonation circuit open. With its removal, the detonation circuit was now closed and ready for testing.

"Two minutes. Test detonation circuit." The officer at the control board switched the detonation circuit knob to TEST and pushed the detonation button. The green light below the detonation switch flashed.

"Detonation circuit tested and ready, sir."

"Turn detonation switch to DETONATE."

"Detonation switch to DETONATE, sir." The next time the detonation button was pushed, the world would change.

"One minute to detonation and counting."

"… fifty."

"Johann, I need some assistance. You've had so much to do with making this moment possible. Would you honor me by helping me push the button?"

"… thirty."

"Of course, Werner. But—" Their eyes locked. "But there is one other person who has made this moment possible, but it is he whose name cannot be mentioned."

"Yes, Johann."

"… ten seconds. Start all high-speed cameras and data recorders. Shields up, gentlemen."

"… five."

"… four."

"… three."

"… two."

"… one."

"… *DETONATE!*"

Werner and Johann, their eyes still locked, pushed the button. For an instant, a heart-stopping nothing. Then the whole room filled with the whitest, most intense light the world had ever seen.

There was a collective gasp in the bunker, and the light subsided after only two seconds. Everyone forgot about the professor's warning, put down their eye shields, and rushed out of the bunker to witness the blast.

Even at a distance of fifty kilometers, the sight was overpowering. The roiling, boiling, rising fireball was a morass of colors—gold, red, green, purple, violet, blue—every color imaginable, each at its most intense. It illuminated every peak and crevasse of the Harz Mountains and created a mushroom cloud of immense height. Forty seconds later, the roar and shock wave from the blast reached the men at the bunker. It was louder than anything they had experienced on the battlefield and several of them had difficulty keeping their balance.

The entire group was shocked and stunned in disbelief at what they had just seen. They stared in silence and awe as the cloud continued to rise. Finally Air Marshal Galland spoke. "You did it! You crazy bastards really made this goddamn thing work."

Yes, we did, thought Johann. *We made this goddamn thing work. Now we'll win the war, but at the cost of our souls.* He was still numb when he realized that people were shaking his hand and slapping him on the back. Grown men were crying, and even the chancellor was smiling.

"Well," said Stauffenberg, his composure completely restored. "Congratulations, Major. When can we get this into production?"

"Right now, Chancellor," mumbled Major Rinehart, struggling to recover himself. "Right now." He went inside the bunker and picked up a telephone.

"Production. Metz here."

"This is Rinehart. Our test was successful, Heinrich. Start the assembly lines."

"Yes, Major. We saw it. We heard the roar, and we felt the shock wave from here."

"Even at that distance? My God!"

"Yes. Some of us went outside to watch. It was quite spectacular. We'll win the war now, won't we?"

"Yes, Heinrich, we'll win the war."

"We will start production right now, Major. As you ordered, the first eleven devices will be for the V-1 and the next twenty will be gravity bombs. The V-1 devices should be ready for shipment by tomorrow afternoon and the remaining weapons will follow a couple of days later. Will this be satisfactory?"

"Yes, Heinrich. That will be most satisfactory." He was barely whispering now. *Most satisfactory, indeed. It has started. This terrible thing that I have helped create is now going to be produced on an assembly line just like so much sausage, and then used to bomb nations into submission. But if we hadn't done this first, the Americans and British would have won the race, and they would have shown no reluctance to use it on us. But, my God … my God … what have I helped to let loose?*

The cloud from the nuclear explosion was beginning to lose its mushroom shape. Werner and Johann had retreated to a quiet corner of the bunker to reflect on what they had just seen. Their conversation was interrupted by Chancellor Stauffenberg, who paused for a long time before quietly asking, "how did you do it?"

Werner and Johann looked at each other, and both nodded their heads in agreement. "Come with us," Werner said to the chancellor. "We'll show you."

Niedersachwerfen
June 15, 1945 6:00 a.m.
German Nuclear Weapons Assembly Facility

The three men arrived at the entrance to the assembly plant and were cleared through security. The first part of the tour was at a railroad siding inside the mountain.

"This is where the steel drums of uranium hexafluoride are unloaded and brought into the plant," explained Werner."

"What's uranium hexafluoride?" asked the chancellor.

"It's a gas—the basic material we work with to make U^{235}, Chancellor. The ore from the mine in Czechoslovakia is processed into uranium oxide. This is a yellow powder which we code-named

'Preparation 38.' After a lot of chemistry, it is transformed into uranium hexafluoride, which is pumped into steel drums and shipped here. This is highly corrosive stuff, and we have to handle it very carefully. Let's go inside, and I'll show you how we make an atomic weapon."

The inside of the plant was surprisingly quiet, the most noticeable sound being the low hum of electric motors—lots of them. "Once the uranium hexafluoride is inside the plant, it is pumped into these centrifuges," explained the Professor. "We have fifty thousand of them right here, arranged in twenty-five arrays of two thousand centrifuges each."

"Why do you need so many?" asked Stauffenberg, somewhat incredulously.

"Because of the properties of uranium hexafluoride and the way a centrifuge works, Chancellor. Uranium hexafluoride contains a lot of U^{238} atoms, which we don't want, and only a few U^{235} atoms, which we do want. The centrifuge separates the two by spinning the uranium hexafluoride at a very high speed — on the order of one hundred thousand rpm. The heavier U^{238} atoms are forced to the outside of the cylinder, where they are collected and recycled through the system. The lighter U^{235} atoms, the ones we want, collect in the middle of the cylinder, where they are sent on to the next centrifuge. Each centrifuge removes more of the U^{238} atoms, and this increases the concentration of U^{235} atoms. It takes two thousand centrifuges to get U^{235} with a purity level of 90 percent, which is what we need to make the fissionable material that goes into our nuclear weapons."

"How do these centrifuges achieve such a high speed, Professor?"

"We worked with the people at Siemens on this. They came up with a system that actually 'floats' the rotating part of the centrifuge on air bearings. Most of these centrifuges have been in continuous operation since 1936, happily spinning away at one hundred thousand rpm."

They walked down the aisle separating two arrays of centrifuges. "Here we are at the end of the separation process, Chancellor. We were initially stumped at this point. We had our U^{235} at 90 percent purity, but in a gaseous form. We couldn't figure out how to turn it into a useful metal. Then Otto Hahn, one of our most brilliant chemists, suggested that we expose the gas to calcium. We tried that, and the result was a reaction with the fluorine in the uranium hexafluoride, which created a salt and left us with the 90 percent pure U^{235}. We then developed procedures to safely collect the U^{235}, divide it into fifteen kilogram units, and store it until it's needed."

The chancellor was clearly stunned by everything he had seen so far. "This is alchemy, Professor. And at the highest level. You've turned gas into atomic weapons. I'm really impressed! But tell me — what is the output of each of these arrays?"

"Each of these arrays can produce about thirty kilograms of U^{235} a year, Chancellor. That's enough for two nuclear weapons like the one that was tested earlier today. There are twenty-five arrays, so each year we can produce enough U^{235} for fifty weapons. These centrifuges have been spinning for eight years, so we have enough fissionable material on hand right now to produce four hundred weapons. And more uranium hexafluoride is coming in from our facilities in Czechoslovakia all the time."

"Have you had any problems with the centrifuges, Professor"

"Nothing serious, Chancellor. Since we began full-scale operations in 1936, we've had to replace only forty-three due to malfunction. That's a failure rate of less than one-tenth of one percent.

"What happens if one fails at one hundred thousand rpm?"

"We designed the centrifuge casing for exactly that eventuality, Chancellor. It's twenty millimeters thick and made of steel alloy, so when a centrifuge rotor fails, the damage is limited to only that unit. We have an elaborate system of sensors that can detect a centrifuge failure and shut it down before it becomes catastrophic. When the sensors detect a rotor that is out of line, the electric motor is automatically turned off and the gas lines are closed."

"Doesn't this disrupt the operation of the other centrifuges in the array?"

"Not at all, sir. The way we have things set up, one or more of the centrifuges in the array can go down without affecting the others. We can actually remove a damaged centrifuge and replace it in a couple of hours without disrupting the operation of the other centrifuges in the array—or the quality of the product at the end of the process. We have a stock of new centrifuges, electric motors and gas lines ready to go at all times. The broken centrifuges are stored in a safe place, along with the other waste products from this operation. Once a centrifuge breaks, there's not much that can be salvaged from it because of the radioactivity."

The party moved into the next chamber of the assembly plant, which was separated from the centrifuges by a series of large steel doors.

"I'm beginning to understand why you felt it was necessary to build this facility inside a mountain, Professor. Much more secure from enemy air attacks."

"Yes, Chancellor. That was our main concern. We also wanted to keep our work away from prying eyes. Actually, we've done quite a bit to disguise what's happening here. The air in the entire installation is changed and filtered every few minutes, and every bit of waste from the process is collected and buried in another part of the complex inside the mountain. This is only temporary, because we hope to find a more suitable location for permanent burial somewhere in Russia once the war is over. This process generates some very dangerous by-products that have to be disposed of with great care."

"Excellent, Professor. That's good thinking."

"Thank you, sir. Now this is the part of the process where the U^{235} is turned into the nuclear components for our weapons. This is one of four assembly lines we have in the complex. The fifteen kilograms of U^{235} is divided into two parts, one smaller part and one much larger part.

"So one part of the nuclear weapon is quite a bit larger than the other. Very interesting, Professor."

"Yes, it is. And at the risk of embarrassing my old friend, the Major, I'm going to tell you the story of how this discovery was made, since I'm sure he hasn't told you about it himself. We had been working under the assumption that the two pieces of fissionable material had to be the same size the shape, and this was getting us nowhere. It was the Major who suggested that we use two masses of dissimilar size and shape to achieve the reaction we wanted."

"Is this true, Major? You never told me this before."

"Well, Chancellor … most of the work was done by Professor Heisenberg and his team, and I just …"

"Come now, Johann," interrupted the Professor. "No false modesty allowed here. It was your idea that put us over the top, and I want to make damn sure that the chancellor knows of your contribution to our success."

"Major, you never cease to amaze me," said the chancellor, actually smiling. Not only a revolutionary, but a nuclear scientist as well." But before Rinehart could respond, Stauffenberg, looking at him directly, added, "And I'm very glad you're on our side and not theirs, Johann."

At this point, all that a thoroughly embarrassed Johann Rinehart could manage was a mumbled "thank you, sir."

Professor Heisenberg salvaged this awkward moment for his friend with a continuation of the tour.

"We're at the beginning of the assembly line for the nuclear components, Chancellor. Here the U^{235} is put into a crucible and heated up to 1,135 degrees centigrade by an electric furnace. The impurities driven off by this process are captured by a ventilation system that leads to a system of high-efficiency filters so that there is no evidence of what is going on from the outside.

"This entire process occurs in lead-lined rooms with double doors and ventilation systems at each end so there is no danger of any exposure to radiation. Everything is done by mechanical arms manipulated by technicians on the outside. Television cameras mounted inside the assembly rooms are used by the technicians to guide the mechanical arms. We've been perfecting our equipment and procedures since 1936 when we first began to produce U^{235} in usable quantities, so we've had eight years to get it right.

"The stress on these technicians is very high, and for this reason, each team works only one six-hour shift a day. Each nuclear device takes about four hours to make, and an additional two hours are required for decontamination before the next nuclear device is assembled.

"Now, here we can see the molten U^{235} being poured into a mold. When the U^{235} has solidified, the mold is opened, and the 'tamper' is removed. At the other end of this assembly line, the same thing is happening with a much smaller piece called the 'bullet.' These are the two main components of the nuclear weapon. Look at the base of the 'tamper,' Chancellor, and you'll a little round hole in the middle. That's where the 'bullet' enters at the time of detonation.

The three men moved to the center of the assembly line. Professor Heisenberg continued, and the excitement in his voice was quite apparent. "This is the final step in the process here at the factory, Chancellor. The 'tamper' is placed at one end of a lead casing, and the 'bullet' is attached to a lead cylinder of the same diameter and placed at the other end. Both are firmly secured in the casing. Now we see a tube being installed between the 'bullet' and the 'tamper.' When the bomb is detonated, a charge of C-4 goes off in back of the 'bullet,' propels it down the tube and into the hole at the bottom of the 'tamper,' which is exactly the same size and shape as the 'bullet.' This makes the nuclear explosion.

"All the nuclear components are now in place, and here we can see the top part of the lead casing being put in place, with a highly-machined lead gasket between the two halves of the casing to insure that there is no radiation leakage. Temporary safeties are installed to keep the two pieces of fissionable material apart in case of an accident during transport. Once this is done, the air in the assembly room is changed, the assembly room itself is decontaminated, and the nuclear component is removed and prepared for shipment. It can now be handled just like any other piece of ammunition—but in actual practice, nobody does.

"This nuclear component is then shipped by train to either the submarine base at Wilhelmshaven or one of our forward bomber bases for final preparation. Just before this nuclear component is to be used, it is loaded into either a gravity-bomb casing or a warhead for a V-1 missile. At this point, the C-4 detonator, the fusing mechanism and the radar altimeter, which is pre-set for detonation at 580 meters, are added, the permanent safeties are installed, and the nuclear component we have seen produced here is now part of an atomic weapon ready to go to war."

"And Hitler initially approved this program ..."

"Yes, Chancellor," replied Johann. "In 1934. And then he abandoned it in 1940 when he thought we could win the war with conventional weapons. After that, well ... we all know what happened after that."

"Yes, we do," replied the chancellor. "We certainly do." *Yes,* he thought, *but we don't know __why__. Hitler had this weapon within his grasp, and with it, certain victory. But he threw it away! And that bothers me. There's so much about this man that we don't understand. I'm going to have to look into this.*

"Gentlemen. This has been an incredible morning. Now we all have work to do, both here and in Berlin. Thank you for everything you have done, and I assure you that there will be an opportunity at a later date for a more formal recognition of your accomplishments."

Near Ohrdruf, Thuringia
June 16, 1945 9:00 a.m.
German Nuclear Research Center

During the next few days, a complete analysis was made of the effects of the blast. The results were staggering. The blast was estimated to be the equivalent of 13.6 metric kilotonnes of high explosive. Within a radius of 1.6 kilometers from ground zero, destruction was total. Even the strongest reinforced concrete structures had been blown away. Almost every building within five kilometers of the test tower had been damaged.

The blast shattered glass up to a distance of almost twenty kilometers. Radios and radars were knocked out, and those closest to the site not destroyed in the blast had their electrical components damaged by the electromagnetic pulse produced by the explosion, which shut down radars as far away as Munich. Aerial observations made shortly after the blast indicated that a huge cloud of smoke over the test site was visible from a distance of 160 kilometers.

All the animals that took part in the test faired very badly. Those closest to the explosion died instantly, their bodies turned to black char. Animals that were indoors were usually spared flash burns, but flying glass from broken windows filled most rooms, killing many that may have otherwise survived the blast. Within minutes, nine out of every ten animals within a kilometer or less from the center of the blast were dead. Radiation sickness among those that survived would peak three to four weeks after the blast and would not taper off until two months after the test.

Heinrich Metz and his technicians worked quickly and carefully, and soon the bombs and missile warheads began to come off the assembly line at the rate of sixteen per day. The missile warheads were transported by rail to Wilhelmshaven, where they mated with V-1s. The missiles, with their wings folded against their fuselages for storage, were then loaded onto the submarines that would carry them close enough to be launched against targets in the United States.

The bombs were also transported by rail, but their destinations were Luftwaffe bases at Orsha and Zaporizhzhya. Still others found their way to Oldenburg in northern Germany.

The pacing element was the strike against the American naval base at Norfolk, Virginia. All the other strikes would be timed to coincide with Norfolk. The chancellor wanted the first use of Germany's nuclear force to be overwhelming and shocking in its destructive power, so all the strikes were synchronized to occur within a fifteen-minute period. This would demonstrate that Germany not only had the atomic bomb and was willing to use it, but that they could control to a very high degree the timing of its use, even over long distances. And this power was about to be unleashed.

Chapter 5

The Bright Light of Darkness

Berlin
July 19, 1946 3:15 a.m.
Spandau Prison

"So everything went off just as you expected it, Professor."

"Yes, Oppy. Just what we expected and more. We were so confident in this design that we had completed 90 percent of the assembly of the first group of atomic weapons before the test. These were the warheads for the V-1 missiles, and since they had the farthest to go, we produced them first. After the test, all we really had to do was close them up and get them ready for shipment."

"So your earlier choice to go with uranium instead of plutonium—"

"Yes. That turned out to be the right choice. We could have produced a more powerful bomb using plutonium, and it might have been easier to make, but we went with uranium because it was easier to handle and much more stable during the ignition phase. We decided to wait until the war was over before turning our attention to plutonium."

"What kind of reaction did the test cause in Washington? We didn't hear a thing. Not even rumors. I'm not even sure they told General Groves ... they sure as hell didn't tell me."

"We were able to piece a few things together from second- and third-hand sources, Dr. Oppenheimer," replied Johann, "and it looks like it happened this way ..."

Washington, DC
June 26, 1945 7:30 a.m.
The Oval Office of the White House

President Truman had only been in office since April 12. It had just been two and one-half short months since the tragic death of President Roosevelt.

Truman had inherited a war on two fronts. The Japanese were being driven back, but at a fearful cost. But things were not going well with the Germans.

We can still beat them as long as we get the atomic bomb first, Truman thought. *But will we? We know they're working on it, but we don't know how far along they are. And that's a problem.*

Truman had not been told about the Manhattan Project until thirteen days after becoming president. Now it seemed that this was the only weapon the United States had left that would give them victory over the Germans. And once they had been beaten, it would be all over for the Japanese, too. *But now this meeting with Vannevar Bush. And why so early?* he wondered. *But then, my secretary said he sounded very worried. Well, I'll see what Vannevar has to say. He's bringing along someone I haven't met before, fellow named Tolman, who works for General Groves. Must be important.*

"Mr. President, Mr. Bush and Mr. Tolman are here to see you."

"Fine, fine. Send them in."

"Good morning, Mr. President," said Vannevar Bush. He was the director of the National Defense Research Committee, and he reported only to the president. He was effectively the president's science advisor.

"I don't believe you've met Richard Tolman before, sir. He's Leslie Groves' personal scientific advisor."

"Nice to meet you, Mr. Tolman. Please sit down, both of you. Coffee? I'm no good in the morning until my second cup."

"No, thank, you, Mr. President," said Bush.

"Now, what's all the urgency, and why the long faces, gentlemen?"

Vannevar Bush took a deep breath. He knew this was going to be difficult for the president to hear, but he had to know. "Mr. President, we believe the Germans exploded an atomic device on June 15."

Harry Truman put down his coffee cup. "Are you sure about this, Vannevar? If this is true, it's grave news, indeed."

"We're about as sure as we can be, Mr. President. This came to us from the people we work with at MIT. They've been monitoring air samples on an experimental basis for some time now, and they think that the Germans have developed a uranium bomb."

"How can you be so sure of the date, Vannevar?"

"Several different locations recorded a major seismic disturbance on June 15, and by using triangulation methods, they placed the site of this disturbance near the German town of Ohrdruf in Thuringia. We confirmed this a few days later when MIT detected traces of nuclear debris in the air. This is a new science, Mr. President, but they said they were pretty sure about it. We know that the Germans have a nuclear research and test facility at Ohrdruf, but that's about all we know. No one has been able to get close enough to tell what they're doing."

"Any idea how big a blast it was?" asked Truman.

"We think it was on the order of fifteen thousand tons of

high explosive, Mr. President. That's about the size of the bomb Oppenheimer is working on at Los Alamos. We also have some reports of an electromagnetic disturbance coming from that area on June 15, and that would be consistent with the other reports we have regarding an atomic explosion."

"Fifteen thousand tons!"

"Yes, Mr. President. That's enough to wipe out a good-size city and everyone in it. And that doesn't count the people who will die afterward because of heat and radiation burns. If the Germans can figure out a way to deliver it to targets here, we could be in a lot of trouble."

The president remained silent for a long time, obviously very troubled, but trying not to show his emotion. "Vannevar, is it possible that this explosion was the result of an accident?"

"We have no way of knowing, Mr. President."

"Hmm. I see. Tell me, where are we on our own nuclear program? How far away are we from a test?"

Richard Tolman spoke up. "Mr. President, I spoke with General Groves about this yesterday, and his estimate is three weeks to a month, assuming we don't run into any last-minute roadblocks."

"How could the Germans have gotten so far ahead of us? When did they start their program?"

Vannevar Bush again. "Mr. President, the Germans have been very secretive about their nuclear program since Adolf Hitler came to power in 1933, so their research could go back as far as that time and we wouldn't have known anything about it. All the information we have is from the scientists who were driven out of Germany because of Hitler's anti-Jewish policies. They've all told us the same thing, which is that the Germans are working on a bomb and that they have some very capable people, particularly Professor Werner Heisenberg. He's their leading nuclear physicist. Smart, too. He was awarded the Nobel Prize for Physics in 1932 for the creation of quantum mechanics. So it is quite possible."

"So we have this probable atomic test by the Germans. How long do you think it will be before they have an operational weapon?"

"Hard to say, Mr. President," replied Tolman. "General Groves and Dr. Oppenheimer estimate that the time it will take to make an operational weapon after the test could range between one and three months. Our own weapon should take a month."

"I see. But what about delivery systems? How could they get it here?"

"Mr. President," Vannevar Bush began, "we know that the Germans have never developed anything like a long-range bomber or an aircraft carrier. Hitler had no use for either, so no programs were funded for their development. They have made some advances in submarines, but how that could translate into delivering a nuclear weapon—well, quite frankly, sir, you'd have to talk to someone else about that."

"I understand, Vannevar. Well, I think that's about all we know for now, gentlemen. Keep me informed about anything new, would you? Thank you for coming in and don't be concerned; we'll be all right. Good morning."

Both men rose. "Good morning, Mr. President." They exited the room and left behind a very worried Harry Truman.

My God, thought Truman. *Just when things couldn't get worse, they have. And we were doing so well as long as Hitler was in charge. That fanatic was our best general. He did everything wrong, but now that he's gone, it looks like the Germans have the bomb, which means it's all over for us and the British. And God knows what they'll do to the Soviets. God knows what they'll do to* us*!*

The president flipped the switch on the intercom. "Get Bill Donovan at OSS. Tell him I want to see him as soon as possible. And have George Marshall come in, would you please? Thanks."

Maybe these two men will have some ideas. I hope so. I'm fresh out.

Harry Truman felt very tired. *I'm not going to get too much sleep now.*

July 3, 1945 4:00 a.m.
North Atlantic Ocean
About 200 miles east of Norfolk, Virginia

Captain Carl Emmermann
U-796N

1.
Upon receipt of these orders, proceed to 36.93°N on 3 July 1945.
You will remain submerged at this location until time to launch
your missiles.

2.
You will attack the following targets with nuclear missiles in this
order:
    American Naval Air Station located at 36.93°N 76.28°W
    American Naval Port at Hampton Roads located at 36.58°N
    76.21°W

3.
You will time the launching of your first nuclear missile so it will
strike the American Naval Air Station at 5:00 a.m. local time.

4.
You will coordinate your attack with the launching of a radar-
jamming missile from U-797N, which will launch its missile before
you launch yours. Your first launch should take place as soon as
possible after the launching of the missile from the U-797N.

5.
Following each launch, you will communicate with the chancellor's
office in Berlin regarding the status of the launch.

6.

Following completion of your second launch, you will submerge and remain on station to receive further orders.

7.

At all times during this mission, you are to regard the safety of your boat and its crew as your highest priority. While risks are inherent in any combat situation, you are to weigh carefully any risk you might take in carrying out your mission against the possible loss of your boat and its crew.

Raeder

Captain Carl Emmermann couldn't be more pleased. *The first nuclear strike against the Americans and I was chosen to make it! This means at least a mention in the history of this war, and I will see to it that it's our side, not theirs, who does the writing.*

Now it was time. Navigation had placed the boat right on 36.93°N, thanks to the SINS, the Ships Inertial Navigation System, which although new, had proved to be exceptionally accurate because of its precision-made gyroscopes and accelerometers. And right on schedule for launch time, which he calculated to be 4:38 a.m. local time.

"Sonar, where is 797?" he asked.

"Captain, I make him just north and east of us. There are also three Type 21s in the area.

"Very well. Periscope depth. Radar, make a sweep as soon as the radar mast is up. I want to see if we have any company."

"Periscope depth, Captain."

"Very well. Up periscope and radar mast."

Captain Emmermann made a quick 360-degree sweep and saw nothing.

"Captain, radar shows a patrol plane about ninety kilometers south of us. She's heading away from us at about 440 kph. We should be out of range of his radar."

"Very well, radar. Periscope and radar mast down." *Damn! This was going to complicate things. Let's see, if we launch at 4:38 a.m., which is about twenty minutes from now, he'll be about 200 kilometers out, and he's sure to see the launch. He'll turn around and head straight for us at full throttle, which is about 500 kph. It'll be close for the second missile, but we should be able to launch and still have enough time to submerge and get out of here.*

"Surface. Battle stations missile." Emmermann was conscious that this was the first time such a command had been issued in anger aboard a submarine. The crew below deck unchained the missile from its storage rack, positioned it on the hydraulic lift that would bring it to the surface, and installed a fresh battery to provide power for the missile's systems.

Captain Emmermann took up his position on the bridge. Two lookouts with high-powered binoculars were to his right and left, keeping a 360-degree watch.

"Submarine surfacing just off our starboard bow, Captain."

"Very well." *That would be the 797.*

"Radar, I want constant updates on that American patrol plane."

"Aye, Captain."

Emmermann unlocked and opened the missile launch control cover. He would have final responsibility for launching the missiles.

"Missile Launch Officer, proceed with missile launch check list," he said into his microphone.

The missile launch officer saluted the captain and began the checklist leading to launch.

"Open missile access hatch."

The large hatch in front of the coning tower opened, revealing a V-1 missile on its launching sled with its wings folded.

"Elevate missile to launching ramp."

The hydraulic lift elevated the missile and its sled until it was flush with the end of the launching ramp.

"Position missile on launching ramp."

The launching sled beneath the missile was pushed forward until it engaged the slot of the launching rail.

"Retract missile lift and close missile access hatch."

The hydraulic lift that had brought the missile up to deck level was lowered and the missile access hatch was closed.

"Install retaining bolt."

The retaining bolt that held the missile in its position was installed. The bolt would be sheared when the pulse-jet was brought to maximum power and the booster rockets were fired.

"Unfold wings."

The missile's wings, which were flush against the side of the fuselage, were unfolded, brought out to the sides of the missile, rotated ninety degrees, and locked into place.

"Spin up gyros."

The gyroscopes that would keep the missile on course for its twenty-two minute flight were activated. This would take the missile right over its target. Its final descent would be triggered by a signal generated by the Type 21 submarine U-3207, which was located about thirty kilometers off the American coast just north of Emmermann's sub. Upon receiving a high-frequency signal from the missile submarines, the 3207 would generate a beam right across the target, which would shut off the fuel in the missile as it intersected the beam. This would cause the missile to pitch over, shed its wings, send a signal back to the 3207, and dive on its target. At an altitude of 580 meters, a barometric altimeter would detonate the warhead.

"Fuel the missile."

A hatch right beside the missile was opened and a fuel hose was unreeled. The end of the hose was coupled to a receptacle in the missile, and 577 liters of fuel were pumped into the fuel tank.

"Install booster rockets."

Four booster rockets were installed to the rear of the missile's launching sled. This is what the patrol plane would see.

"Radar, where's that patrol plane?"

"Still heading away from us, Captain."

"Very well. Keep me informed of any change in its course."

"Aye, Captain."

The countdown continued.

"Install booster rocket igniters."

The igniters were installed in the booster rockets. These were twitchy things that had to be handled with extreme care; there was no room for a slip-up.

"Install main engine control cable."

The cable that supplied power to start the Argus pulse-jet and control its speed was plugged into the missile.

"Remove safeties."

The three safeties were removed. The missile was coming to life.

"Navigation, where are we?"

"Right on target, Captain, at 36.93 degrees north. About one minute to launch."

Emmermann checked his watch. *Good. We should launch right on time.*

"Blinker, contact 797. Tell him we have about one minute to launch."

"Aye, Captain."

The blinker light flashed the message to the U-797. There was an instant response.

"Captain, the 797 says she will be ready to launch in about forty seconds."

"Very well."

The missile was his now.

Emmermann elevated the launching ramp. Next, he started the Argus pulse-jet, which would power the missile once the booster rockets fell away. The cable controlling the speed of the engine would remain attached to the missile until it was launched. Once the missile launched, it would disconnect from the cable, freeing the missile for its twenty-two minute flight.

The noise of the pulse-jet was shattering. *My God, they could probably hear that racket all the way in Norfolk.*

"Missile launch crew, clear the deck."

The missile launch officer turned, saluted the captain, and then ordered his men into the safety of the coning tower.

"Navigation, where are we?" Emmermann had to shout into the microphone because of the noise from the missile's engine.

"Very close now, Captain. Still right on 36.93."

"Very well." *It was up to U-797 now.*

Emmermann inserted the key into the panel. He didn't have to wait long. There was a flash of light and a roar from the U-797's deck as its missile flew into the night sky.

It was loaded with equipment to jam the radars protecting the facilities at Norfolk. He knew this launch also said to the American patrol plane, "Here I am! Come and get me!"

He counted to five slowly. He barely remembered to duck behind the protective wall of the bridge before he turned his key to the LAUNCH position. He pushed the throttle forward, bringing the pulse-jet to its maximum power and igniting the booster rockets. He was rewarded with the same flash of light and roar he had seen from the U-797 as his own missile sped down the launching ramp.

The first nuclear strike against the enemy! And it was mine!

"Radar, where's that patrol plane?"

"He's turning around, Captain. We've got about twenty minutes before he gets here."

"Very well." *Twenty minutes.*

"Radio, tell the 3207 that our missile is on its way." *Should be enough time for the second missile, but it will be close.*

"Radio, raise Berlin and tell them that the first missile has been launched. Also tell them we have an American patrol plane headed in our direction about twenty minutes out, but we will launch the second missile before they get here."

"Aye, Captain."

"Missile launch officer, prepare the second missile for launch." He pushed the button that lowered the launching ramp.

"Aye, Captain." Below deck, the second missile was moved to the hydraulic lift.

"Navigation, set a new course. Put us on 36.58 degrees north."

"Aye, Captain."

He felt the boat change direction very slightly. *Just a few hundredths of a degree, but it will put our second missile right over the American navy's docks at Hampton Roads.*

The countdowns were going very smoothly on board both Emmermann's boat and the U-797. Then the executive officer's voice came on the earphones.

"Captain, we just received a message from U-3207. They had to submerge because of enemy patrol planes in the area. They won't be able to make the engine cut-off signal for our first shot. Probably be twenty to thirty kilometers long."

Damn! The first nuclear missile to be fired at an enemy from a submarine. My submarine. And it's going to miss. I can't worry about that now. It's out of my hands, so concentrate on the second missile.

"XO, did 3207 say anything about being ready for the last two shots?"

"No sir. Captain Bleichrodt said we were to stand by."

"Very well, XO."

Fucking American planes! One coming right at me, and another one on the trail of the 3207! Damn! Okay.... steady, now. This is not the time to lose it.

Then he saw the missile launch officer's salute. He ordered them off the deck. It was now his responsibility to launch his second missile and then submerge. It was going to be tight, and probably in violation of his orders regarding the safety of his boat and crew, but he wanted one more chance to get it right!

"Captain, we just heard from the 3207. They're ready with their cut-off beam. They'll be able to switch from the missile launched from the 797 to ours one minute after they receive the signal from the 797's missile that it is diving on its target. So we should time the launch of our missile for one minute after the 797 launches its missile."

"Very well, XO. That will be our procedure. Right after we launch and get the ramp stowed, make your depth one hundred meters. I'll want maximum speed and a ninety-degree right turn. We have a patrol plane closing in on us, and they're probably carrying those damn sonar-homing torpedoes. I want our boat to be running parallel to them when they drop their torpedoes. We should be able to outrun them."

"Aye, Captain. Depth of one hundred meters, maximum speed, and a ninety-degree right turn."

"Very well, XO."

Now to the business at hand. Elevate the launch ramp and wait for the 797's launch. Wait ... wait. There it goes! Looks like a good bird. If the 3207 can keep its beam going, that'll be all for the American navy at Norfolk. Now just a few more seconds to allow enough time for the 3207 to turn its beam to the right heading for his last missile. Turn on the engine. Twenty seconds ... ten seconds ... five seconds ... now!

He turned the key in the control panel, pushed the throttle forward, and the boosters ignited, propelling the missile into the still-night sky. He remembered to duck this time. He pushed the button to lower the launching ramp into its stowed position.

"Lookouts below! Clear the bridge! Dive! Dive!"

The diving Klaxon sounded as he locked up the missile launch control panel. The launching ramp was stowed. The missile boat captains had insisted on this; they wanted to be able to get that ramp lowered and locked down quickly in case something like this happened.

The water was just covering the deck as he slid down the ladder and secured the hatch.

"Radio, raise your mast to its maximum height and send this to Berlin: 'Second missile launch successful. Am diving to escape enemy patrol plane.' Then send a message to 3207 that our second missile is in the air."

"Radio mast raised to maximum height and—both messages sent, Captain."

"Very well. Radar, where was the range on that plane when we submerged?"

"About twenty-five kilometers and closing, sir."

"Very well. Anything from Berlin?"

"They're just confirming, sir. And they added a 'well done,' Captain."

"Very well. Lower radio mast."

More time.

"Coming up on one hundred meters, Captain."

"Very well, XO. Level out and maintain maximum speed on present course." He wanted to be right in front of the torpedo when it came. He didn't have long to wait.

"Captain, sonar. Splash in the water, high-speed screws. Right in back of us. About three hundred meters."

Okay. Stay cool. We should be able to outrun this sucker. Just don't make any turns or try anything fancy. This boat wasn't built for high-speed maneuvers like the Type 21, or, for that matter, my Mercedes roadster. I wish I was driving her now; I'd make short work of that torpedo, just as I did with the police the last time I was on the autobahn.

He shook his head and returned to the present. *No police behind me now, but something much more deadly. Wait a minute ... there was only one splash, and those planes carry two torpedoes!*

It seemed like an eternity before sonar came back on the line. "Three hundred fifty ... four hundred ... four hundred fifty ... five hundred meters, sir. Screws fading, sir. I think we've lost him."

"Very goo—" he didn't get to finish, because sonar was screaming into earphones.

"High-speed screws in the water, Captain! Dead ahead!"

"Reverse course! Sound collision alarm!" *There's the second torpedo! Very clever, flyboy!*

The big ship protested and began to turn. The huge prop cavitated as it floundered in the water. His crew and anything not tied down were flying all over the place.

"How far, sonar?"

"Three hundred meters and closing, sir."

"Keep those distance readings coming, sonar."

"Aye, Captain. Now two hundred fifty ... two twenty-five ... two hundred meters, Captain ... one-fifty ... one hundred ... I can't track it now, sir... too close."

C'mon, baby. Do this for me just one more time. He could feel the big boat's prop biting into the water.

Maybe there's a chance. Yes! Picking up speed! We might do this! That fucking pilot guessed right and flew around me, got in front, and then dropped his fish. Smart guy! Like to buy him a drink sometime when this war is over, but first, we have to get through this.

"Sonar, anything?"

"Just coming up on the scope now, sir. One hundred meters ... one hundred fifty ... now two hundred meters, sir ... screws fading, sir. I think we've outrun him."

"Very well, sonar. And good job. XO, ninety-degree left turn. Maintain maximum speed for the next hour." *God, that was close! Now head out into open water and get as far away from the coast as possible. The American plane that has been chasing us will soon have lots of friends in the air, and they'll all be very angry. But what about my boat and crew?*

"This is the captain. I want damage and injury reports from all compartments as soon as possible."

The damage reports came in, but nothing that would prevent them from remaining on station as their orders specified. The missiles, with their deadly warheads, had remained firmly chained down. There were no ruptures in the pressure hull, and the motor and batteries were all functioning properly. The boat was safe.

The reports on the injured came in next. At first, nothing serious, just a few bruises and sprains. Then the report from the galley came in.

"Captain." It was the XO. "It's Cookie. Looks like a pot of boiling water spilled on him when we made that turn. Scalded him real bad. We gave him some morphine and took him to sick bay."

"Very well. Thanks, XO. Keep me informed on his condition. Captain out."

Cookie! How many times had he been told to knock off that kind of stuff while we were under attack! Can't be too hard on him, though. He was the only one of the crew who had served with me on all of my boats, and he had asked to be on this one. I told him he was over-age and could retire with honor, but he said no, he wanted to make this one last deployment with me, and I couldn't turn him down. I'll have to visit him when I have a chance. Cookie, of all people! Damn! Damn!

Okay, relax. Wait awhile, and then go to periscope depth and look around to see if there are any more patrol planes in the area, and if there were any reports from Berlin on our missile strikes. I know our first missile missed, but what about the others ...

Benns Church, Virginia
July 3, 1945 5:00 a.m.
Benns Church and cemetery

The first missile launched against the American naval base at Norfolk landed in Batten Bay, just a few kilometers west of the naval air station. This was the radar-jamming missile launched from the U-797N, and it had done its job. The radars protecting the Naval Air Station were completely disabled for a few critical minutes, allowing the second missile, with its nuclear warhead, to penetrate the base's defenses.

With its fuel spent, the first missile automatically pitched over and began a vertical dive toward the water. The wings tore off, and a powerful charge blew it apart on the way down so that no one would be able to salvage anything worthwhile from its watery grave.

The second missile launched against the base had over-flown the Naval Air Station because the U-3207 had to submerge to avoid detection by an American patrol aircraft. With no signal to interrupt its flight, the missile had kept on flying until it was directly over the small community of Benns Church, about twenty-four kilometers west of its intended target. When it ran out of fuel, the missile had pitched over, and at an altitude of 580 meters, the nuclear warhead had detonated with a force of almost fourteen thousand metric tonnes of high explosive.

Ground zero was located between the historic St. Luke's Church and its cemetery. The church vaporized in the explosion, and there was nothing left of the cemetery.

Everyone in Benns Church, Virginia, was killed instantly. Most of them, with names like Jordan, Hodsden, Driver, and Morrison, were the direct descendents of the people who had founded the town in 1789. Their names had been inscribed on the tombstones in the St. Paul's Church cemetery.

Now there was nothing left of the town, its people, its church, and its cemetery—nothing but radioactive dust.

East of Norfolk, Virginia
July 3, 1945 5:30 a.m.
B-24 patrol plane at 1,000 feet altitude

It had started a little less than one hour ago when the tail gunner reported he had seen "something that looked like two Roman candles going off" in the middle of the ocean north of them. Captain Jim Monroe had turned his plane around immediately.

Now what? he wondered. *We're getting our asses kicked out of the Atlantic by these new German subs. I've sunk a couple of them, but they just keep coming. They've sunk a lot of our ships and blockaded our ports, so nothing is getting through to England, and those poor bastards are starving. And what was that bright light we all saw to the west about thirty minutes ago? Got a bad feeling about that …*

They were about thirty miles out when the third and fourth missiles were launched from the German submarines. Captain Monroe and his crew saw everything.

"Get me the Naval Air Station on the radio, right now."

"Can't raise them, Captain. Lots of interference. Could be related to that lightning we saw earlier, sir."

"Captain." It was Jones, the radar operator. "I've got them on radar. There are two of them, and it looks like they're submerging."

"Very well. Let's get those fuckers before they go too deep." *That wasn't lightning. Much too bright for that. I wonder if Linda and Jimmy are okay. Can't worry about them now. Find those subs and get them.*

Still, the horrible feeling that things were very bad in Hampton would not leave him, even as he tried to concentrate on sinking the German submarines that would destroy his life.

Hampton, Virginia
July 3, 1945 5:00 a.m.
Home of Linda Monroe

The roar and shock wave from the bomb that destroyed Benns Church jolted Linda Monroe awake. Instinctively, she checked on her baby, Jimmy, to make sure he was okay. The noise had also awakened him, and he was crying very loudly. She picked him up to comfort him, and then headed for the front yard to see what was happening. This was not the usual kind of storm for this time of year.

What she saw astonished and shocked her. To the west, there was a bright cloud rising higher and higher into the night sky. *My God! This is horrible! What can it mean? It looks like the end of the world!*

Her neighbors had also gone outside to see what was going on, and they seemed just as frightened as she was. They stared at this phenomenon for quite some time and worried not only about themselves, but also for their husbands and sons. They all knew the war was not going well and wondered if this had anything to do with it.

The light from the bomb that exploded over Newport News at 5:45 a.m. blinded Linda Monroe and all of her neighbors. The shock wave knocked her viciously to the ground, breaking her arm and killing Jimmy.

She could not see the bomb that exploded over Hampton Roads a minute later, but she could feel the flesh searing off her bones. She died quickly and in terrible agony, trying, but failing, to scream, and barely being able to wonder what had happened, or why.

Norfolk, Virginia
July 3, 1945 5:00 a.m.
U.S. Naval Headquarters

The detonation of the nuclear warhead that destroyed Benns Church and woke up Linda Monroe created an electromagnetic pulse that disabled every radar within a radius of one hundred miles, permitting the second and third nuclear V-1 missiles to complete their mission unimpeded. They detonated above their intended targets at Hampton Roads and Newport News, destroying or disabling those ships of the United States Navy's Atlantic Fleet that had not already been sunk by Admiral Dönitz's Type 21 submarines. Altogether, three escort carriers, six heavy cruisers, thirty-five destroyer escorts, twelve submarines, plus various support vessels were either sunk outright or severely damaged, and everyone on board them was killed.

The fireballs and shock waves from the nuclear warheads destroyed all dockside structures and exploded all the nearby fuel and ammunition stocks. The Naval Air Station where Captain Jim Monroe's B-24 had been stationed was blown away and all the airplanes sitting on the tarmac were incinerated.

It would take many weeks to add up the misery inflicted on the people in the area of the blasts. More than 150,000 perished immediately, almost all of them service personnel or their families. Over the ensuing months, that many and more would succumb to severe burns, as well as to injuries caused by radiation, which no one yet knew how to treat. Still others who had escaped physical harm were scarred for life by what they had seen and experienced immediately after the explosions. The impact on the United States had yet to be felt, but it was soon in coming.

Washington, DC
July 3, 1945 6:00 a.m.
The presidential quarters in the White House

"Mr. President. It's General Marshall on the phone. Something about the naval base at Norfolk."

President Truman had just finished breakfast and was getting ready for his morning walk. *That'll have to wait. Can't be good news from George Marshall this early in the morning.*

"George? What's happened?"

"Mr. President, we're not completely sure, but it looks like the Germans have bombed the naval base at Norfolk. Everything there is just … gone. Could be nuclear weapons, Mr. President."

"Are you sure about this? My God, George, if this is true, then it's all over for us. Do you have any reliable confirmation?"

"No, we don't, Mr. President. We're still trying to get some people down there to see what happened. Things are a real mess between here and Norfolk, sir. All the phone lines are down, and radio communications are out all the way up to Baltimore. We have reports of a bright flash seen as far away as Richmond, so we're pretty sure that something big happened down there."

"Okay, George. Keep trying, and as soon as you get some reliable reports, let me know."

"Of course, sir. Good-bye, Mr. President."

"Good-bye, George."

The president had a horrible, sinking feeling in the pit of his stomach. So bad he could hardly move.

"Who was that?" his wife Bess asked. *No sense in hiding anything from her.*

"George Marshall, dear. It looks like the Germans have destroyed our naval base at Norfolk, probably with atomic weapons."

"Oh my God! That's terrible! Isn't there anything we can do to stop them?"

"No, there really isn't. They've chased our navy out of the Atlantic with their submarines, and the only thing we have between them and us is a handful of patrol planes armed with torpedoes and depth charges. And it looks like they got past those easily enough."

A silent gloom enveloped them.

"What are we going to do, Harry?"

"I don't know. I just don't know."

The two of them, now feeling very old and very tired, held each other closely for a long time and cried.

London
July 3, 1944 1:00 p.m.
Churchill's bunker at 10 Downing Street

"Prime Minister, it's Admiral Cunningham on the phone for you, sir. He sounds very agitated."

"Very well." The prime minister picked up the phone. "Admiral … What's that? … The Germans have attacked Scapa Flow? I see … what's the damage? Nothing left of the fleet? Nothing left of *Scapa Flow*! You're sure about this, are you? Yes, I see … just flew over it … nothing but three big clouds … I see … reports of some bright flashes and then three huge explosions.

"So they get past our radar network … yes, I see … lots of jamming before the explosions. Yes … yes, that would account for those German planes that were nosing around the base a couple of months ago. Probably taking pictures and sniffing out our radar frequencies.

"So you put everything up when the radars were jammed ... yes ... See anything? Yes ... that makes sense ... six planes at 32,300 feet, coming in very fast from the southeast. Probably three carrying bombs and three carrying radar jamming equipment ... we gave chase, but couldn't catch them.

"What about the interceptors, Admiral? ... almost all destroyed in the blasts ... only two returned to base ... most unfortunate.

The prime minister paused. Few people in England besides himself knew of the American's concern about the German's atomic bomb, but he felt it was now appropriate to tell Cunningham.

"No, Admiral, it's not. I spoke with the American president a few days ago, and it seems that his scientific people had just told him that they believed the Germans exploded an atomic device on June 15. Yes, only three weeks ago. Damn short time to move from test device to operational weapon, but it looks like that's what they've done. Yes ... yes ... This could be most serious. Yes, try to get some people in there to see what things look like and then call me back. Thank you, Admiral."

Most serious, indeed, thought the prime minister. *I warned them about this possibility, but no one has trusted me since Gallipoli. I had raised the alarm when Hitler came to power and started rearming, but to no avail. "That's just Winston, and he's got his war paint on again," they said. Even after Hitler marched into Austria and Czechoslovakia, no one lifted a finger.*

What fools they had been, Baldwin and Chamberlain. And Chamberlain had been the worst. Waving that silly piece of paper around and proclaiming, "Peace for our time!" What nonsense! Any idiot could see that Hitler was getting ready for war, but no one wanted to believe it. You don't give a man like Hitler everything he wants and not expect him to want more.

And now we're paying for it. Years of unpreparedness interspersed with moments of supreme stupidity has led to this. Now, all I can do is wait for the Germans to present their terms. I'll have to accept them, of course, no matter what they are. The alternative would be an England reduced to radioactive rubble. I'll bluff and bluster, but in the end, I'll accept their terms. Then I'll submit my resignation to the king. Let someone else toady up to those Nazi bastards in Berlin.

His cigar had gone out. He started to light up another Romeo y Julieta, but before he could do that, he was seized by a rare fit of despair. He put the unlit cigar down, realizing that he would be the one who will go down in history as the man who precipitated the breakup of the British Empire and brought about the downfall of England. He who had fought so hard and so ineffectually against the rising tide of tyranny that had swallowed up Europe and now threatened England with total destruction; he would be blamed.

But there's still work to do, he thought, as he rallied himself for the task at hand. *Must get the best possible deal from the Germans. Then summon the muse of oratory once again and try to explain to a people who have seen more than their share of suffering that their sacrifices have been in vain, and that they would now be under the heel of the German boot.*

I know that Stauffenberg and his government have renounced Nazism, but I don't believe it. Not for a minute. Not even after they stopped the murder of the Jews and said they would be held accountable for it. No, they're all Nazis, every damn one of them!

Perhaps my friend across the pond would have some words of advice and solace. Yes, that's it. Call my new friend Harry Truman and see what he has to say. I need a brandy before this call … it is going to be very difficult. Yes, I must talk with Harry."

Winston Churchill felt very old and tired as he reached for the bottle of Hine brandy. The youthful radiance that had astonished and buoyed up England and the rest of the world was now gone, and in its place was the burned-out hulk of a once great man who had given it his best, but who, in the final analysis, had failed.

The connection with the White House was instantaneous. "Hello, Mr. President," said the Prime Minister. "I thought I'd better bring you up to date … what's that? You've been attacked, too? Yes … Scapa Flow and the fleet are gone, Mr. President. German atomic bombs, I'm afraid. And Norfolk as well? Nuclear missiles fired from submarines? My God, Harry, what are we going to do now? What *can* we do?"

Moscow
July 3, 1945 1:00 p.m.
Red Square

It was a perfect day for a parade, and the Soviets knew how to do this better than anyone. All the graduates from the military academies were parading before Stalin and the Politburo, honoring them with their salutes and shouts of "Hoo-*RAH*" as they marched past the reviewing stand on top of Lenin's mausoleum.

There must be ten thousand of them, Stalin thought. *Let's see … there's the Frunze Military Academy; the J. V. Stalin Academy of the WRPA, named after me; the F. E. Dzerzhinsky Artillery Academy in Leningrad; the Budyonny Military Academy of Communications, and the oldest one, the Mikhailovskaya Artillery Military Academy, which goes back to 1698!*

Joseph Stalin took great pride in these tall, straight and eager young men and women. He knew they worshiped him as their father and spiritual leader, because they believed that it was by his will alone, "Stalin, the Man of Steel," that the Germans had been hurled back at Moscow and Stalingrad. He did not disagree with this. And he knew that they would gladly give their lives for the Rodina, the Motherland, and he drew strength from this.

Enough strength to carry this fight all the way to victory in Berlin, he thought. *But how many of the men and women that I am reviewing today will still be alive at the end of the war? What a strange and wonderful people Russians are. Oppressed for centuries by Czars and the church, but still so willing to defend with the last drop of their blood the sacred soil of their country.*

So many have already died, he thought. *We're still pushing the Germans back, but at a fearful cost. The cowardly Americans and British did not keep their promise to invade from the west, because they didn't have the stomach for it. I'll finish the job, all right, and after I crush Germany, I'll—*

"Comrade Stalin … *Comrade Stalin!*"

"Yes, what is it?" Stalin didn't appreciate the interruption, and the tone of his voice clearly showed his displeasure. He turned and saw an extremely agitated Captain Boris Malinovsky, his personal aide and secretary.

"Comrade Stalin, Major Gribkov reports that our early warning radar is being jammed. He thinks it might be a German attack. Comrade Stalin, I think you and the members of the Politburo should go inside."

"Nonsense, Captain," Stalin said tersely. "The radar is just broken again. Tell Gribkov to either fix that damn thing and quit bothering us with these false alarms or I'll send him to the western front. Now get out!"

Captain Malinovsky shivered, as he always did, at Stalin's wrath. He had learned the hard way not to argue with him when he was in one of his moods.

"Yes, Comrade Stalin. As you wish, Comrade Stalin."

Damn right, "as I wish." Too many false alarms. Yes, the radars protecting Moscow are second-rate, but the Germans haven't caused us too many problems before, so why should they now?

He silently cursed himself. *Why did I purge all those radar scientists back in the thirties? Maybe they could have developed better protection for us that didn't break as often. Our radars are not nearly as advanced as the Allied models, but they're the best we have. I'll have to talk with my espionage people about stealing some of their designs. But now, there's this wonderful parade to review.*

He had turned around just in time to receive the salute from Marshal Semyon Timoshenko Military Academy of Chemical Defense when the first Arado flew overhead at an altitude of one thousand meters. It carried jamming equipment that easily overwhelmed the radars that were charged with the protection of the Soviet capitol. Following behind the lead plane were five more Arados, each carrying a 13.6 kilotonne nuclear weapon. All dropped their bombs at the same time.

The nuclear weapon that detonated over Red Square at an altitude of 580 meters killed Joseph Stalin and everyone else on top of Lenin's mausoleum, along with the ten thousand troops who just a few minutes before had been shouting themselves hoarse in celebration of their leader. Lenin's mausoleum, the most sacred shrine in the Soviet Union, was blown away, as were the sacred shrines of another era: St. Basil's, the Cathedral of the Archangel, the Cathedral of the Annunciation, and Dormition Cathedral. The four other bombs were spaced evenly to the north, east, and west of the Kremlin, and all found their mark. Moscow ceased to exist.

Stalingrad
July 3, 1945 1:00 p.m.
9,855 meters altitude, 150 kilometers west of the city

Lieutenant Heinrich Gilkrest sat in the bombardier's position as the Arado approached its target, Stalingrad, the Soviet Union's major city on the Volga River. Even though the city was in ruins, it still gave the Soviets control over the southern part of the Volga River, so it remained a target of strategic importance.

He was no stranger to this place, having fought in the epic struggle waged during the winter between late 1942 and early 1943. That battle had almost cost him his life.

He remembered that time with bitterness. Hitler's "no retreat" order had doomed the Sixth Army to defeat. Göering had rashly promised him that Stalingrad would be supplied from the air and Hitler had believed him. It was an impossible task from the beginning.

He had been the pilot of one of those cargo planes, and luck was with him until January 5, 1943. He had made it through the gauntlet of Soviet fighters and antiaircraft guns while carrying quite a bit more cargo than was specified for the plane. He had managed to land safely, and with the aid of many willing hands, his plane was unloaded in only a few minutes.

His trip back to the Luftwaffe base at Zverevo was harrowing. He had taken on as many wounded men as he could carry, but after the door was closed and he was about to begin his takeoff run down the shell-holed runway, his plane was overrun with soldiers desperate to get out. They climbed on the wings and held onto the landing gear. It was all he could do to get into the air. One by one, he watched them drop off the plane to their deaths.

Poor bastards, he thought. *No one could blame them. At least they died trying to escape this freezing hell-hole, or worse, being captured by the Soviets.*

But that was just the start of his problems. The Red Air Force had been gaining in strength and now they seemed to be everywhere. He had always counted on the slow speed of his Ju-52 "Auntie Ju" to keep him unnoticed and it had almost worked again. He had the airstrip at Zverevo in sight when two Soviet fighters jumped him.

They each managed to make one pass at him before being driven off by a couple of Fockers, but the damage had been done. His plane was all shot up and so was he. The memory of how he had landed his crippled plane had not yet returned to him.

When he regained consciousness, it was a month later, and he found himself in a Berlin hospital. The doctors and nurses attending him had said it was a miracle he was alive. Recovery was slow and painful, and only made worse when the doctors told him he would probably never walk again. He had proved them wrong on this and many other things. His determination was fueled by one thought: revenge.

He had willed himself back into shape, and when he heard that three new squadrons were being formed for the Luftwaffe's newest bomber, the Arado 234C-2, he pulled all the strings he could, including favorable letters of recommendation from his commanding officers at Stalingrad. It worked, and soon he was on his way to flight training.

His injuries kept him out of the pilot's seat, so he happily settled for being a bombardier. And he had a wonderful piece of equipment to work with. The Lotfernrohr 7 bombsight, made by the Carl Zeiss people, was a superb example of German craftsmanship. It had originated in America, but was stolen from the Carl L. Norden Corporation by a German agent in 1938.

Bomb release was normally automatic in order to reduce timing errors. *But no*, he thought. *I'm going to release the bomb manually. I'm not going to surrender the pleasure of dropping an atomic bomb on Stalingrad to a machine.*

Now they were getting close. He heard the pilot order the other four planes to break formation and spread out so the five targets could be bombed at the same time. The target for his plane was the October Tractor Factory in the middle of the city. This factory had attracted worldwide attention during the battle of Stalingrad, because of the heroics of its workers who kept producing T-34 tanks under the worst possible conditions. It was eventually shut down by German bombs, but not until it was too late. The Sixth Army was surrounded and starving and there was no way out but surrender. Field Marshal Paulus and almost 100,000 men had gone into captivity.

Now Stalingrad lay before him, undefended by either planes or antiaircraft fire that would cause any problems. He grimaced as the plane shook, aggravating his recently healed wounds and forcefully reminding him of that terrible day two years ago. *Strategic reasons, like hell*, he thought. *This is revenge for my broken body.*

"Almost there, Heinrich. Time to remove the safeties so our little surprise will go off."

Heinrich removed the three safeties and got three green lights. The bomb was ready to go.

"It's all yours, now. You will be in direct communication with the bombardiers of the other planes, so when you say 'bomb release,' we will all drop our bombs at the same time. That should make quite a nice explosion. We're at 9,855 meters, and as soon as the bombs are gone, we'll make a one-eighty-degree turn and head for home. We'll be well out of the way when they go off."

Lieutenant Heinrich Gilkrest peered into the bombsight's eyepiece and easily placed the October Tractor Factory in its crosshairs. *Payback time.*

Washington, DC
July 3, 1945 10:00 a.m.
The Willard Hotel

Special Ambassador Hans Bernd von Haeften had arrived in Washington on July 25, just ten days after the successful test of

Germany's nuclear weapon. He and his party had been the only passengers on the *Europa*. It was a quick passage; the ship averaged almost twenty-eight knots, which had been fast enough to capture the Blue Riband in 1931. After they landed in New York, they were met by a fleet of limousines and enclosed trucks that immediately transported them and their equipment them to Washington.

His trip had been the result of secret negotiations between American Secretary of State, Edward Stettinius, and Erwin Planck, the newly appointed minister of foreign affairs under Chancellor Stauffenberg. Planck had replaced Joachim von Ribbentrop, one of the most fanatical Nazis in Hitler's regime.

Ribbentrop had gained international infamy by giving the Nazi salute to George VI of Great Britain when he presented his credentials to him as the newly appointed ambassador from Germany in 1937. He had conducted his business mostly by screaming at subordinates, and it seemed to the ambassador very appropriate that Ribbentrop was now rotting in solitary confinement in a jail cell at Spandau.

Haeften and his party were the only guests in the 372-room Willard Hotel. At his insistence, and over many objections from many very important people, all of the other guests in the hotel had been compelled to leave. Haeften occupied a suite on the top floor that was adjacent to the suite that housed the latest communications equipment and Enigma machines. His staff occupied all the rooms surrounding these two suites, including the next floor down. The intention of this arrangement was to prevent the installation of any listening equipment by the Americans. Even so, every room occupied by the Germans was electronically swept twice a day to preclude this possibility.

Washington was in a state of near panic. Word of the attack on the naval base at Norfolk had spread like wildfire throughout the city and up and down the East Coast. People were leaving the major coastal cities as quickly as possible in fear of additional attacks. Every road leading west was jammed with cars, buses, and any other means of transportation. Trains and planes were filled to capacity. Gasoline and food were in short supply, and liquor stores had long since been emptied out. There were rumors that London had been bombed and that something terrible had happened in the Soviet capital. Riots had broken out at gas stations and supermarkets, and the police in most cities were simply overwhelmed.

Excellent, thought the ambassador. *This will make my job a lot easier.*

Haeften went to the phone and dialed a number that rang in the office of the president's private secretary.

"Office of the President."

Keep it professional. I know how Ribbentrop would act in this situation. But this is no time for German histrionics.

"Yes, good morning. This is Ambassador Haeften. I would like to see President Truman at one o'clock this afternoon … Yes … It is most urgent. Would this be a convenient time?" He had rehearsed his calm, evenly measured tones many times.

"Please hold, Mr. Ambassador."

Haeften knew she was consulting with the president, and he knew what the response would be.

"Very good. I would also request that Secretary of State Edward Stettinius, Secretary of War Henry Stimson, and General George Marshall also be present. Can this be arranged? Very good. Thank you."

Washington, DC
July 3, 1945 1:00 p.m.
The Oval Office of the White House

"Mr. President, Ambassador Haeften is here to see you."

"Show him in. And please see that we are not disturbed."

"Yes, Mr. President. Mr. Ambassador, the president will see you now."

"Good afternoon, Mr. President ... gentlemen."

"Will you have a seat, Mr. Ambassador?"

"No, thank you, I prefer to stand."

"Very well ..."

"Gentlemen, as you know by now, we have the atomic bomb. We have used it on your naval base at Norfolk, the British naval base at Scapa Flow, and the Soviet cities of Moscow and Stalingrad. All these attacks occurred simultaneously at five o'clock this morning, Washington time. All of these targets have been completely destroyed."

So it was true, Truman thought. *Churchill told me about the devastation at Scapa Flow. News of the attacks on Moscow and Stalingrad was coming in slowly, but nothing had been confirmed. Now there was confirmation. But why waste bombs on Stalingrad? Must have been purely for revenge.*

"Gentlemen, Chancellor Stauffenberg has instructed me to present to you a list of terms. The unconditional acceptance of these terms is the only way you can prevent more nuclear attacks on your East Coast cities and military installations. May I read these terms to you, Mr. President?"

They intend on attacking our cities! And we can't do a damn thing about it. Truman felt numb, but he managed the correct response.

"Of course, Mr. Ambassador."

Ambassador Haeften distributed copies of the terms and then began.

"First, the American government will cease its program of nuclear weapons research and development. All the scientists and technicians involved in this program will be brought to Washington, DC, and turned over to representatives of the German government. All—"

"Excuse me, Mr. Ambassador," the president interrupted. "What do you intend to do with these people once they have been turned over to you?"

"Mr. President, they will be transported to New York, put on the ocean liner *Europa*, and taken to Germany. What will happen to them after that, I do not know. May I continue?"

Truman nodded his assent. He looked at his list of the scientists to be handed over to the Germans, and at the top were the names of J. Robert Oppenheimer and Edward Teller. *My God, if they could get those two to work for them ...*

"All equipment and facilities associated with your Manhattan Project will be destroyed under our supervision, and all notes and journals pertaining to this project will be turned over to us. All fissionable material produced to date from any source will be placed in our custody.

"Second. All offensive and defensive actions against the German nation by your armed forces will cease, and all military and civilian personnel, and all equipment engaged in these actions will be returned to the United States. All military and civilian bases involved in such actions will be closed under our supervision, and all military and other governmental espionage operations against the German nation will cease."

"Does that include our operations against Japan?" asked George Marshall.

"No, General Marshall, it does not. As of this morning, we have broken diplomatic relations with the empire of Japan and withdrawn from the Tripartite Pact signed in 1940 between us, the Japanese and the Italians. The Italians have withdrawn from the present conflict, so this leaves only the United States and the empire of Japan in an active state of war. Let me emphasize that we will give no further assistance to the empire of Japan in this conflict, and we will do nothing to hinder your military operations against them."

Very clever. Truman felt a pain in his gut. *Stab the Japanese in the back and leave the two of us to grind each other into powder in the Pacific. And we were counting on the atomic bomb to end that conflict without having to invade Japan. Now that will not be possible, and it's likely that more than one million of our men will die in the invasion. We'll probably have to kill every damn Jap before it's over. The biggest diplomatic betrayal in modern history, and very clever.*

"Third. Upon completion of its military operations against the empire of Japan, the United States will evacuate all of its possessions of any kind in the Pacific Ocean and cede them to Germany. All military and civilian personnel will leave these possessions intact and without any damage and return to the United States. This will be accomplished under the supervision of the German Kriegsmarine. All military equipment will be similarly evacuated to the United States, except for the ships of the United States Navy, which will be scuttled in the ocean under our supervision. Exceptions to this operation are all South Dakota, North Carolina and Iowa-class battleships and all Essex-class aircraft carriers, which will be turned over to the German Kreigsmarine. In addition, all medium and long-range bombers and fighters, such as, but not limited to, the B-17, B-24, B-25, and B-26, and the P-38 Lightning, will be destroyed under our supervision. All remaining B-29s will be turned over to the German Luftwaffe."

George Marshall felt sick. *That means Pearl Harbor and Corregidor. And we shed so much blood over them in those first dark days of the war.*

"Fourth. Upon completion of its war with the empire of Japan, the United States of America shall cede to Germany the Panama Canal, including all of the facilities in the Panama Canal Zone."

"Why do you want the Panama Canal?" asked Harry Truman.

"Mr. President, let me assure you that under our jurisdiction, the Panama Canal will be open to all maritime nations. Our sole purpose in acquiring it is to construct new facilities that will permit the next generation of commercial cargo vessels and warships passage. At present, all ships are limited to a width of one hundred and ten feet. We intend to construct new locks that will permit the passage of ships with a beam of over two hundred feet."

My God, thought George Marshall, *now they'll control the Suez Canal, the Strait of Malacca, and the Panama Canal. They'll have a stranglehold on all maritime commerce.*

"Fifth. The government of the United States will turn over to the government of Germany all weapons of war in development and experimental stages, including but not limited to ships, tanks, planes, and all forms of electronic equipment including radar, radar-jamming technology, and the like.

"Sixth. Following the completion of its military operations against the empire of Japan, the United States will cease the production of all military equipment that could be of any possible use against Germany. This includes nuclear and thermonuclear weapons, long-range bombers, aircraft carriers of any size, submarines of any type, and all surface ships above three thousand tons displacement. No ship in the United States Navy shall be equipped with sonar of any kind. All existing sonar units are to be removed from ships of any size under the supervision of the Kriegsmarine. All ballistic missile research, development, and production will be prohibited. Any other weapon developed by the United States, at any time in the future that the German government deems a threat is to be immediately discontinued at our discretion and under our supervision.

"Seventh. The United States shall cease teaching nuclear physics at all private and public institutions. In addition, no one from the United States shall either attend or conduct meetings of any kind related to any phase of nuclear physics. No articles or reports of any kind shall be published or distributed on any aspect of nuclear physics."

The Germans had thought of everything. The United States of America, once the strongest and most advanced nation the world had ever seen, was to be reduced to a second-rate power. There would be only one great power left in the world, and it would be the Germans. The ambassador told them that similar discussions were being held with the British Prime Minister.

"What about the Soviets? Are you talking with them?" asked the president.

"Mr. President, do not be concerned with the Soviets. We have other plans for them," came the uncharacteristically testy reply from the ambassador.

Truman knew what that meant. The Soviet Union was to be destroyed with nuclear weapons. Their leadership, including Stalin himself, had probably died in the attack on Moscow, so God only knows who's in charge now. The Germans obviously did not intend to talk with them unless it was to accept their unconditional surrender, and knowing the Russians, they would all die before they let anybody, especially their ancient enemy, the Germans, take their country from them.

The ambassador spoke for another half hour, outlining the terms for the American capitulation. "And that, gentlemen, completes our terms. Are there any questions? Does anything that I have said need clarification?"

There were no questions. Everything was painfully clear.

"Gentlemen, I want to emphasize a very important point. You will notice that there is no mention of an occupation force. There is no intention of having German troops marching down Pennsylvania Avenue and occupying the capitol and the White House. This state of affairs will prevail only as long as you adhere to both the letter and the spirit of the terms that I have just presented to you. Should you choose to be less than cooperative in the implementation of these terms, then our position on the military occupation of your country will be reevaluated.

"One last thing, gentlemen, and then I will leave you to your deliberations. I must have your answer of unconditional acceptance of these terms by six o'clock tonight. If I do not have such an answer, nothing will prevent the resumption of our nuclear attacks on your East Coast cities and military installations. I must make a positive communication with Berlin to stop these attacks. In the absence of such a communication from me personally, the attacks will be made. I urge you—"

"Like the one on Benns Church in Virginia, Mr. Ambassador?" the president interrupted, finally boiling over with anger.

Ambassador Haeften had expected this remark. The report he had received from Berlin indicated that the first atomic missile fired from their submarines had detonated in the Virginia countryside twenty to thirty kilometers west of its intended target. Now he knew the name of the unfortunate target.

Keep your tones measured, thought Haeften. *Elicit no emotional response.* "Mr. President, the destruction of Benns Church was not intentional. To be quite honest, we missed our target, which was the Naval Air Station. Please believe me when I tell you that we deeply regret the destruction of this town and the loss of civilian lives."

Most certainly. But of course. They "deeply regret it." But not enough so they won't do it again, only on a much larger scale. President Truman was still seething, but this time he kept quiet. He did not want to antagonize this man who now held the fate of the United States in his hands.

"If that will be all, gentlemen, I will take my leave. I urge you, as strongly as I can, to accept these generous terms without delay. Our missile boats are still on station. It is my hope and my prayer they will not have to be called back into action. Whether this happens or not is now entirely in your hands."

And you're damn lucky about that, thought Haeften. *If Hitler had been in possession of the bomb, there would have been no discussion, just total destruction, followed by an impossible ultimatum. But I'm sure they know this.*

The five men sat in stunned silence after the door closed behind the ambassador. It was now four o'clock. They had two hours to decide the fate of their country and probably the free world. Finally, Edward Stettinius broke the silence.

"This is outrageous! It flies in the face of all civilized conduct! They're threatening our cities with atomic destruction if we don't surrender! That violates all the rules of war!"

"Yes, that's all true, Edward," said George Marshall. "And if our positions were reversed, we'd do the same thing. In fact, we already have. The targets we have chosen for nuclear destruction in Japan are all heavily populated areas, so our hands aren't entirely clean. Now we're on the other side, and we have to accept the situation for what it is. We know they have the technology to do this, and now they have shown us that they also have the will."

"George, do we have anything that can stop them?" asked the president. "Anything at all?"

George Marshall considered his answer carefully before saying, "No, Mr. President, we don't."

George Marshall was as depressed as he had ever been, but he managed to continue. "Our fleet, what's left of it, is bottled up in port by the German blockade. We could put everything we have to sea in hope of getting something past the blockade and sinking their submarines, but it's very likely that anything we try to get out would be sunk by their new subs.

"In reality," he continued, "all we've got at the moment are some B-24s with sonar-homing torpedoes, and now that everything at Norfolk is gone, we probably have a lot fewer of these planes than we did earlier today. We might be able to sink some of their missile-firing submarines, but we don't know how many of them there are or where they're located. We know they have at least two, because that's what the pilot of the patrol plane said. We don't know where they're going to strike next, and we'd be lucky to get all of them even if we did. They could launch from anywhere within one or two hundred miles of their next target, Mr. President, and that's a lot of ocean for us to cover, even with ten times the number of planes we have left. From what the patrol plane reported, two subs can launch four missiles in less than thirty minutes, and if even one of those monsters gets through, it's all over for whatever it hits."

"So you're advising me to accept their terms. Is that it, George?"

A long, heavy silence enveloped the Oval Office.

George Marshall continued. "I see no alternative, Mr. President. If we try to find their missile launchers and fail, they'll hit us with everything they have, and the destruction would be incalculable. Most of our population lives on the East Coast, and most of our industry and financial institutions are here as well. They would all be destroyed, and our nation would be finished for a hundred years. There would be Germans occupying every major city, and the presidency and Congress would be replaced by a military dictatorship run from Berlin. No, as hard as it might be for us to accept this, I think we have no choice. I'm sorry, sir, but that's the way I see it."

"What do the rest of you think?" Truman asked.

They sat in stunned silence. No one could disagree with Marshall's argument and no one offered alternatives. It seemed as though the greatest and longest-lived democracy the world had ever seen was about to capitulate to a much smaller nation, but one with a single-minded leadership who had stolen a technological march on them and the rest of the world.

It was almost too much for Truman to bear. Now he would go down in history as the president who had to surrender to the Germans in order to save his country from total destruction.

The discussion now became angry and heated. The four other men became very agitated. Everyone was blaming someone else for the debacle, and accusing each other of incompetence.

All of this is completely irrelevant , thought the president. *I need ideas, not this.*

"All right, gentlemen, that's enough. The way I see it, we have no choice but to accept their terms if we are to survive as a nation. The Germans have the power to destroy us, and I'm not going to let that happen, even if it means surrendering to them. Does anyone have another idea?"

Silence.

"Then I'm going to see Ambassador Haeften. I will tell him that I accept their terms unconditionally and have him call off the nuclear attacks. Any objections? Any alternatives?"

There were none.

"Before I go to see the ambassador, this is what I want you to do ..."

Washington, DC
July 3, 1945 4:30 p.m.
The Willard Hotel

Ambassador Haeften was trying his best to remain calm, but he couldn't. He knew that in less than two hours, orders would go out from Berlin for the second strike against an American city, and he could do nothing to prevent this unless Truman agreed to their terms.

He hoped and prayed the president agreed, because the next target for atomic destruction was Boston. The ambassador loved that city and knew it well. He had been an exchange student at Harvard in 1921, only three years after the end of the First World War. He had encountered no problems and no resentment, due in no small part to his easy-going manner, dashing good looks, and continental accent. He was immediately accepted as a "good" German.

Von, as they had called him, had been very honest about his part in the First World War. He had been disqualified from military service for health reasons, but he'd pulled enough strings and used his family's name in the right places to get into the war. He had desperately wanted to fight but had to settle for the assignment of driving an ambulance for the medical corps. The crowd he ran with enjoyed his stories about action at the front lines. Some of the older students at Harvard had actually fought in the war, and it was from them that he sought, and received, acceptance. After all, they agreed, they were all soldiers serving their countries.

The year 1921 had been magical for him. He had fully enjoyed everything that his adopted city had to offer. He had discovered major league baseball and became an avid Red Sox fan, reveling in the time he spent in that most famous of all big-city baseball temples, Fenway Park. He went to as many games as his classroom schedule permitted and cheered himself silly rooting for the home team. There was always lots of beer, Polish sausage, and good times with his new friends.

Alas, the Red Sox finished second in their league that year behind the hated New York Yankees. It was all because of "the curse" that had been placed on the Red Sox since that infamous day in 1920 when Babe Ruth was sold to the Yankees for a paltry $100,000.

Harry Frazee, the owner of the Red Sox, had needed the money to finance his Broadway production of *No, No, Nanette,* so he sold The Bambino to the Yankees to raise the money. The Sox had finished the season with a record of seventy-two wins and eighty-one loses, a below .500 season, and this was a source of national shame and disgrace. *And all because that schmuck of an owner needed money for his miserable show,* he thought.

Then there was Caitlin O'Connell, she with flaming red hair, a face full of freckles and a laughing, smiling, ruby-red mouth that had found his own mouth on many a cold winter evening. He had been a virgin before meeting her at a Harvard fraternity party, but that was soon taken care of by this charming creature who found him irresistible.

But all too soon his happy days at Harvard and his languid nights with Caitlin came to an end and he had to return to Germany. He wondered if she was still alive and living in Boston; the city for which he could now do nothing for but wait and pray.

A steward interrupted his reverie. "Mr. Ambassador! *Mr. Ambassador*! President Truman is here."

"Show him in immediately! Mr. President—"

"Mr. Ambassador. I accept your terms. With no conditions."

Right to the point, thought the Ambassador. *Good.*

"Gerhard, get me Berlin. I wish to speak to the chancellor immediately."

"Mr. Ambassador, I would like to remain here while you make this call. I need absolute assurance that the attack has been called off."

"Of course, Mr. President. I understand your concern. Elisabeth, plug in your earpiece and interpret for President Truman everything that is said."

"Yes, Mr. Ambassador," Elisabeth responded.

Then only a few seconds later, Gerhard said, "Mr. Ambassador, I have the chancellor now. The connection is loud and clear."

"Chancellor, I have wonderful news," began Haeften. "The Americans have accepted our terms unconditionally. President Truman is here with me now, and he wants your absolute assurance that there will be no more nuclear attacks on American cities. Yes, sir, we'll hold."

Now it was Elisabeth. "Mr. President, the chancellor is ordering Admiral Raeder to communicate with the captains of the missile-firing submarines and order them to stand down."

Minutes now seemed like hours to the president.

"Yes … yes … Mr. President, I can hear the admiral talking with the submarine captains giving them the order."

The president felt more agonizing minutes pass.

"The admiral is now confirming with the chancellor that the order has been received and understood. And now the chancellor is telling the ambassador that … there will be no nuclear attack launched, sir."

A relieved President Truman was visibly crying. Ambassador Haeften was also crying. The city he considered to be his second home, the city of fond memories and his first love, would be spared.

The two men shook hands. Both wanted to embrace the other, but Midwestern reserve and German correctness would not let this happen.

Finally the ambassador spoke. "Mr. President, we have survived a disaster for your country, and I believe, for ours as well. Now there is much work to do. First—"

"I know, Mr. Ambassador." said President Truman, now recovering his composure. "It's already started. I have ordered General Marshall to secure all the facilities involved in our Manhattan Project and to bring the scientists and technicians on your list to Washington as you instructed, along with all the fissionable materials produced by our enrichment facilities. I have put the full might of the United States Army at his disposal to do this, just in case there is resistance. I have also ordered him to communicate with the general staff of your country to begin the disengagement of our troops who are in combat against Germany and to make plans to have them and all their equipment shipped home."

A man of action, thought Haeften. *I will communicate this observation to Berlin and tell the chancellor that I believe we can work with him.*

"Mr. President, these are most prudent and correct actions. We will, of course, provide your staff with some of our own people to assist you and your staff with the implementation of the terms we agreed to this afternoon. Now, I'm sure that you have a lot of work to do, as do I. So, if there is nothing else we need to discuss, Mr. President ..."

"Thank you, Mr. Ambassador. For my part, sir, my staff and I will do everything we can to see to it that the terms of our agreement ... Oh, I almost forgot. Here's my copy of the agreement with my signature at the bottom. You'll probably want this for your governmental archives."

The ambassador accepted the proffered document as though it was a sacred offering, bowing slightly to the president.

"As I was saying, Mr. Ambassador, my staff and I will do everything we can to implement both the letter and the spirit of the agreement. We want no more of those terrible things to strike our cities. Now I'll bid you a good afternoon, Mr. Ambassador. I have a speech to make to the American people this evening, and I need to start writing it."

Yes, we'll be able to do business with this man, thought the ambassador. *But right now, I wouldn't want to be in his shoes. What an awful thing he has to do tonight.*

Washington, DC
July 3, 1945 8:00 p.m.
The Oval Office of the White House

"Thirty seconds, Mr. President."

Harry Truman became vice president only because he was acceptable to both the conservatives in the party and the New Dealers. Roosevelt could have been elected again with anyone as vice president, but it was Truman's fate to have been chosen when Henry Wallace was dropped after his first term. "Wallace is too strange," some people had said. "We need someone more stable, someone like Harry Truman." So here he was, now President of the United States, and with the most difficult task any president had ever been given: to tell the American people that they had lost the war and would now be subject to the will of a foreign power.

The irony of the date had not been lost on him. It was July 3, and tomorrow the country would normally be celebrating its one hundred and sixty-ninth anniversary of independence from foreign rule. A massive fireworks display had been planned for Washington. The president would now have to tell his fellow citizens that the start of their next one hundred and sixty-nine years would be under the domination of a new and very dangerous foreign power. He doubted there would be fireworks in the skies of any America city tomorrow night.

Now he called on his stern Southern Baptist upbringing for the strength he needed to tell the American people, who had never seen defeat in war, that they had lost the biggest and most important conflict in history. The optimism of FDR's "… we will gain the inevitable triumph, so help us God," which had aroused the American people's fury just a little over three years ago, was now gone. And he hoped he had the wisdom and the character to tell them so.

"Fifteen seconds, Mr. President."

Everyone was watching him. All those movie cameras out there would record every word and every twitch. *Please, God, please: help me get through this.*

The lights were turned to full brightness and the cameras began to whir. He saw the director pointing at him. It was time.

"My fellow Americans, I come to you this evening with a heavy heart. This is a very dark time in our history. You have probably heard of the destruction of our naval installations at Norfolk,

Virginia. I must now tell you that this destruction was brought about by an attack by German submarines firing nuclear missiles. This is a new and very destructive weapon that is thousands of times more powerful than the largest weapon available to us or any other nation. Every ship at Norfolk was destroyed, as well as every shore installation for many miles in all directions. The loss of human life is incalculable, but we believe it to be in excess of 150,000, most of them service personnel and their families. During the coming weeks and months, tens of thousands more will die from heat and radiation burns.

"The Germans have made it clear that unless we accept their terms, every city and military target on our East Coast will suffer the same fate. We have heard from our British allies that their naval base at Scapa Flow has also been destroyed by German nuclear weapons, and that Prime Minister Churchill, faced with the reality of the complete destruction of his country, has capitulated. Nuclear attacks by the Germans have also been made on the Soviet cities of Moscow and Stalingrad, but as of yet, we have no information on the damage caused by these attacks.

"Now it falls to me as your president to inform you that I have accepted the terms presented to us this afternoon by the German ambassador. I have done this to prevent any further loss of life and the certain destruction of our East Coast cities. Pursuant to these terms, I have issued orders that our own program for the development of nuclear weapons be discontinued, and that all the scientists and technicians involved with this program be brought to Washington and turned over to the Germans. All of our nuclear research and development facilities are to be dismantled under the supervision of the Germans.

"At present, we are engaged in a major conflict on two fronts: against Germany in Europe, and against the empire of Japan in the Pacific. In accordance with the terms that we accepted from the

Germans, our war with them in Europe is finished, and all of our troops and equipment in this theater will be brought home. The war against Japan, however, will go on, and we remain confident that we will prevail in this struggle. The Germans are no longer allied with the Japanese, and they will not assist them in their war with us. The war against Japan will continue to be a difficult and costly struggle, but we know that we have both the means and the fortitude to see it through to a successful conclusion.

"After we defeat the Japanese, more sacrifices have been demanded of us by the Germans. We will have to cede to them all of our possessions in the Pacific, including the Hawaiian Islands, the Philippine Islands, and the Panama Canal. I know this will be very difficult, because so much of our blood was shed in defense of these islands beginning on December 7, 1941. It will not be easy to give up these bases without a fight, but the alternative, which is the destruction of our East Coast cities by nuclear weapons, is something we cannot accept. In addition, I have been assured by the German ambassador that all maritime nations that currently use the Panama Canal, including the United States, will continue to have access to this important waterway.

"This is the first time in our history that we have ever been forced to capitulate to a foreign power. This will not be easy for us to bear. We have been a confident and victorious people throughout our existence. We are also a tough and resilient people, and we will get through this time of trial no matter how long it lasts. I am certain that the forces of tyranny and oppression that now reign will one day be overthrown, and we will once again enjoy the freedoms that we have had for so many generations.

"Let us, therefore, conduct ourselves with courage and dignity, even in this, our darkest hour. Let our conquerors know that while they have defeated us with arms, they have not, and never will, defeat us in spirit. Let us retain the assurance of a better tomorrow, even though we are now bowed down under the yoke of oppression. Let us show the world what Americans are made of. Let us set the example for other conquered nations, so that one day, we may all rise up and throw off the chains of slavery that now bind us.

"Good night, God bless you, and may God bless the United States of America!"

Chapter 6

To the Last Bullet

Berlin
July 9, 1946 4:15 a.m.
Spandau Prison

"So that's how you got us out of the war. How did you do it with the British, Colonel?"

"Well, Dr. Oppenheimer, we needed someone just as hard-nosed as we knew Churchill would be. We looked around a bit and came up with Count Albrecht von Bernstorff, who was an embassy councilor and part of our plot to kill Hitler. Tough guy, hard as nails, and wouldn't rattle easily.

"We sent him to see Churchill right after Scapa Flow had been bombed. He listened for a full forty-five minutes while Churchill went on about how '… we will fight you on the beaches and in the streets, we will never surrender ….' When he finally stopped, Bernstorff simply took a map out of his briefcase and placed it before Churchill. On this map were two hundred circles. Bernstorff told him that each circle represented the area of total destruction that a fifteen-thousand-ton atomic bomb would create, and that if two hundred of these bombs were used against England, there would be nothing left to scrape up. Churchill looked at the map and saw that most of the circles were over their major cities. Now, we didn't have two hundred bombs at that time, but Churchill didn't know that. He only knew that Scapa Flow and the fleet had been destroyed by atomic bombs. Bernstorff said that Churchill folded without further discussion, and England was out of the war. He said that Churchill almost seemed relieved, which isn't too surprising, given the state that England was in even before Scapa Flow."

"Yes, we heard," said Dr. Oppenheimer. "Pretty damn near starvation because nothing was getting through the submarine blockade. But what happened after we and the British were forced out of the war? We heard the Soviets were taking a real beating."

"That's right, Dr. Oppenheimer. After we got the Americans and the British out of the war, our field commanders went crazy with their new nuclear weapons. They were blowing the hell out of everything the Soviets had, but they still kept coming.

"What finally happened was that our scientists were able to persuade the high command that all of these nukes were poisoning the land and the air, and if we didn't stop using them, we would inherit a very dead Soviet Union, and possibly poison the air for the entire planet. With a lot of grumbling, we decided to limit the use of nukes to special, high-value targets that simply would not yield to conventional weapons.

"The problem with the Soviets was that after our raid on Moscow, we couldn't find anyone to talk to. We didn't know who was in charge or where he was. We kept calling them on all frequencies until we finally received a reply. Yes, they would be willing to talk to us if we would come to them in Kurgan. Chancellor Stauffenberg asked me if I would like to volunteer to head up a delegation to Kurgan, and I said, 'Of course, sir,' as he knew I would. Besides, I was the logical choice. I spoke Russian better than anyone else on the staff. I was also promoted to full colonel because, as the chancellor said, 'The Soviets might respect that rank more than a mere major.'"

"Lucky you."

"Yeah, lucky me. So, we all set off for Kurgan, using the chancellor's Condor and not knowing whom we would be meeting with or what would happen. We told the Soviets about the time we would arrive. We refueled at Zaporizhzhya, our most forward Luftwaffe base at the time so that we would have enough for the round trip. We didn't know what kind of aircraft support facilities the Soviets would have at Kurgan, so we decided to take no chances. Turned out to be the best thing we did on the entire trip. The whole story of that trip is still under wraps, so I'm going to have to raise your security classifications to Top Secret. This is what happened when we met with the Soviets ..."

Kurgan
November 3, 1945 2:00 p.m.
Soviet Military Headquarters

"Chairman Beria will see you now."

About time, thought Colonel Rinehart. *He'd kept us waiting in this goddamn freezing room long enough. Okay, let's do this.*

Lieutenants Westphal and Weiss, both proficient in Russian and who had volunteered for the mission, accompanied him.

What the men saw when they entered the meeting room was a long table littered with cigarette butts and empty vodka bottles. Seated in the center was Lavrentiy Beria, former head of the NKVD, the People's Commissariat for Internal Affairs, and responsible for the massacre of millions of people under Joseph Stalin. To his right sat Georgy Malenkov, a secretary of the Central Committee, and rumored to have been instrumental in the downfall of Nicolai Yezhov, the former head of the NKVD. The ties between him and Beria were very strong.

To Malenkov's right was Nikita Khrushchev. He had supported Stalin's purges of the 1930s, and had been rewarded with the post of governor of the Ukraine. Hundreds of thousands more had died under his rule. He had been in Stalingrad as a political officer during the winter campaign between 1942 and 1943, and had barely escaped death on several occasions.

At the opposite end of the table were Generals Ivan Konev and Georgy Zhukov. Both were very hard men who had seen many battles and were not to be trifled with. Rinehart wondered how he had let himself be talked into this.

Rinehart removed some papers from his briefcase, but before he could begin, Beria was screaming at him. "You think you can make us surrender and take our land away just by reading us a piece of paper?"

"Mr. Chairman," Rinehart protested, "if I may be permitted to present our terms to you, I—"

"Terms! *Terms?* You dare to come to us with *terms?*" Malenkov leaned over and whispered something into Beria's ear.

Beria calmed down. But just a little. "Very well, *German!* Let's hear your fucking *terms.*"

Here we go, thought Rinehart. *In bocca del lupo or something like that—in the mouth of the wolf.*

"First. The armed forces of the Soviet Union will cease all military operations against the armed forces of Germany.

"Second. All members of the armed forces of the Soviet Union and all citizens of the Soviet Union shall withdraw to an area bounded by latitude sixty north and longitude eighty-five east as far east as the city of Iret on the Zaliv Shelikhova. The peninsula of Kamchatka south of the city of Anapka will be included in this new—"

"*What!*" Beria shrieked. "You dare to tell us where we can live? Who the fuck do you think you are, you goddamn hun bastard! This is our land! You understand that, you miserable piece of German shit? You want an answer? Here's your fucking answer!"

Beria picked up an empty vodka bottle and hurled it at Rinehart, missing his head by not more than a centimeter.

Colonel Rinehart took a deep breath and somehow managed to remain calm. "I take it that the chairman rejects our proposal."

"*Get out! Get the fuck out of here!*" Now both Malenkov and Khrushchev were forcibly restraining Beria, but just barely.

"I think we can leave now, gentlemen. We have our answer." Colonel Rinehart got no argument from Lieutenants Westphal and Weiss.

The men hurriedly drove back to the quarters provided to them by the Soviets, and had just settled in when they heard a furious knock at the door. Rinehart opened it and saw a very agitated Fyodor Alexandrov, Nikita Khrushchev's aide.

"C-C-Comrade C-C-Colonel," he stammered. "It-It-It is im-im-imperative that you l-l-leave im-im-immediately!"

"Calm yourself, Fyodor. What do you mean?"

Alexandrov managed to compose himself. "Chairman Beria is working himself into a drunken rage. Comrade Khrushchev says if you do not leave right now, your lives are at risk. Beria means to come out here and kill all of you!"

Colonel Rinehart didn't need to be told twice. "Gentlemen, we're leaving! Right now! Don't bother to pack. Get into the car and head to the airport. We've got to leave immediately, or we'll all be dead."

He turned to Alexandrov. "Now listen very carefully, Fyodor. Your country is headed for annihilation as long as Beria is in charge. There are many in our high command who would like nothing better than to kill every single Russian with nuclear weapons and take over everything. Your one chance is for someone like Khrushchev to replace Beria. That's the only way your country can be saved. Go back to Khrushchev and tell him that I can promise him three weeks without nuclear strikes. However, he must replace Beria within those three weeks, or all hell will break loose over you."

"I understand, Comrade Colonel. But how will we let you know that we have succeeded?"

"Call us on the same frequency you used earlier. Khrushchev's call sign will be Mountain Bear and mine will be Cheese Monger."

"Cheese Monger, Comrade Colonel?"

"It's a long story, which I hope to be able to tell you some day. Now go and good luck."

"You too, Comrade Colonel."

This is a long shot, thought Rinehart, *but it's the best chance that the Soviets have for survival. Either Khrushchev will succeed and we won't have to exterminate them, or he will fail and then God help us all.*

The men jumped into the car and sped off toward the airport, and not a minute too soon. The car carrying Beria and his aides had stopped at their quarters, and not finding them there, correctly guessed they were headed for the airport.

Colonel Rinehart and his men were about five minutes ahead of Beria. They reached the airport and drove straight onto the runway to where the Condor was parked.

"Let's hurry this up. I think they're right behind us," said Rinehart. "We need to get airborne as soon as possible." *It's going to be close, but at least I had ordered that the plane be turned around after it landed.*

The checklist for a take-off in a Condor usually takes about ten minutes, but this time it was completed in thirty seconds. The four engines started in rapid succession, and the plane slowly made its way down the runway.

We might make it, he thought. *We just might make it. Shit! Those drunken bastards are right beside us and they're shooting at us! Come on! Faster! Faster! We might make ... Christ! ... I've been hit!*

Lieutenant Weiss immediately came to his aid. "This could be bad, Colonel. Here, let me help you." Rinehart felt himself getting dizzy and losing control, but he knew he had to hang on until he completed his mission.

Weiss reached for the first aid kit, which contained bandages, a disinfectant, a tourniquet, and a morphine ampoule. He tore off the colonel's left pant leg and tightened the tourniquet, rather expertly, Rinehart thought. Weiss applied the disinfectant and then the bandage. He was about to inject the colonel with the morphine, but the colonel held up his hand.

"Not yet, Lieutenant. I have to talk with Berlin first."

"Yes, Colonel. Let me know when you need it."

I need it now, he thought, *but it would put me out, and I can't let that happen yet.* "Get me Berlin on the radio."

Seconds later, the connection was made.

"Eagle's Nest, this is Eagle. Come in, Eagle's Nest."

"Eagle, this is Eagle's Nest. I read you loud and clear. This is Keitel. Is that you, Colonel Rinehart?"

"General, it's good to hear your voice."

"Yours too, Colonel. How did things go with the Soviets?"

"It was a disaster, General. They wouldn't even listen to us. Lavrentiy Beria is running things now. He's a terrible drunk and refused to let us present our terms. He chased us down the runway, shooting at us as we took off."

"My God, Colonel! Is everyone all right?"

"I'm afraid I stopped one, General, but I'll be all right."

Keitel started to say something, but Rinehart continued. "General, please listen very carefully. Beria will accept no terms that involve giving up territory. The only hope for the Soviets is for him to be replaced. I told Nikita Khrushchev's aide that he, Khrushchev, had three weeks to replace Beria with himself, or it would be all over for Russia. So here's the deal, General: we are to hold off on any more atomic strikes against the Soviets for the next three weeks to give Khrushchev time to kill Beria and take his place. If he succeeds, he will call us on the same frequency that they used earlier. His call sign is Mountain Bear and mine is Cheese Monger. And no nuclear bombs for three weeks."

Rinehart was in real pain now.

"I understand, Colonel, and I will pass this onto the chancellor with my own recommendation that we proceed exactly as you have instructed. Now, can you make it back to Zaporizhzhya?"

"Thank you, General. I think I can make it."

"Good luck, Colonel. Keitel out."

Rinehart sagged back into his seat, dropping the handset. He had completed his mission, knowing that it might cost him his leg, if not his life. "Lieutenant, now would be a good time for that morphine."

Weiss was at his side immediately, making the injection. At last. The drug surged through his veins and brought him relief from the agony in his left thigh. Before he passed out, his last thought was *Oh, God … please don't let them take off my leg … please.*

At German headquarters in Berlin, General Keitel sat back in his chair, lit a cigarette, and reflected on the events of the last few minutes. *I have never particularly liked Colonel Rinehart,* he thought. *Promoted much too fast by the chancellor. He's a very capable man, to be sure, but he's not one of us, not one of the German warrior elite … like me and some of the others. And up until the time he killed Himmler and Bormann, he had probably never fired a shot in anger. Still … he had acquitted himself most admirably then. And just now … most admirably. Perhaps I should revise my opinion of him, at least a little. Yes … enough to make sure he is well taken care of. His bravery today is most deserving of special care, and I'm going to see that he gets it.*

He picked up the phone and dialed a number. "This is General Keitel. Get me the Luftwaffe base at Zaporizhzhya. Yes, immediately! Yes, this is a priority." He heard a lot of static and switching of circuits, but finally the connection was made.

"This is General Keitel from staff headquarters in Berlin. Connect me with the commanding officer. I don't care what he's doing; get him on the phone immediately! With whom am I speaking? Major Flächsner, this is General Keitel." He could hear the clicking of boot heels. "A plane will be landing at your base very shortly. This is the chancellor's plane that departed your base earlier today. Yes, Major, that one. There is a wounded officer on board the plane, a Colonel Johann Rinehart. That's right, Rinehart. He's been shot while carrying out a dangerous mission, and he is to be given the very best medical treatment available at your base. Yes … yes, your best medical officer is to attend to him personally. Yes … This takes priority over everything else, do you understand, Major Flächsner?" The major understood.

"Once Rinehart's condition has stabilized and he is capable of travel, I want him transported to St. Luke's Hospital just outside of Innsbruck. You know the one I mean … Yes, that one. I hold you personally responsible for his condition, Major. Keitel out."

The general had one more phone call to make. "Get me St. Luke's at Innsbruck. Yes, the one for general officers." He heard the switching of more circuits.

"This is General Keitel in Berlin. Connect me with General Liebel." This time the connection was instantaneous.

"General Liebel, this is General Keitel. I want you to prepare to receive a Colonel Johann Rinehart. Yes, I know that, but it's on my authority. Do you understand, General Liebel?" The general understood.

"I can't be certain when he will be coming to your facility, but when he gets there, he is to receive the best care available for as long as it takes for him to make a full recovery. Yes … yes. That will be most satisfactory. Keitel out."

Kurgan
November 3, 1945 4:00 p.m.
Soviet Military Headquarters

Major Dimitri Stepanovich had been listening all day to the standard German radio frequencies hoping to pick up something that might be of use to Comrade Beria and the other members of the committee. They had chosen well when they gave him the assignment, because he was fluent in German.

A filthy language, he thought, *but I learned it well enough in happier days when I was posted to Berlin right after the Molotov-Ribbentrop Pact was signed in April 1939.*

That pact was such a farce, he remembered with disgust. *It had but one purpose, and that was to buy time for Hitler to build up his strength so he could attack us, and that's exactly what happened. I damn near didn't get out before they invaded.*

He turned the dials on his radio and got nothing but static and the hum of coded messages being sent. *Maybe something on higher frequencies. Yes, I'll try that.*

He removed the cover from the high-frequency radio receiver, a rig of his own design, and switched it on. He was actually startled when he heard the transmission coming in so clearly; it couldn't have been more than a few kilometers away.

He listened intently as two German officers spoke, and immediately realized the importance of their conversation. He turned off the radio, sat back in his chair, lit his pipe, and thought for a very long time. *If I do the right thing,* he reasoned, *it would be good for my country and perhaps for Dimitri Stepanovich as well.*

Maybe even a promotion and a medal. That would be nice. But if I guess wrong, well ....

He got out a pencil and paper and began to write, very carefully, everything he had heard on his high-frequency receiver. Then he put the correspondence in an envelope, sealed it, and wrote the name of the person who would receive the precious intelligence.

"Lieutenant! *Lieutenant!*" *Where is that lazy s.o.b.?*

A breathless Lieutenant Yakovlov finally appeared in the radio shack and saluted the major.

"Lieutenant, you are to take this to headquarters right away. Make sure no one else sees this." Dimitri showed him the name on the envelope. "It is for his eyes only. Do you understand?"

"Yes, Comrade Major! I understand, Comrade Major! Am I to wait for a reply, Comrade Major?"

"Wait and see if there is a reply, and if there is, bring it to me immediately, otherwise, return here at once."

"Yes, Comrade Major!"

This Yakovlov's a fool, an ass-kissing fool. Should be transferred to a combat unit on the western front. But not now. More important things to do.

Berlin
November 15, 1945 8:30 a.m.
The Old Reich Chancellery

The radio operator interrupted the morning staff meeting.

"Chancellor, there is a call coming in for Cheese Monger from Mountain Bear."

Maybe he's done it, thought Stauffenberg. *Maybe Nikita Khrushchev's really done it. Maybe he's killed Beria and we won't have to destroy the Soviets after all.*

"Put it through in here. And find the interpreter."

"Yes, Chancellor."

The communication was transferred from the radio room to the conference room where the German high command was meeting.

"Mountain Bear, this is the chancellor. Cheese Monger is not available. What is your situation?"

"Chancellor Stauffenberg, so we finally meet." The voice was slurred and difficult to understand. Stauffenberg had a bad feeling about this.

"This is not Mountain Bear, *Chancellor*, this is Beria. Lavrentiy Beria. And I've found out about your little plot to overthrow me, *Chancellor*."

Chancellor Stauffenberg was stunned. He started to speak, but was interrupted by a blast of profanity from the speaker.

"You fucking hun son of a bitch! Did you really think you could do this to *me*? I ran the NKVD, remember? And we know *everything*! Do you know what we did when we found out? Well, I'm going to tell you, *Chancellor*."

Stauffenberg and the others in the room couldn't believe what they were hearing.

"We got them both, Khrushchev and that aide of his, Alexandrov. Pathetic little man. Not worth any trouble, so we shot him in the back of the head, just as we did at Lubyanka.

"But Khrushchev put up a fight, *Chancellor*. Too bad for him. I gave him to my bodyguards. They told me he had a nice, tender ass. Then what was left of him was brought to me. Know what I did to him then, *Chancellor*? I shot him. Once in each knee, and then once in each collarbone. Slowly. He was still alive, *Chancellor*, so I shot off his balls … *one at a time*! Tough, peasant son of a bitch; not dead yet, *Chancellor*! But I'm a man of mercy, so I shot him in the back of the head, just like Alexandrov."

Chancellor Stauffenberg and the others were too horrified to speak.

Beria continued. "You motherfucking, shit-eating, sons of whores. Do you really think you can defeat us? Never! We laugh at your atomic bombs! You will have to kill the last Russian firing the last bullet out of the last rifle before you defeat us, and then the ghosts of all the Russians you have killed will rise up out of their graves and smash you! We'll kill all of you, and when we get to Berlin, I will personally cut your dick off and shove it down your throat, you worthless—"

Stauffenberg drew his hand across his throat and the transmission ended in mid-sentence.

Silence filled the room. Then Stauffenberg found his composure. "There seems to be a new leader in the Soviet Union. And a not very stable one, at that."

"Agreed, sir," said Keitel. "What should we do about him?"

"Kill him," Jodl responded. "We'll never be able to deal with him."

Silence. Then Stauffenberg said, "I must agree with you, General. But how?"

"The obvious answer would be to drop an atomic bomb on him," said Galland.

"No. We have to be certain that we got him," replied Stauffenberg. "An atomic bomb would leave nothing to verify that he's dead."

"I would suggest a coordinated air and ground attack," said Rommel. "Send in some Arados, bomb the hell out of the place, and then follow up with paratroopers to make sure we get him. Pick up the paratroopers at the airfield with the same transports used for the drop."

"Sounds like a good plan, Erwin," said the chancellor. "We'll need some reconnaissance first so we'll know what to expect when our paratroopers land. Get busy with the details right away. If I were the Soviet leader, I'd be thinking about moving right now, because he knows that we know where he is."

"Right away, Chancellor. But before we do that, sir, today is November 15, and that makes it your birthday." Rommel clapped his hands, the conference room doors flew open, and food and bottles of champagne miraculously appeared and took the place of the papers and charts on the table.

The chancellor smiled and almost reluctantly accepted the good wishes of his staff officers. After a couple glasses of champagne, even he unwound a little and enjoyed the occasion of his thirty-eighth birthday.

How fortunate I am to be here, he thought. *By all rights, I shouldn't even be alive, so thank you, God, for preserving my life for another year.*

Berlin
November 18, 1945 10:30 a.m.
The Old Reich Chancellery

It was the second anniversary of the assassination of Adolf Hitler. No special ceremonies were planned in Berlin or anywhere else in Germany. His assassination was still too fresh in everyone's mind, and because many people were still fearful of what others might think, any outward expression of joy, any hint of a celebration, was muted, very private, and conducted among only the closest and most trusted of friends.

At the Reich Chancellery, plans were underway for a combined assault on Kurgan. A radio operator interrupted with a call for the chancellor.

"It's Georgy Malenkov, sir. He wants to speak to you."

"Chancellor Stauffenberg here. What—"

He was interrupted by the voice of a very confident Georgy Malenkov. "Chancellor, this is Premier Georgy Malenkov. Beria was executed right after your party left because he was no longer capable of leading us. General Zhukov, General Konev, and I are now running the Soviet Union, and before you think about dropping one of your atomic bombs on us, you need to know that we are no longer at Kurgan.

"Beria was a drunk, but he was right about one thing, Chancellor, which is that we will never surrender. The next time we talk, it will be when you come to us on bended knee to offer your surrender. That's right, Chancellor, *your* surrender, not ours."

He paused to let this sink in.

"You know that you are a long way from home, and your supply lines are stretched thin. The Russian wilderness will swallow you up, Chancellor, and then we will fall on you and annihilate you. So we offer you this one chance: turn around and go home now. Leave our country in peace and we will not slaughter you. If you don't accept this offer, then may God help you, because no one else will. Malenkov out."

Silence pervaded the room.

Finally Stauffenberg spoke. "Gentlemen, it looks like we have a war on our hands with a determined enemy who will not listen to any talk of surrender."

"Yes," said Keitel, "but we can still beat them. Our machines are superior to theirs in every respect except numbers, and Speer has some plans to address this issue, which I think you might find most interesting. We've been holding these ideas in reserve in case it became apparent that we would be in for a long war. Now it appears this time has come. Albert, tell us what you've come up with."

"It goes like this, sir," Speer began. "Our industry is working at full capacity. Everybody in Germany is contributing to the war effort. We can't produce any more tanks or planes than we are now. But there is plenty of industrial capacity in other countries, Italy and France, in particular."

"The Italians *and* the French? Most intriguing," said Stauffenberg. "Please continue."

"It's simple. I suggest we contract with them to build all our front-line fighters and bombers. They both have airplane assembly lines and skilled workers who have been sitting idle since they got out of the war. We can set up multiple lines for the 262s and Arados, and within a few months, we'll be able to overwhelm the Soviets in the air. Their economies are in the tank, so they should be eager for the work.

"Malenkov is right about our supplies," Speer continued. "We're stretched pretty thin, and the longer we stay in Russia, the more vulnerable we will become. To overcome this, we need to build a network of railroads, highways, and pipelines that will follow our troops wherever they go. We can hire engineers and workers from the former Soviet colonies to do this. They'll jump at this as long as we pay them well and promise them complete independence."

"Sounds like you've been giving this some thought, Albert," said the chancellor. "Get rolling on all these ideas right away. Work with the foreign ministry when you present these proposals to all the governments involved. I'd like this to be done through diplomacy, if possible, but we'll always have the military option available if that fails. Have the diplomats hint at this without making any overt threats—they'll get the message. We have to keep up the momentum of our attack on the Soviets. Thank you, gentlemen. That is all."

Berlin
March 4, 1946 8:00 a.m.
The Old Reich Chancellery

The plan for the conquest of the Soviet Union was prepared by the German general staff and presented to Chancellor Stauffenberg for his review. This was in sharp contrast to the way Hitler had run the war, which was to dictate strategy, and then compel his generals, however unwilling, to prepare plans to accommodate his wishes.

"Gentlemen, let's see what you have."

General Keitel unrolled a large map of the Soviet Union which indicated the position of all German units and their opposing Soviet forces.

"Chancellor, our plan is to create three large armies, each consisting of about three million men, each to be supported by three thousand planes of all types, ten thousand tanks, and twenty thousand pieces of artillery. Since we have been successful in negotiating with the Italians and French for the use of their assembly lines and workers for the production of our 262s and Arados, they should be coming into service in substantial numbers within the next few months."

"Nine million men!" exclaimed the Chancellor. "Can we really raise a force that large?

"Yes, Chancellor, we can," replied Keitel. "We have extended the draft to all of the territories we have brought into the Reich, and we are certain that we can both raise, and sustain, an army of that size for as long as the war lasts. And with no lowering of standards."

"Very good," replied Stauffenberg. "Please continue."

"These three large armies are to be led by experienced field marshals. Kesselring is recommended for Northern Command. He was the only early field marshal not sacked by Hitler. He's had experience in Russia, and he led the Second Air Fleet in support of Army Group Center during Operation Barbarossa.

"Field Marshal Rundstedt is recommended for Central Command. He's also had experience in Russia. He was responsible for the successful encirclement of large Soviet forces in the battle of Kiev. Rundstedt is seventy-one years old, but he's still very sharp, Chancellor. He wants this very badly, and we think he's up to the job. He knows this will probably be his last campaign, so he'll put everything he's got into it.

"For Southern Command, we recommend Erwin Rommel. He told us he's itching to get back into the fight, and although he has no experience in Russia, the tactics he used while commanding the Afrika Corps should be most effective in the coming campaign. Also, his reputation as a successful commander should prove to be a great asset."

Albert Speer spoke next. "We've taken Malenkov's warning about being a long way from home very seriously, Chancellor. Each of these three armies will be supported by an extensive network of double-tracked rail lines, pipelines, and paved roadways. With our own workforce stretched to its limits with war production, the construction and protection of the road, railroad, and pipeline networks will be contracted out to former colonies of the Soviet Union—Georgia, Belarus, the Baltic States of Latvia, Lithuania, and Estonia, and Poland, Hungary and Czechoslovakia. The promise of complete independence was very appealing to them, and they all signed up, probably as much out of fear of the consequences if they didn't as anything else. Payments will be made not only in the form of hard currency, but also commodities, particularly wheat from the Ukraine and petroleum from the Middle East and Russia. If these pools of workers prove to be insufficient, then we'll start recruiting in other countries, including Italy, France, Greece, and maybe even Canada."

Admiral Wilhelm Canaris, head of Abwehr, the German military intelligence service, spoke next. "Since each of the field marshals will operate with a large degree of independence, with the overall strategy for the campaign being directed from Berlin, communications will become of paramount importance. The wisdom of your order to find a successor to the Enigma machine is now becoming quite apparent, sir. We've developed a new coding-decoding device, based solely on electronics, and we're now distributing it to all combat units. The number of variations possible with this new machine is so many orders of magnitude greater than anything possible with Enigma that we are confident that even the most brilliant Russian cryptographers and mathematicians won't be able to crack it until it's too late."

Chief of Staff Jodl now spoke. "The overall strategy for this campaign will be to remain on the offensive and keep the Soviets from concentrating their forces for a massive counterattack. We will achieve this through dominance of the air, which will permit us to do just about anything we want on the ground. Our reconnaissance over the battlefield and rear areas has improved to the point where we can detect almost all enemy movements and then bring the necessary forces to bear to prevent a surprise attack. With our superior fighters and bombers, we are confident we can strike enemy formations at will very shortly after they have been detected. Our air-to-ground communications have improved, so battlefield conditions can be accurately transmitted to field commanders in a timely manner.

"With regard to refugees, Chancellor, we propose relocating them to Kazakhstan, which is comparatively sparsely populated at the present time. If there proves to be a large number of refugees, then we may have to enlarge the boundaries of this country to accommodate them. We will use our railroad network to move most of them so they won't clog up the roads used by our armies."

At the end of the discussion, Chancellor Stauffenberg addressed his staff. "Gentlemen, we have prepared a plan which I believe will lead us to victory. We now have to see how well it holds up in battle. We must be prepared to make changes as necessary to accommodate the realities of combat, and unlike my predecessor, I promise you that I will be open and receptive to your recommendations. One more thing: Unlike Hitler, there will be no 'no retreat: fight to the last man' orders coming from me. Now there is much work to do. You know what your assignments are, so for now, you are dismissed."

Berlin
March 18, 1946 8:00 p.m.
The Old Reich Chancellery

"One minute, Chancellor."

This is the one part of being chancellor that I really don't like, thought Stauffenberg. *I know what I look like, with the eye patch and everything—a stiff and unsmiling, stereotypical German autocrat giving orders and expecting them to be obeyed. Nothing to be done about that.*

Now I'll be on television, brought right into people's homes. Someone told me that Hitler had been on television in 1936 when he was at the Berlin Olympics. I know I'll be compared to him, and I'll come in second. But never mind that, just do your best ... now.

"People of Germany. The last time I addressed you, I promised I would tell you the truth about the war. A lot has changed since I became chancellor. We have developed and used atomic weapons against the United States of America and England, and I am happy to inform you that they have accepted our terms and are no longer in the war.

"We are, however, still at war with the Soviet Union. I have spoken with their new leader, Premier Georgy Malenkov, and he told us most forcefully that they will never surrender. In fact, he said the next time he speaks to us, he expects it to be when we offer him *our* surrender.

"This means we are in for a long and costly struggle. The Soviet Union is a vast country, its army is large and well led, and its people are very tough. I foresee a struggle that will last for years, not months.

We have already been through a lot, and more sacrifices will be asked of us. Almost every family in our nation has been touched by the war. Nevertheless, I believe that as long as the goal of complete victory over the Soviets is kept in sight, we will be able to sustain the national effort necessary to achieve this."

The chancellor paused.

"Many will want us to end the war as quickly as possible through the use of our atomic weapons. If we follow this path, however, we would make the lands that we conquer, if not the entire world, uninhabitable because of the radioactive poisons released every time an atomic weapon explodes. So while I am not totally ruling out the use of atomic weapons in the coming campaign, I am cautioning our commanders to use them sparingly, and then only when all conventional methods have failed. We do not want to turn our planet into a radioactive wasteland unfit for human habitation.

"I am happy to tell you that other nations have joined our cause. Lithuania, Estonia, Latvia, Belarus, Georgia, Poland, Hungary, and Czechoslovakia have agreed to provide workers for the construction and security of the railroads, highways and pipelines that will supply our troops. For this assistance, we are most grateful. They will be well paid and then rewarded with complete independence from the Soviet Union.

"Two other nations, Italy and France—a former enemy—have also agreed to help us achieve victory. All of our industrial capacity is being used, but given the scale of the task that confronts us, more is needed. The Italians and French have taken on the job of building many of the machines of war that we need to ensure victory. Workers in these two nations will produce our newest jet-powered fighter planes and bombers in great quantity. These highly skilled men and women will also be well paid, unlike the slaves used by the Nazis. We are grateful to the governments of Italy and France for assisting us with their industrial might."

He paused for a moment.

"Refugees from this war will be treated humanely. It will be necessary to remove everyone from the areas that we conquer to prevent sabotage and to give us the space necessary for our population to expand. This will be done in such a way that minimizes the loss of their lives. We must always be mindful of what the world thinks about the way that Germany conducts this war.

"The deeds of the previous government are stained with the blood of millions who were exterminated by the most brutal means imaginable, and this will be attached to us for generations. We must not add to this shameful record by mistreating people who are unfortunate enough to be in the wrong place at the wrong time, and who, through no fault of their own, have to be relocated.

"We have all worked very hard to arrive at this point in the conflict. We are assured of final victory. Let this sense of inevitable triumph keep us dedicated to our work so that with even greater determination, we may arrive at that happy time when we can say that the war is finally over and that our sons, brothers, and husbands will be coming home.

"Good night, God bless you, and may God continue to bless our holy Germany."

Chapter 7

The Nurse and the General

Berlin
July 9, 1946 4:35 a.m.
Spandau Prison

"Sounds like you had a close call, Johann. You never told me about this before."

"I couldn't because of the classified nature of our dealings with the Soviets. I'm violating security regulations now by telling you this, but I think I can trust you both."

"I'm sure the professor won't tell anybody," said Oppenheimer. "And in a few minutes, you won't have to worry about me, either, Colonel."

Neither the colonel nor the professor laughed at the condemned man's gallows humor.

"What happened to you after that, Johann? They must have done a pretty good job patching you up at the Luftwaffe base."

"They did as good a job as they could have, Werner, but they missed something that almost cost me my left leg, and possibly my life. Fortunately, General Keitel's intervention delivered me into the hands of much better doctors, and they were able to turn things around for me. It happened this way … "

Outside of Innsbruck
November 17, 1945 8:30 a.m.
St. Luke's Hospital

"Open your eyes, Colonel!"

Got to do it now! Got to do it now!

"Colonel Rinehart! Open your eyes!"

She sounded so far away, but he felt her touch on his shoulder.

"Come on, Colonel! Wake up!" He felt her gently shaking him into consciousness.

Must do it this time! There! Eyes open! Everything blurry, but oh! The pain!

"Welcome back, Colonel. Don't try to move or speak. Just listen. You're going to be okay. We didn't have to amputate your leg."

My leg! My leg is okay? But I can't feel it … or anything else.

She took his hand and placed it on his left leg. His leg hurt badly, but he felt it. *Thank God! It was still there.*

"You're in St. Luke's Hospital, Colonel. General Keitel arranged for you to come here. You've been away for two weeks, but you're going to make a full recovery."

Two weeks! Has it been that long? He tried to speak, but couldn't. He winced. His whole body was on fire.

"You're still very weak, Colonel. And it's time for your shot. You'll feel better after you've had this."

He felt a little prick, and then a flood of pure bliss washed over him. *Thank you,* he tried to say, but couldn't.

Outside of Innsbruck
November 19, 1945 3:30 p.m.
St. Luke's Hospital

It was two days later, and he had managed to remain awake for longer stretches of time; however, he was still having trouble speaking clearly.

"Awake again, Colonel?"

His eyes focused a bit better this time, and he saw her sitting next to him.

"Hello," he said, his voice barely audible.

"Hello to you, too, Colonel. I'm Connie, and I'll be your nurse for as long as you're here. I know you have a lot of questions, so be still and I'll see if I can answer them for you." She very gently placed her two fingers over his mouth. He could feel their warmth.

"You came to us on the afternoon of November 4. The doctors at the Luftwaffe base had done a fairly good job on you, but you were still running a very high temperature, and there was some infection. We took an X-ray and found that they didn't quite get everything, so we had to go back in and remove what they had missed. The doctor will explain it all to you. It was a narrow escape, but we didn't have to amputate your leg. You should heal up just fine after some physical therapy, and then we'll send you back to Chancellor Stauffenberg as good as new."

The colonel wanted to ask her what had happened after he left Kurgan, but she was one step ahead of him.

"You have a lot of friends who are very concerned about you, Colonel. There are several letters for you, including one from General Keitel."

His voice rasped. "Open that one … read it to me."

"Are you sure, Colonel?"

He nodded; she opened the letter and began to read.

My dear Colonel Rinehart:

I send you the greetings of everyone here in Berlin. We wish you a speedy recovery and a swift return. You are sorely missed at the table.

I have some sad news about your trip to Kurgan. It appears to have been in vain. Beria found out about our plot to have him replaced with Khrushchev, and he killed him in a most brutal manner. Beria then called here to inform us of what he had done.

We were making plans to have him eliminated when we received a call from Georgy Malenkov. He told us that Beria had been removed and that he had taken his place as premier. He said that he, Zhukov, and Konev were now running things.

We're in for a long war, Johann, and it's going to take everything we have to defeat the Soviets, so please return to us as soon as you can.

I have some leave time coming, and I shall spend some of it in Innsbruck with a visit to you.

Until then, I remain

Yours,
Keitel

Oh, my God! Khrushchev's dead and it's my fault! He probably didn't even want to be involved in a plot to overthrow Beria, but I

*did that for him! What an idiot I was! But how did they find out?
Alexandrov! That must be it. He must have betrayed Khrushchev to
Beria. General Keitel didn't say anything about Alexandrov in his letter,
so that's the only explanation. I didn't even know Khrushchev, and he
has been killed because of my stupidity!*

"I'm sorry, Colonel, sounds like bad news. Are you all right?"

"Yes, Connie. I just want to be left alone right now."

Connie left the room, and he started crying.

*I should have waited until we got back to Berlin and then Westphal
and Weiss could have reported on what happened. But no! I had to
make a decision right on the spot, and it turned out to be a very bad
one. Now every Russian will pay for my blunder. Oh, my God, my
God, can you ever forgive me for this?* He cried himself back into
unconsciousness.

Later that day, Colonel Rinehart had a visitor.

"Colonel, I'm Dr. Weitzel. How are you feeling today?"

"Much better, Doctor, thank you."

"Let me take a look." Dr. Weitzel gently removed the bandages
and examined the wound.

"You're healing nicely, Colonel."

"Well, that certainly is good news, Doctor."

"We'll start you on physical therapy in a few days. This is a very
important part of your recovery, Colonel. How well you do with
your therapy will determine how well you will be able to use your
leg for the rest of your life."

"I understand, Doctor."

"The bullet that got you had a flat head, and when it went
through the skin of the airplane, it took some pieces of the aluminum
with it. This is what the doctors at the Luftwaffe base missed when
they removed the bullet. We had to go back in and remove the
aluminum."

"Ouch!"

"Yes, I'm sure. But at the same time, that aluminum skin probably saved your life by slowing the bullet down. If it had done any more damage, it might have severed your femoral artery, and you would have bled to death. As it is, you have a very nasty wound, but we were able to patch you up. So now the rest is up to you, Colonel."

"Thank you, Doctor."

The rest is up to me! But now I've doomed the Russians to atomic extermination! What's the point of it all?

Outside of Innsbruck
November 30, 1945 10:00 a.m.
St. Luke's Hospital

"Good morning, Colonel," said Connie. "You have an important visitor here to see you."

"Who is—" He didn't have a chance to finish the sentence before he saw the imposing figure of General Keitel standing next to him.

"General. I'm— "

General Keitel came right to the point. "Colonel, what's this I hear about your lack of cooperation with your physical therapy? Come on now, this isn't like you. What's this all about?"

Rineheart was almost in tears. "General, you can't possibly understand. I'm responsible for what's going to happen to the Russians. How stupid I was to involve Khrushchev in this without first asking him! I cost him his life! Now Russia's going to be turned into nuclear rubble and everybody's going to be killed all because of me! I shouldn't have trusted Alexandrov."

Keitel sat beside his stricken friend and put his hand on his shoulder. Something he rarely did.

"Now listen to me, Johann," he said gently. "It wasn't Alexandrov who betrayed Khrushchev. Beria killed him before he got to Khrushchev. Shot him in the back of the head. We don't know who told Beria, but it wasn't Alexandrov, we're fairly certain about that. We don't know how it happened, and we probably never will.

"Khrushchev was doomed anyway. Maybe he could have turned things around and signed some kind of an agreement with us, but you and I both know better, don't we? Russians rarely surrender, and they never give up their land without a fight. That's the one thing they'll die for—their land. So it's pretty certain that even if Khrushchev had made an accommodation with us, someone would have killed him, and then we would have been right back where we started."

He paused a moment.

"A lot has happened since you've been away, Johann. Beria was assassinated right after you left Kurgan. Malenkov did it, and he is now sharing leadership of the Soviet Union with Zhukov and Konev. He called us right before we were planning to launch a raid on Kurgan. He seems to be a very intelligent and dangerous man, Johann, so it looks like we'll be at war for quite a bit longer than we thought. Just as Beria had said, 'The last bullet fired by the last rifle carried by the last Russian.' And that's why we need you back. You have a good head on your shoulders and a clear vision. Not like us crusty old Prussian types who can't see beyond the next battle."

Keitel stood and sternly addressed the man in the bed. "Now see here! And this is an order, Colonel! No more despair about what happened to Khrushchev; it couldn't have been helped. You made a courageous call at the time, and it's too damn bad it didn't work out. You've got it pretty good here at St. Luke's. I've met Miss Erickson, and she seems very competent and quite charming and beautiful as well, so I'm sure you're in the best possible hands."

"You're right about that, General. And I have you to thank for getting me into this place. I know it's reserved for only generals and other high-ranking officers."

"Don't mention it, Johann. You deserve the best care our nation can give you. You're important to the war, and we need you back as soon as you recover. By the way, did you know that Hermann Göering came to this hospital quite a few times?"

"No, I didn't, General. I know he seemed to take a lot of vacations, but—"

"Well, Johann, and I tell you this in the strictest confidence; they weren't vacations. Göering was a terrible morphine addict. He was, shall we say, 'impaired' most of the time, and every few months he would admit himself here for detoxification, just so he could do his job, which, I think you'll agree, he didn't do very well. He might have been a competent fighter pilot, but he never understood anything about making war."

"You'll get no argument from me on that, General."

Keitel looked at the younger man seriously. "You and the others did Germany a great favor that day, Johann. And I will also tell you this. Right after the atomic bomb test, the chancellor quietly commissioned a team of the foremost psychoanalysts in the country to take a good close look at our former leader. After examining all of his speeches and decisions, and interviewing quite a few of us who were close to him, it didn't take them long to conclude that he was a 'borderline' personality. In short, he was incapable of winning the war, even if he had been given the atomic bomb on a silver platter. He would have taken himself and all of Germany down with him in a blaze of glory, just like in Wagner's *Götterdämmerung*, where Valhalla and all the gods burn up at the end of the opera. That's where Hitler was leading us."

Before Rinehart could respond, Keitel stood and addressed him with mock Prussian sternness. "Now, I must be going. You *will* get on with your recovery, Colonel!"

"Yes, sir, General! I will tend to this immediately!" he said in equally mocking Nazi obedience. He almost gave a Nazi salute but stopped short. From Keitel's amused expression, Rinehart knew the general had seen this gesture.

"Thank you, sir," said Rinehart sincerely. "Oh, yes, there's one more thing. I never apologized to the chancellor for all the bullet holes in his airplane. I feel personally responsible for them. Please convey my sincerest regrets for this damage."

Keitel was laughing out loud now, something Rinehart had never seen him do.

"Colonel, those fucking bullet holes were easily repaired, so don't worry about them. You concentrate on repairing the bullet hole in *you*."

Rinehart had never heard him say 'fucking,' either.

The older man bowed slightly at the waist to the younger man, clicked his heels together, turned sharply and left the room, laughing all the way down the hall to the hospital's exit.

The day was indeed full of surprises, Rinehart thought, *especially the revelations about Hitler. But of course! Everything fit, beginning with the debacle at Dunkirk, where he had allowed so many British troops to escape back to England. Then there was the invasion of Russia, which he started before we had finished off England, and then Stalingrad, with his "no retreat" order that had doomed the Sixth Army to destruction. Yes! He truly was incapable of achieving victory, and this is why he distrusted his generals so much; they could have given him victory if he had listened to them, at least before Stalingrad and Kursk. So what Keitel told me today was absolute confirmation that Hitler had to go. Even if we had given him the atomic bomb, he would have found a way to snatch defeat from the jaws of victory, and all of Germany would have perished with him. And that's the way he had wanted it from the very beginning!*

Shortly after the general left, Rinehart's two physical therapists, "Gort" and "Igor," as he called them, came into his room. He referred to them as his "physical torturers," and they appreciated his humor.

The men were "a couple," but nobody cared. They were very good therapists, and they immediately noticed that their patient appeared to be a changed man. The two men gently eased Rinehart from his bed into the waiting wheelchair.

"Is the colonel ready for his physical therapy today?" The tone of Gort's voice was positively evil. Rinehart saw him rubbing his hands together and noticed a malicious smile on his face.

"Yes, gentlemen, I'm ready. More than ready. We have a lot of work to make up."

It was starting to rain outside—lots of thunder and lightning.

"It will be a fine storm, Colonel. Perfect for what we're going to do to you today," said Igor.

"For what I am about to receive, may I be truly grateful," he muttered.

"What was that, Colonel?" asked Gort.

Then in a commanding voice and pointing down the hallway in the direction of the torture chamber, he cried, "Lead on, gentlemen, and do your worst. For God, for country, and for this poor, miserable, and fucked-up body of mine—lead on, indeed!"

Outside of Innsbruck
February 13, 1946 10:00 p.m.
St. Luke's Hospital

Johann Rinehart had taken the chance remark by General Keitel about Göering's morphine addiction to heart, and with the help of Dr. Weitzel, he had gradually weaned himself off the drug before he became dependent on it.

Instead, and to his great delight, Rinehart was becoming more and more dependent on Connie. When he finally mustered the courage to ask her to tell him something about herself, she replied that she came from a town in Sweden so small that it didn't appear on any maps. He then asked her what people did for entertainment in her town, and she responded with mock seriousness that "we watch ice melt, Colonel." They both laughed at her remark.

Connie had a beautiful, lilting laugh, which he found enchanting. Enchanting, yes, and he found himself falling under her spell.

She told him that since nothing was going on in her hometown, she escaped to Stockholm as soon as she finished high school, leaving behind a string of broken hearts spread across one hundred kilometers in all directions, including Sven Olafsen, who, it had been assumed by everyone except her, would take her as his wife.

"Sven wasn't a bad man," she said. "Quite the contrary. He was a very good man. Just dull and boring, like the town we lived in."

She had begun her studies at the School of Nursing at Charité Hospital in Berlin. When the war started, she found that returning to Sweden was impossible, so she finished her schooling in Berlin. Following graduation, she used some of the connections she had made at Charité to become a German citizen without the usual waiting period. This was helped by the fact that people with her skills were badly needed for the war effort, and so a way was found to cut through the usual red tape associated with foreigners becoming German citizens.

She was immediately hired by Charité, where she befriended General Oskar Dirlewanger of the SS, who had ended up in St. Luke's with a very serious wound. He had requested that he be attended by "that beautiful, blonde Swedish nurse" he had met at the Charité Hospital in Berlin. Whatever the SS wants, the SS gets, so after a hurried phone call from Innsbruck, it was arranged for nurse Connie Erickson to be transferred to St. Luke's.

Her temporary assignment as nurse to the ailing SS general eventually grew into a permanent position, and she quickly found a home at St. Luke's tending to the highest-ranking officers of the Third

Reich. She told Rinehart that these men were all full of themselves, talking endlessly about how they were going to rule the world as gods; at least, that's what they thought at the beginning of the war. Later, they would come back to St. Luke's as tired and defeated old men, looking only for a pretty face and a warm touch to comfort them in what for some would be their last days. Nurse Connie Erickson gave them all of that, for which she had been handsomely rewarded.

Then there was Colonel Johann Rinehart, and she knew immediately that he was different. He wasn't full of himself like so many of the other officers she had met, although, she found out, he had every right to be proud, even boastful, of his accomplishments. She was told that he had personally assassinated Heinrich Himmler and Martin Bormann on that day when the Nazis' world came crashing down. Then, so it was rumored, he had helped design Germany's atomic bomb, and after that, he had been seriously wounded while on a dangerous mission to try to talk the Soviets into surrendering. But he never spoke of these things. He hardly spoke of himself at all, and then only modestly or with his wickedly clever and self-deprecating sense of humor. Connie had come to enjoy his company, and she felt a sense of accomplishment in seeing him regain his strength.

There had been bad times for him at St. Luke's, the worst being when she had read him General Keitel's letter. He had felt responsible for the terrible things that were going to happen to the Soviets, and it wasn't until Keitel himself had visited him that this overpowering feeling of guilt was alleviated. After that, Colonel Rinehart began to live again, and to her delight, he invited her more and more into the innermost circle of his life.

They had spent a very pleasant day watching the snow fall from the heated sitting room. They had talked about nothing, and everything, and they had taken their meals together in the dining hall, completely oblivious to the hubbub around them.

In the afternoon, they played billiards. He hadn't picked up a cue stick in many years, and she proved to be quite expert at making it look like *he* had won the game; but he knew all along that she was letting him win.

Now it was late. Although he could easily walk by himself, she was holding him very close as they found their way back to his room. When the door closed, she stayed inside.

After he came out of the bathroom, he was pleasantly surprised to see that she had turned down the covers and was in his bed. "Time for a different kind of therapy, Colonel Rinehart."

Johann was at the same time exhilarated and anxious. "Connie, it's been a long time, and I'm not sure …"

She beckoned him to come into the bed. "I'm sure it's nothing I can't handle, Johann."

And what wonderful hands she had. Soon he was fully erect. She was on top of him, guiding him between her legs, and then thrusting and squeezing, thrusting and squeezing, until he could hold back no longer. He exploded in a spasm of exhilaration he had never experienced before, only to be followed by her own pleasure.

Later, lying together, she murmured, "My man … my man … is very good … and very kind … my man … my man …."

He whispered in her ear, "And my woman … does the kind of therapy I'd like to have … for the rest of my life."

Leaning over him and brushing his chest with her breasts, she said, "Johann … is that a proposal or a proposition?"

"A proposal, of—" but he couldn't finish the sentence because his mouth was covered with hers.

Again and again she kissed him hard, as she held his arms out straight with her own. He could feel himself getting erect, and then her hands guided him into her.

"Oh, Johann. Oh, my God! Yes!" She thrust her pelvis forward again and again and again and cried, *"Yes, yes, yes!"*

Chapter 8

New Beginnings

Berlin
July 9, 1946 4:30 a.m.
Spandau Prison

"How long were you at St. Luke's, Colonel?"

"About four months, Dr. Oppenheimer. I healed up pretty fast. My therapy went well, and thanks to Gort and Igor, I was able to resume my duties in Berlin in early April. I moved into an apartment on Ku'damm, brought Connie to Berlin, and we were married last May. She immediately found work at Charité, and that's where she is now. She's the Assistant Director at the School of Nursing. There's so much work for her to do. The war has really taken its toll, and the casualties just doesn't let up."

Oppenheimer was quiet for a long time. "Tell me, has anyone given any thought to what Germany will look like after the war is over? What I mean is, you have been under what amounts to a military dictatorship since 1933. That's thirteen years. Are you going to continue this type of government?"

"Good question, Dr. Oppenheimer. The chancellor is very concerned about this. He called me into his office the other day and asked me what I was going to do after the war. This was the first time I'd heard him speak of this kind of thing."

"Well … what did he say?"

"It went something like this, Dr. Oppenheimer …"

Berlin
April 3, 1946 3:00 p.m.
The Old Reich Chancellery

"Come in for a minute, Colonel. Be at ease and sit down. Now, tell me, Johann, have you thought about what you're going to do when this is all over?"

"I've thought about it some, Chancellor. For one thing, Connie and I would like to start a family. We made a decision to postpone this until the war was over. We want some stability in our lives before we take that big step. Beyond that, I really hadn't thought about it too much, sir."

"Here's something I'd like you to think about, Johann. Germany is going to become a very different place once the war is over. Just about everything in the former Soviet Union will be ours. We're going to incorporate it into Germany and open it up to settlement. It's going to need careful planning and management; we don't want to make a mess out of this.

"Also, we will have global responsibilities. We are now the only atomic power in the world, and we will take steps to see to it that it's kept that way, if you grasp my meaning, Johann. And we must deal with this in a rational and responsible way. We can't be so naive as to think this will be the war to end all wars like the First World War was supposed to be."

"I agree with you, sir. I think there will actually be more wars, now that the major colonial powers, and I include the Soviets, are no longer in control. All of the independence movements that they suppressed will probably flare up. I don't see how we can be the world's policemen and try to put all these fires out. Not only would this be impossible, sir, but it would drain our resources and guarantee that we would be in perpetual state of warfare. I don't think this would be acceptable to a nation that's already been at war for seven years."

"That's just the kind of level-headed thinking we are going to need after the war, Johann, and that's why I want you to stay on and help me transform Germany into the kind of nation that can deal with these challenges. Look, we can't go on being a military dictatorship forever. What might have been the right kind of government for wartime doesn't necessarily translate to peacetime. I want to move us in a direction of a representative civilian democracy. I want to work myself out of a job."

Rinehart was stunned. *The most powerful leader in the world and he wants to "work himself out of a job." What an extraordinary man this Claus von Stauffenberg is!*

"I'd be honored to help in any way I can, sir, and thank you for your confidence in me. But ... how do you intend to do this?"

"I want to form a transitional government that will eventually move us from being a dictatorship to a democracy. Yes, Johann, a democracy ... just like the countries we defeated. Ironic, isn't it? We're going to take on the same form of government as the United States and Great Britian, both of whom we bombed into submission."

Before Rinehart could respond, the chancellor stood up and continued. "But as to our own form of government, I'll need the help of people who were involved in politics before Hitler came to power in 1933. I've been making some discrete investigations, and I think I've come up with the right man to help me with this."

"Who's that, sir?"

"Konrad Adenauer. He was Lord Mayor of Cologne when Hitler came to power. He was a ferocious anti-Nazi, Johann, and this almost cost him his life. He's seventy years old now, but from what I've heard, he's still very sharp. He's living in retirement in Cologne, and—"

"Let me guess, sir. You want me to go see him."

The chancellor appreciated the wry humor in his friend's response and returned in kind. "Yes, Johann, but you'll be able to speak in German this time. And I don't think anyone will be shooting at you as you leave."

"I appreciate that very much," said Rinehart with a chuckle. "Now, what do you want me to tell him?"

"Tell him that when the war ends, I want Germany's military dictatorship to end with it. I want us to return to a civilian government so we can unleash the full potential of our people in the two great tasks that lie before us—settling our new lands and assuming our responsibilities as the most powerful nation in the world.

"Also, tell him I want to free our creative and spiritual forces as well. We are the land of Bach, Beethoven, Schiller, Goethe, Martin Luther, and Dietrich Bonhoeffer. Tell him that these voices have been stilled for too long, and that I want his help in creating the kind of German society where a new generation of musicians, writers, and theologians can be heard without fear of reprisal."

"I'll go visit him, sir, and I'll tell him exactly what you told me. It might be best if I wore civvies for this occasion. What do you think?"

"Probably a good idea. And go by yourself for this visit, Johann. I don't want him to feel threatened by a whole bunch of us showing up on his doorstep, even dressed in civvies."

"Consider it done, sir. I'll leave tomorrow."

Cologne
April 5, 1946 10:00 a.m.
The estate of Konrad Adenauer

"Good morning, Herr Rinehart. Please come in."

"Thank you very much, sir. And thank you for agreeing to see me."

"My pleasure, Herr Rinehart. Please, let's sit on the veranda. It's most pleasant this time of the morning. Gussie, please bring us some refreshments."

Konrad Adenauer was tall and distinguished; the map of his life seemed written in bold type on his very Germanic face. The facial injuries he had suffered in an automobile accident many years ago only enhanced his appearance as a man to be taken very seriously.

Adenauer was born into a Catholic Prussian military family, but he was drawn to the study of law rather than to the study of war. He was educated at the universities of Freiburg im Breisgau, Munich, and Bonn, and became interested in politics when he worked for a lawyer in Cologne who was the head of the local German Center Party Organization. Religion played an important role in politics in those days, and the center party had been formed by Catholics to protect their interests against the Protestant-dominated government.

His hard work earned him the post of Assistant to the Lord Mayor of Cologne in 1906, then Deputy Mayor, and finally Lord Mayor in 1917, a post he held until 1933 when the Nazis took over. Since then, he had retired from politics and had narrowly escaped being sent to the concentration camp at Buchenwald. He had devoted himself to his family, and to his garden, of which he was very proud, and which Johann Rinehart now used as an opening gambit.

"You have a lovely garden, Lord Mayor." Rinehart used the title of Adenauer's last position as a sign of respect for the elder statesman. "Is it your own work?"

"Yes, Herr Rinehart, it is. I devote most of my time to my family and to my garden." *Very impressive,* Adenauer thought. *A German officer, to be sure, but a most knowledgeable and respectful one. Let's see what he has to say.*

"Well, Lord Mayor, I am here to lure you away from your garden and entice you back to Berlin. Your talents are once again required, but this time in the service of your country."

Adenauer was at the same time taken aback and thrilled. He sensed things were different in Berlin now that Hitler and his gang were gone. *But different in which way?* he mused. *Germany was still being run by men in uniform, some of them the same men who had served under Hitler. But they were now subordinates to Stauffenberg, who seemed to be quite different from them. Stauffenberg was also a man of faith, and this counted for something. And he had ended the extermination of the Jews. Perhaps this would be the opportunity to make the final chapter of my life a memorable one. But don't give in too easily ...*

"Herr Rinehart. I am seventy years old, and I have been retired from politics for many years. I—"

"Forgive me, sir, but these are precisely the two qualities that attracted the chancellor to you. Your many years in public service give you the experience our nation needs, and your political past and known opposition to the Nazis give you the credibility required for the job. In addition, there is no scandal attached to any of your pre-Hitler political offices. Sir, there is no one else with your unique combination of attributes. You are the perfect candidate for what the chancellor has in mind."

"And just what is that, Herr Rinehart?"

"Lord Mayor, the chancellor is looking forward to the post-war years, and he sees a Germany that must be transformed. From 1933 to late 1943 we lived under a repressive military dictatorship that brought many horrors into this world and shame to Germany. I don't have to detail these facts for you. Our national spirit and our creative energies were crushed under the totalitarian heel of the Nazis, and now that this evil has been exposed, it is being exorcised. This will take time to complete, maybe generations.

"But now, sir, it is time to reawaken our people and set them free. Our land of musicians, artists, writers, and theologians must rise from the ash heap of its dead Nazi past. The chancellor believes that this cannot be done under any form of military dictatorship, so he wants to move Germany toward a government that is truly representative of the people.

"And he needs help in doing this, specifically, your help. He has asked me to inquire if you would be interested in helping him with the formation of a transitional government that would bridge the gap between the present military dictatorship and a democratically elected government."

Rinehart paused, and then added, "Your country needs you, sir. You cannot refuse."

"What would my role be, Herr Rinehart? Would I be an advisor to the chancellor, or would I be a part of this transitional government?"

"Sir, the chancellor will be most receptive to your views on this subject and all the other factors that would go into the formation of this transitional government. He has indicated to me that there would be no limits on what your role might be. He invites you to come to Berlin and talk with him about this with no preconditions whatsoever."

And I tend to believe him, thought Adenauer. *Yes, this might work. I might get into the history books after all—and on the right side.*

Adenauer rose to indicate that the conversation was over. "I will give the chancellor's proposal the most serious consideration, Herr Rinehart. The most serious consideration."

"Thank you, sir," said Rinehart, now also on his feet. "That's all we can ask from you at this time. I'm sure the chancellor will be most gratified by your response."

"Come, Herr Rinehart. Let me see you out. Safe travel, and my best regards to the chancellor."

Adenauer closed the door. He didn't have to think too long about this one. "Gussie, make preparations to close down the house for an indefinite period of time. And start packing for a long stay. We're going to Berlin!"

"I've already started packing, dear."

"What?"

"Yes, Konrad. I was listening to the conversation, and I knew what you would say. Can't keep a frisky old warhorse like you locked in the stable forever. Now, you just leave everything to me. I'll have us ready to move to Berlin in about a week. You call the chancellor and tell him that we're coming, and then find us an appropriate place to stay. You might try Marmorhaus on Ku'damm. We liked that place the last time we were in Berlin, and it's so close to everything … the cathedral, KaDeWe, Wertheim's, and Kranzler's are all right around the corner. So see if you can get that for us again, won't you?"

"Yes, dear." *I'm about to become one of the most powerful men in the most powerful nation in the world, and I'm … oh, never mind. Just go ahead and get it done as ordered.*

Chapter 9

Loose Ends

Berlin
July 9, 1946 4:50 a.m.
Spandau Prison

Oppenheimer was quiet for some time before he spoke.

"Professor, there's one more thing I must know. You started your nuclear program in 1934. Yet by 1940, when your team was broken up by Hitler, you still hadn't produced a bomb—six years and just a lot of research. We started our program a lot later, and after only three years, we were less than two weeks away from a test. What I want to know is this: did you intentionally hold back the completion of your work so Hitler wouldn't get the bomb?"

Without hesitation, Werner Heisenberg answered. "Yes, Oppy, that's exactly what we did. I've never told this to anyone before, but under the circumstances, I think … I know that it's appropriate. Yes, we could have had the bomb before 1940 and the breakup of our team. Even with all of the problems we had with the Gestapo removing our Jewish scientists, we could have done it. All the elements were in place. We had the high-speed centrifuge technology we needed to produce U^{235}, and we had all the basic research done. All that was lacking was a design, and I'm certain that somebody would have come up with the 'atomic cheese' idea, or something better, that we needed to build the bomb.

"But we didn't, Oppy, and the reason is that we didn't want Hitler to get his hands on the atomic bomb. God knows what he would have done with it! There was never an overt conspiracy to slow things down, and there was never any open discussion about this; we just did it. We didn't want that megalomaniac to have it within his power to destroy the world, which is what we were afraid he would have done.

"So we slowed things down. I kept telling the Nazis that it looked like a nuclear bomb would require two tons of fissionable material, and we couldn't possibly produce that much and neither could the Allies. That was all it took to convince Hitler and the other Nazis that we didn't have to worry about atomic bombs being dropped on Germany. So when he broke up our team in 1940, it was a tremendous relief to all of us. Now we really couldn't make the atomic bomb for him even if we had wanted to.

"At the time, this meant certain defeat for Germany and occupation by the Soviets. But we couldn't be worried about that. Hitler mustn't get the bomb, and that was all there was to it. We'd worry about the Soviets' getting the bomb later. Fortunately, this never happened.

"When the change in government took place, and we saw the kind of people who were in charge, things became quite different, especially after the new chancellor visited Auschwitz and spoke the way he did about what had happened to the Jews and how Germany would hold itself accountable for this. We all knew that we had to get back to our research and make an atomic bomb as soon as possible. We were fewer in number because of the Gestapo, but we were determined to see this through. So when Johann gave us the design breakthrough, we felt confident we could finish in time to win the race. And you know the rest of the story."

"Yes, I do. And I thank both of you for telling it to me. I am at peace now."

Then Johann said, "Dr. Oppenheimer, I think there's one more thing you might be interested in knowing."

"And what's that, Colonel?"

"Shortly after Stauffenberg became chancellor, he quietly gathered together our leading psychoanalysts and asked them to take a look at Hitler's personality. They examined all his decisions and speeches, and interviewed quite a few people that were close to him."

"Interesting, Colonel. So what did they find?"

"Their unanimous conclusion was that Hitler was what might be called a 'borderline' personality, which means that he—"

Rinehart was interrupted by the arrival of the guards. "Now *I* will give the orders, Colonel," said the captain. "You and the professor are to leave immediately! Dr. Oppenheimer, prepare yourself. It's time."

Epilogue

The war with the Soviets dragged on at a terrible cost to both sides. The Soviet army continued to decline, but kept fighting, determined to give up their land only grudgingly to the Germans. But by early 1948, the technological superiority of German arms had pushed the Soviets into the northeastern part of their country. The Germans gave them an ultimatum: stop fighting and live here in peace, or continue to fight and die. The offer was met with a thunderous artillery barrage that lasted eight hours.

The German strategy that evolved was to outflank the Soviets on the north, push them to the south, surround them, and finally annihilate them somewhere north of the Kamchatka Peninsula. To accomplish this, they sent in their mountain troops, who had gained fame for clearing the Soviets out of their not-so-impregnable fortresses in the Ural Mountains. After weeks of sustained fighting in bitterly cold conditions, they succeeded in pushing the Soviets out of the northern reaches of their country southward toward the Kamchatka Peninsula.

At the same time, the bulk of the German army moved up from the south to close the trap. A few Soviet units managed to escape down the narrow strip of land connecting the Kamchatka Peninsula to the Russian landmass, but most of their forces were encircled at the village of Chuvanskoye.

Two months of furious fighting, much of it at close quarters, resulted in the complete annihilation of the remnants of the Soviet forces. When the battle was in its last stages, the Soviets were reduced to a single, strong fortress, defended by a lone artillery battery, firing at point-blank range at the overwhelming numbers of German tanks advancing on them. When it was finally silenced, the Germans who stormed the position found that one of the pieces had been manned by General Zhukov, killed while carrying an artillery shell, and General Konev, killed while opening the breech to receive the shell. Both men had fought to the last with the troops they had commanded for so many years.

Inside the final redoubt, it was brutal hand-to-hand fighting, but the Soviets were finally overpowered. When the Germans entered the command center, they were met by a barrage of withering fire from a single brave soldier, who refused all offers of surrender. After he was silenced with grenades, the victorious Germans discovered that this lone defender was Georgy Malenkov, premier of the Soviet Union. He was indeed the last Russian firing the last bullet from the last rifle, just as Levrentiy Beria had predicted. When Chancellor Stauffenberg heard the details of the last battle, he ordered that Zhukov, Konev, and Malenkov be given funerals with full military honors, and that bronze monuments be erected at the places where they had died. The war ended on November 3, 1948.

The cost of the war to the German people was high. During the nine years, two months, and two days of the war, seven million of her sons, brothers, and husbands paid the ultimate price for victory, and another eighteen million were wounded. Almost every family in Germany was touched, many more than once.

A national day of celebration was proclaimed, highlighted by a parade of victorious army units down Kurfürstendamm. Chancellor Stauffenberg and the general staff were there to receive the salutes of the veterans. Similar celebrations were held in other cities and towns, but for the most part, the people remained quiet. They were too tired, the war had gone on too long, and the cost had been too high. The celebrations that mattered most occurred when the veterans came home to their families.

Soviet records, unreliable at best, became worthless in the wake of the atomic attacks of July 1945. It is estimated that more than one hundred and twenty million Soviets perished during the war, including both military personnel and civilians.

The Soviet units that escaped to the Kamchatka Peninsula numbered approximately twenty-five thousand, and it was decided by the German high command not to pursue them. The narrow entrance to the peninsula was blocked with land mines, barbed wire, and guard towers. German destroyers patrolled the waters around the peninsula, but all they ever encountered were fishing boats. It soon became apparent to the German high command that the Soviets who had fled to Kamchatka wanted nothing more to do with the war, and so they were left alone.

Following in the wake of regular German army units were three large groups of government-sanctioned, privately organized groups, each with a different function. Since no regular army units could be spared from combat, these groups drew their numbers largely from German civilians, and they attracted those who, for obvious reasons, had not been accepted by the military. These people found ready employment in units where the strict standards for service in the Wehrmacht did not apply.

The first group was responsible for clearing the battlefield and recycling the machines of war. This was accomplished by loading the destroyed tanks, artillery pieces, and other vehicles onto railroad cars that transported them to strategically located blast furnaces where they were melted down into ingots of high-quality steel. These ingots were then shipped to factories which turned them into everything from nuts and bolts to railroad tracks and tanks. At the end of the war, the Soviets were facing German tanks and artillery made from steel recycled from their own destroyed machines of war.

Casualty rates in this group were high because of the nature of the destroyed equipment they were handling, which, more often than not, contained unexploded ammunition and leaking fuel. Land mines were also a major problem, because no maps had been prepared by either the Germans or the Soviets showing their locations. For this reason, the term of enlistment in this group was limited to three years, which made it very attractive to prisoners, especially those with life sentences. If they died in service, few would care, and if they survived, they would be released and their records wiped clean. There were always many volunteers for service in these groups.

The second group was charged with the task of finishing the destruction wrought by the regular army. Their task was to raze to the ground every structure left standing, dispose of the rubble, and then plant the area with trees and other vegetation. As with the first group, casualty rates were high.

Hard on the heels of the first two groups came a third group, which the Wehrmacht called the "hyena battalions." They took part in the saddest chapter of the war. These irregulars were given the responsibility of relocating the hordes of Soviet refugees to Kazakhstan, so that Germany would not be charged with genocide in the court of world opinion.

The officers and men in this group, more often than not, were drawn from the ranks of the Waffen-SS and the Gestapo. They took out their resentment over their fall from grace under the Stauffenberg government on the Soviet refugees, and nothing of value escaped these predators. Anyone who resisted was shot immediately, just like in the old days when they were the masters of all they surveyed; hardly anyone escaped the sadism of these animals in human form.

When word of these atrocities reached the German high command in Berlin, retribution was swift and terrible. The 502nd

Heavy Tank Battalion, under the personal command of Field Marshal Erwin Rommel, was ordered to hunt down and exterminate these marauders. Having nothing to lose, the Waffen-SS and Gestapo units fought ferociously, and before being slaughtered to the last man, they took down fully one-quarter of the forces sent against them.

But the seeds of resentment and discontent had been sown. With the ill treatment of the refugees who survived their harrowing journey to Kazakhstan, this bitter harvest would last for generations. The population of this country was increased dramatically by the refugees relocated there by the Germans, and soon the predominantly Kazak majority was outnumbered by the Russians.

The law of unintended consequences then took effect, and Germany soon found itself with an openly hostile neighbor on its southern border.

After a series of bloody clashes, the Russians, led by Leonid Brezhnev, a ruthless and dangerous man who understood only the use of force, overthrew the Kazak government. His constant threats to "retake every meter of sacred Russian soil" brought counter threats of swift and massive nuclear retaliation. Large numbers of German troops had to be stationed on this border, and this remains a major challenge for Berlin to this day.

At the end of the war, Germany found itself with a vast number of territories it had inherited from the colonial powers it had conquered. A quick evaluation was made as to which would be kept for raw materials or geographic purposes, and which would be granted independence.

India was granted independence, but not without problems caused by religion. The result was a partition into a predominantly Hindu nation, India, and a predominantly Muslim nation, Pakistan. Pakistan itself was divided into two disconnected parts: West Pakistan, where Islamabad, the nation's capital, is located, and East Pakistan, a heavily populated and desperately poor region. This is an unwieldy arrangement, that will probably result in more problems at a later date.

The Germans retained the British colony of Hong Kong at least until 1997, when the lease with the Chinese for this island expires. Negotiations are underway with the government of Chang Kai-shek for a more satisfactory arrangement. These negotiations are rumored to include the possibility of a trade that would involve German military assistance to the Chinese in their war with the growing communist insurgency led by Mao Tse-tung in exchange for their permanent ownership of Hong Kong.

Germany was now geographically the largest country in the world. The smaller countries of Belarus, Georgia, the Baltic states, and Hungary, Czechoslovakia, and Poland were allowed their independence because of their assistance to Germany during the war. Although the northern part of Poland was incorporated into Germany to provide it with a corridor to its new holdings in the east, that nation retained its ancient capital of Warsaw.

The war between the Americans and the Japanese ground on in the Pacific, and neither side showed any willingness to negotiate. The animosity generated in the Americans by their defeat at the hands of the Germans was transferred to the Japanese. In November 1945, Operation Olympic was launched with the American invasion of Kyushu, the southernmost main Japanese island. Fierce resistance was encountered during all phases of this attack, including waves of kamikazes that sank many troop transports and war ships. The invading troops were met with suicidal resistance all over the island, even from grandmothers carrying sharpened bamboo spears and children throwing hand grenades. The island took six months to secure and cost the Americans 350,000 killed or wounded. The major test, Operation Coronet, the invasion of the main island of Honshu, would be launched from Kyushu.

Following four months of around-the-clock bombing from its bases in Kyushu, the Americans invaded Japan on Monday, May 13, 1946, taking dead aim at Tokyo. They expected a long and bloody fight with more than half a million casualties. However, when it became obvious to Emperor Hirohito that the Americans meant to press on regardless of cost, he committed suicide. When this news reached the remaining armed forces of the empire, the shock was so overwhelming that most of its commanders followed his example, leaving the ordinary Japanese soldier leaderless. Most civilian leaders also took their own lives rather than suffer the humiliation of occupation by a foreign, and racially inferior, country. Resistance soon crumbled, and the war was over within two months, leaving both sides battered, and Japan a smoldering ruin.

It was Toshikazu Kase, from the Foreign Ministry, who led the small delegation of Japanese civilian and military officials that signed the document of surrender. This was presented to them by General Douglas MacArthur on July 29, 1946, on the deck of the battleship USS *Missouri*, which was anchored in Tokyo Bay.

Kase was the highest-ranking civilian official left in Japan. The fact that he had not committed suicide like so many other Japanese leaders was attributed to the American values he had been exposed to when he attended Amherst College, and later, Harvard University, where he graduated as a Research Fellow in 1927. He said the reason he did not take his life was that he felt it was his sacred duty to help guide Japan through its post-war years.

This was a pledge he kept, and over the next forty years Toshikazu Kase held many high governmental positions, including the office of prime minister, to which he was elected four times. By the time he retired from public life in 1986 at the age of eighty-three, Japan had become an economic powerhouse renowned for its high standard of living and the quality of its industrial products. Its gross domestic product, as measured by the worth of all of its manufactured goods and services, placed it third among the nations of the world, surpassed only by Germany and the United States.

Pursuant to the terms of the agreement with the Germans, the Americans abandoned their bases in the Pacific, and by May 31, 1947, they had left forever places with names such as Pearl Harbor, Wake Island, and the Philippines. All the fighters and bombers that had been used in the campaign against the Japanese were destroyed, except for the B-29s, which were turned over to the Luftwaffe. All ships of the United States Navy were towed out into the middle of the Pacific Ocean and scuttled, with the exception of the South Dakota, North Carolina and Iowa-class battleships and Essex-class aircraft carriers, which were turned over to the Kriegsmarine. Resentment in the United States over these actions was high, particularly among veterans who had shed their blood in the defense of these places, flown these planes, and served on these ships. In some cities, the National Guard had to be put on alert as a deterrent to the possibility of civil unrest.

Shortly after the end of hostilities in the Pacific, the Germans took possession of the Panama Canal and began construction of new locks of an advanced design capable of accommodating ships with a beam of two hundred and fifty feet, one hundred and forty feet wider than the locks available to shipping before and during the war. The major reason for the construction of these new locks was to give the German navy the flexibility it needed to move its new aircraft carriers, which had a beam of over two hundred feet, between the Atlantic Ocean and the Pacific Ocean as strategic considerations dictated. This expansion also permitted the next generation of supertankers and large cargo ships to make the transit between the oceans more quickly and efficiently than by going around Cape Horn at the southern tip of South America.

Germany now had the United States flanked on both its western and eastern borders, having taken control of the Bahamas from the British at the time of its capitulation. Several Luftwaffe and Kriegsmarine bases were established in the Bahamas and the Hawaiian islands, providing facilities for Germany's new fleets of ballistic missile-firing submarines and long-range bombers, which ensured that the United States would continue to live up to the terms of the agreement it had signed on July 3, 1945, with the Stauffenberg government.

The Germans retained the island of Bermuda as a playground for its officers, who soon fell under the spell of the local population and the pink and blue atmosphere that pervaded everything. No military bases would be established there, and the more casual and leisurely way of life on the island soon softened even the most severely disciplined Prussian armor. Many of Germany's top-ranking officers soon purchased property on the island, and several spent their remaining time in a pleasant alcoholic daze, doing nothing more strenuous than ordering up "one rum punch, maybe two rum punch …"

Even before the last shot had been fired at Chuvanskoye, the Germans began to move aggressively into their newly conquered territory. One of their main objectives was the large Soviet port of Vladivostok on the Pacific Ocean. The facility had been severely damaged by both aerial and artillery bombardment, as the Soviets had fought to the last man and sabotaged the port. Once under German control, they began to clear away the wreckage so that the port's antiquated facilities could be updated. This was to become the major shipyard for the Kriegsmarine's Pacific Fleet, which would include submarines, some of which had ballistic missile launching capabilities, aircraft carriers, and other surface ships ranging from fast destroyers to heavy battleships. A new generation of ships, many powered by nuclear power plants designed by Professor Heisenberg's group, was being planned, and with the abundant supplies of coal and iron ore in the area, they would soon be realized.

And they would be needed more quickly than anyone expected, for with the defeat of the major colonial powers, the lid was off, and civil wars erupted all across the Southeast Asia area. While most were not serious, the German government took immediate notice of the one in the former Dutch colony of Indonesia because of its proximity to the Strait of Malacca, one of the most important navigation "choke points" in the world.

This turned out to be Germany's first foreign adventure, and many of its retired soldiers who thought that they had finished fighting for their country were dismayed when they found themselves recalled to duty. But this time it was a markedly different kind of warfare involving twentieth-century pirates living in jungles and making war with not only machine guns, but with blow guns as well. Many hard lessons in this kind of warfare were to be learned quickly, and the cost was high.

The Adenauer government was hard pressed to justify the presence of German troops in a place so far from home. The cost of the last war had been so great that the thought of more sacrifices in distant lands was more than most Germans could bear. As a consequence, the Grand Old Man of post-war German politics was forced to resign in 1963 in favor of his vice chancellor, Ludwig Earhard.

The new chancellor, responding to the mood of the public, began a reassessment of Germany's role in Indonesian affairs. This led to a gradual withdrawal of German combat forces from the area. However, a sufficient force remained in place as trainers to ensure that when Indonesia attained independence, it would have the forces necessary to protect not only itself but its vital waterways as well.

Wehrner von Braun finally built his rockets, but not for military purposes. He had always dreamed of space travel, and with the blessing of the Adenauer government, he initiated a program that resulted in a Moon landing on November 18, 1968, the twenty-fifth anniversary of the assassination of Adolf Hitler. The captain of the two-man ship that made the landing was Karl von Richthofen, grandson of Lothan von Richthofen, who with his brother, Manfred, the famous Red Baron, had accounted for 120 victories in the First World War.

The dream of Chancellor Stauffenberg for a healing of the rift between the German nation and the Jews was never completely realized. The reconciliation and forgiveness that he sought with this persecuted race did not suit the German post-war mood, and the nation that had turned its back on the Children of Abraham during the war continued to do so afterward. Indeed, Germany seemed more interested in forgetting everything in their history of the last forty years than in learning any lessons from it.

Many steps were taken in an attempt to integrate the Jews back into German society, including the formation of Jewish regiments for the army, Kriegsmarine, and Luftwaffe, and all fought bravely and with great distinction. But even the shedding of their blood in common cause with the rest of the youth of the Reich was not sufficient to ensure the integration of the Jews into a post-war Germany. While both the Stauffenberg and Adenauer governments passed strict laws that forbade all forms of discrimination, serious problems remained that defied all attempts at resolution. Many Jews sought refuge in other countries, such as Poland and the United States. Several groups tried to immigrate to Palestine, but they were all turned away, sometimes at gunpoint.

For many years, no Muslim government would admit Jews to any part of the Holy Land. Finally, after lengthy negotiations, they agreed that a small permanent Jewish presence, not to exceed five hundred carefully screened people, would be allowed in Palestine to ensure the safety of the holy sites sacred to the Jewish people. Scholarly research was permitted, but only as long as it didn't interfere with Muslim traditions. Small groups of Jewish visitors, no more than fifty at a time, were also allowed into Palestine. Equally restrictive arrangements were made for Christians through negotiations with the Vatican, the Greek Orthodox Church, the Church of England, and other Protestant denominations.

Public sentiment in Germany against the Nazis was too strong for anything but the most severe punishment, as though by pursuing this course some sort of atonement could be achieved in the eyes of the world. Several spectacular trials were held, the most notable being that of Lieutenant Colonel Adolf Eichmann, who had been in charge of transporting the Jews to the death camps. He was tried and found guilty, but escaped the hangman's noose by committing suicide with the cyanide capsule he always kept hidden in his clothes for use in such an eventuality.

With the end of the fighting in the Soviet Union, Colonel Johann Rinehart resigned his commission in the army and took the civilian post of Minister of Strategic Assessment in the Adenauer government. This ministry was charged with making an evaluation of the strengths and weaknesses of every nation in the world and their potential impact on Germany. From the reports prepared by Rinehart's ministry, the size and strength of Germany's strategic forces was determined and foreign bases were established, modified, or abandoned according to need.

Rinehart remained politically neutral, even when asked by Adenauer himself to take a more active role in Christian Democratic Party affairs. Johann and Connie finally started a family, and she gave birth to twins in late 1950. She gave up her position as assistant director of the nursing school at Charité Hospital to devote herself totally to her family.

Professor Werner Heisenberg continued his research on nuclear weapons. His efforts resulted in the development of a lightweight plutonium warhead for ballistic missiles capable of being launched from depths exceeding thirty meters by Germany's new fleet of atomic-powered submarines. These missiles could reach any part of the United States with untold destructive power, and they were instrumental in keeping the uneasy peace between these two nations.

In 1952, when Professor Heisenberg went to Chancellor Adenauer with a proposal for the development of thermonuclear weapons, Edward Teller's H-bomb, he was turned down flat by the chancellor. "Don't we already have enough weapons to destroy everything a hundred times over, Heisenberg? No! No more! We've terrorized the world enough already." When Ludwig Earhart came to power, however, he quietly told the professor to "have a design ready to go into production in a few months, just in case we need it for persuasive purposes."

Johann Rinehart served Germany as a civilian for twenty years after the end of the war. His first position was that of Minister of Strategic Assessment. However, when a wave of anti-militarism swept the country in 1957, he was removed from this position and the ministry itself was reduced to a line department within the government bureaucracy. Rinehart soon found work as the director of the Museum of Military History in Dresden, and under his leadership it became the foremost repository of German and Allied military equipment from World War II. He remained in this position until his retirement in 1968.

Connie Rinehart devoted herself to her family, and only after her children were safely launched in their respective careers did she return to nursing. She secured a position at Charité in the School of Nursing, where she easily absorbed all the technological advances that had been made during the previous twenty-plus years. She was a gifted teacher, and quickly made the transition from nurturer of her own children to nurturer of future nurses.

Johann Rinehart celebrated his seventy-seventh birthday on February 11, 1987, with a trip to the Matterhorn. This was something he and Connie had always planned to do, and with the opening of the cable car lift almost all the way to the summit in late 1979, they felt that now was the time. So, in spite of warnings from some of their friends about making this trip in winter, they set off in high spirits for Zermatt, Switzerland, on February 8.

The trip to the summit was breathtaking. The view from all sides was so magnificent that Connie almost forgot to take the pictures that she had promised their friends. They had just reached the end of the cable car lift and made their way to the summit when they were ordered to return to the cable car because of the approach of an unexpected—and very powerful—storm. About halfway down, the cable car came to an abrupt halt, slightly injuring three of the passengers. Connie provided first aid as best she could, and was able to make them somewhat comfortable. They assumed that whatever the problem was, it would soon be fixed.

But this was not to happen. All attempts to repair the broken machinery failed, and it was finally determined that the only way to rescue the marooned passengers was by helicopter. By now, news of the impending tragedy had reached the newspapers, and dozens of reporters descended on the scene, further complicating the rescue effort.

The storm was one of the worst the area had experienced in years, and all rescue attempts had to be postponed. The storm lasted for three days with wind speeds approaching one hundred kilometers per hour and temperatures that dropped to -40°C. Halfway through the storm, the cable car's on-board heating system failed, leaving the passengers at the mercy of the elements.

When the rescue party finally reached the cable car, the found the eight lifeless bodies of the passengers, many of them almost naked, huddled together in what appeared to be a last attempt to keep warm. The tabloids made much of this, implying that in their last moments of life, the passengers had degenerated into a sex orgy.

The local medical examiner said that the cause of the death for all the passengers was extreme hypothermia brought on by prolonged exposure to sub-zero temperatures. He said that what appeared to be huddling together by the passengers for warmth was more properly described as burrowing, which is a characteristic behavior of people in the last stages of extreme hypothermia, He added that it is not uncommon for people suffering from hypothermia to become confused and start shedding their clothes, a phenomenon known as paradoxical undressing.

A team of engineers took apart the cable car machinery and soon determined that the cause of its breakdown was the use of a "light-duty" greasing compound in an area where a "heavy-duty" product was specified. This occurred when a new employee picked up the wrong grease gun before making his rounds. This employee was red-green color blind—something he had not disclosed when he interviewed for the job— so he could not tell the difference between a green heavy-duty grease gun and a red light-duty grease gun. He chose the red grease gun, to fatal effect for the eight passengers on the aerial cable car.

In its final report, the panel of engineers recommended that additional fail-safe and back-up systems be made a part of all future aerial cable car installations, and that all existing systems be retrofitted with these improvements. With regard to the problems pertaining to the grease guns, the major recommendation of the panel was that all greasing operations be carried out by teams of two or more technicians to minimize the chance of human error.

All these recommendations were enthusiastically embraced by the aerial cable car industry, and within a few years, these new safety standards were in worldwide use. After 1987, the number of deaths attributed to aerial cable car systems dropped dramatically.

Following a private service at St. Nicholas Lutheran Church in Berlin, Johann and Connie Rinehart were interred in the Hall of Heroes. This is a marble mausoleum in the National Cemetery in Berlin reserved as a final resting place for those men and women, and their spouses, who participated in the November 18, 1943, assassination of Adolf Hitler. It is often referred to derisively by the tabloids as "Germany's Valhalla."

Johann and Connie Rinehart left behind two children, born

as twins, in 1950. Wilhelm Rinehart was named after General Wilhelm Keitel, the man who saved Johann Rinehart's life after he was seriously wounded while on a secret mission during World War II. Keitel also became Wilhelm's godfather, an honor the old soldier greatly treasured.

Wilhelm Rinehart repudiated his father's military career early in life, and as an adult, he became a radicalized politician. He cast his lot with the newly-ascendant anti-war, pro-environment Green Party, and was elected to the Bundestag in 1998, the same year the Greens formed a coalition with the Social Democrats. He became an outspoken advocate for reducing both the size of the military and Germany's role in world affairs; making free housing available to poor people; closing all nuclear power plants, and providing free higher education for all. He took part in many demonstrations organized by those who championed these causes and was arrested several times, only to be released after identifying himself as a member of the Bundestag. Throughout his turbulent public career, he never lost touch with his parents, who, although sometimes amazed at his behavior, never withdrew either their love or support from him.

Anna Rinehart chose a more conventional lifestyle, graduating in 1974 with a Master's Degree, *magna cum laude*, from the Dessau Institute of Architecture. She secured a position with the prestigious firm of Gerkan, Marg and Partners, and by 1985, she had been promoted to the position of senior project architect. She and her brother rarely spoke, and they acknowledged each other only briefly at the 1987 funeral and internment of their parents.

This estrangement ended in 2002 shortly after the death of Claus von Stauffenberg. The government announced that there would be a national design competition for the monument to be erected in his honor. This attracted all the leading architects in Germany, including Anna Rinehart, who was surprised and delighted when Wilhelm offered to collaborate with her. They and their parents had spent many pleasant weekends at Claus and Nina Stauffenberg's Bavarian estate, and in spite of their political differences, the twins were united in their genuine affection for this man.

Anna designed a structure that drew heavily on the monuments of other famous leaders, particularly those honoring the American presidents Thomas Jefferson and Abraham Lincoln. Her final design, although strongly influenced by these American monuments, also incorporated the simpler and cleaner lines associated with more contemporary buildings.

But how was Stauffenberg himself to be depicted? The newspapers and pictorial magazines were filled with drawings of the sculptures proposed by the great artists of Germany. But while they all emphasized his heroic side, very few of them showed the human qualities that Anna and Wilhelm remembered so well.

It was Wilhelm who recalled the story that Stauffenberg told about the trip he and the general staff made to Auschwitz the day after he became chancellor. He particularly remembered the part about the old Jewish woman who had hugged Stauffenberg and thanked him for liberating her, even though she knew she was very ill and would never leave Auschwitz alive.

With this in mind, the submission from Anna and Wilhelm Rinehart featured a bronze statue of Stauffenberg, one and one-half times life size, hugging an anonymous, old Jewish woman dressed in rags. This was to be placed in the open center of the monument. Surrounding the statue and chiseled deep into the marble floor of the monument were the words Stauffenberg spoke during his first address to the German people as chancellor: "we have a lot to be accountable for."

The Rinehart's design was presented to a committee that included two of the Stauffenberg children, Heimeran and Konstanze. The committee immediately perceived that their submission showed not only Stauffenberg's heroism, but his humanity and humility as well.

The decision of the committee was swift and unanimous, and the brother and sister team of Wilhelm and Anna Rinehart won the competition.

Claus Schenk Graf von Stauffenberg, once the most powerful man in the world, retired from public life after the installation of the government of Chancellor Konrad Adenauer in April 1949, five months following the end of the war. Stauffenberg returned to his estate in Bavaria and devoted himself to raising his family and writing his memoirs. He was often approached by those seeking his endorsement for political office, and all were politely, but firmly, refused. He enjoyed the company of companions from the old days, particularly Johann and Connie Rinehart and their children, whom he doted on almost as much as he had his own children when they were toddlers.

Stauffenberg died peacefully a few days after Christmas in the year 2000, having lived long enough to see Germany enter the twenty-first century as a world power far beyond anything his predecessor had ever dreamed of. He was troubled in his last years by the resurgence of the authoritarian side of the German character, particularly its manifestation in the disaffected youth who would wear swastika armbands and defiantly shout "Heil Hitler" at the world. He often said they didn't have any idea what real Nazis stood for, and therefore they were to be pitied even more for their ignorance.

He was given the largest state funeral Germany had ever seen, and it was televised around the world. Few people remembered the name Stauffenberg; most connected Germany with Adolf Hitler. Nevertheless, it was Stauffenberg who had the gleaming white marble monument dedicated to his honor in the mall in front of the Reichstag, and not Adolf Hitler, whose ashes remain forever silent in the still, clear waters of a lake on the outskirts of Berlin.

Author's Notes

Both real and fictional characters populate this book. On the German side, the only fictional character with a major role is the German officer Johann Rinehart, the thread of whose life from 1934 to the end of book holds the story together. The remaining major German characters are real, and many of them perished in the aftermath of the failed attempt on Adolf Hitler's life on July 20, 1944.

Although there were fewer than two hundred people involved in the plot, Hitler cast his net wide, and many times that number were rounded up, then either summarily executed or brought to trial, humiliated, and *then* executed. Of the 184 persons identified in the plot, all but three were executed, some in remarkably brutal fashion. One exception to this was General Ludwig Beck who, because of his high standing within the German military, was given the opportunity to commit suicide rather than face trial and certain execution. He made two attempts at suicide but only succeeded in wounding himself. He was then executed in the office of General Friedrich Fromm by a sergeant who was brought in to administer the coup de grâce. General Beck was to have been Germany's new führer had the plot to kill Hitler been successful.

Field Marshal Erwin Rommel was also a member of the July 20 plot to kill Hitler. Because of his great prestige, however, Hitler allowed him to commit suicide rather than bringing him to trial, where he almost certainly would have been found guilty and then executed.

All of the Soviets are real with the exception of Major Dimitri Stepanovich. Lavrentiy Beria was head of the NKVD, the Soviet security apparatus. Beria never became premier, and he was executed in December 1953 shortly after Joseph Stalin's death. Georgy Malenkov succeeded Stalin and held power from March 1953 to February 1955. He was forced to resign because of his close ties to Beria. Both General Ivan Konev and General Georgiy Zhukov served the Soviet Union with distinction in World War II and both were there at the end in Berlin when the Germans surrendered.

The following is a list of the major characters in the book, in order of appearance, that indicates whether they are real or fictional, and if real, who they were.

Name of Character	Real or Fictional	Who They Were
Prof. Werner Heisenberg	Real	Head of German nuclear weapons program
Johann Rinehart	Fictional	
Dr. J. Robert Oppenheimer	Real	Head physicist of American nuclear weapons program
Adolf Hitler	Real	Führer of Germany, 1933 to 1945
Colonel Claus Schenk Graf von Stauffenberg	Real	Led failed plot to assassinate Hitler
Lieutenant Georg Müeller	Fictional	
Hans Dieter Müeller	Fictional	
Field Marshal Wilhelm Keitel	Real	Supreme Commander of the German armed forces in World War II

Name of Character	Real or Fictional	Who They Were
Chief of Operations Staff Alfred Jodl	Real	Deputy to Wilhelm Keitel
Grand Admiral Erich Raeder	Real	Commanded German Navy in World War II
Grand Admiral Karl Dönitz	Real	Commanded German submarines in World War II
General Adolf Galland	Real	Luftwaffe general in World War II
Albert Speer	Real	Reich Minister of Armaments and Munitions, 1941 to 1943, then Reich Minister of Armaments and War Production, 1943 to 1945
Harry Truman	Real	American President, 1945 to 1953
Vannevar Bush	Real	Science advisor to American presidents from 1939 to 1953
Richard Tolman	Real	Science advisor to General Leslie Groves
Korvettenkapitän Carl Emmerman	Real	Commanded German submarine U-172 during World War II
Captain Jim Monroe	Fictional	
Linda Monroe	Fictional	
General George Marshall	Real	U.S. Army Chief of Staff during World War II
Winston Churchill	Real	British Prime Minister, 1940 to 1945
Joseph Stalin	Real	Soviet leader during World War II
Lieutenant Heinrich Gilkrest	Fictional	
Ambassador Hans Bernd von Haeften	Real	Member of plot to assassinate Hitler

Name of Character	Real or Fictional	Who They Were
Edward Stettinius	Real	American Secretary of State, 1944 to 1945
Henry L. Stimpson	Real	American Secretary of War during World War II
Fyodor Alexandrov	Fictional	
Levrentiy Beria	Real	Head of Soviet NKVD (secret police) during World War II
Nikita Khrushchev	Real	Soviet leader, 1955 to 1964
Major Dimitri Stepanovich	Fictional	
Georgy Malenkov	Real	Soviet leader, 1953 to 1955
Georgy Zhukov	Real	Marshal of the Soviet Union during World War II
Ivan Kovev	Real	Marshal of the Soviet Union during World War II
Connie Erickson	Fictional	
Konrad Adenauer	Real	German Chancellor, 1949 to 1963
Leonid Brezhnev	Real	Soviet leader, 1964 to 1982
Toshikazu Kase	Real	Member of Japanese Foreign Ministry during World War II

The advanced German airplanes—the Messerschmitt 262 and the Arado 234—were real, and had they been produced in sufficient numbers and introduced at an earlier date, they might have delayed, but not changed, the final outcome of the war. The Messerschmitt 262, the world's first operational jet fighter, was deployed as an interceptor too late in the war to make a difference. At Hitler's insistence, this remarkable plane was operated as a bomber, not a fighter, until almost the end of the war.

One of the main problems with the 262, and every other German jet aircraft, was the lack of suitable engines. The Jumo 004, the world's first operational turbojet engine, powered the 262. It produced a thrust of 1,980 pounds, was sluggish in acceleration, and had a life of between ten and twenty-five hours, depending largely on the skill of the pilot. This was due to the shortage of critical materials such as nickel, cobalt, and molybdenum, resulting in the use of aluminum-coated steel for temperature-critical parts of the engine. Even with all these shortcomings, the 262, and the other jet planes developed by the Germans, maintained a substantial speed advantage over their Allied counterparts.

The Arado 234C-2, a four-engine derivative of the original two-engine plane, which had the distinction of being the world's first jet-powered bomber, was just in the planning stages when the war ended. By the end of the war, however, only about two hundred 234s of all models had been built.

The Lotfernrohr 7 bombsight was the primary bombsight used in most Luftwaffe level bombers. It was derived from the American Norden bombsight, which was stolen from the Americans by the Germans in 1938.

The Type 21 submarine was by far the most advanced submarine of World War II. Although 120 were built, only two entered operational status. The submarine could dive to more than 900 feet and had a hull made of inch-thick aluminum coated with synthetic rubber to reduce its acoustic signature. It had a submerged speed in excess of 17 knots and could remain under water for up to eleven days before having to resurface. Constant Allied bombing of submarine construction yards, logistical problems, and shortages of materials and labor caused this deadly submarine to have little influence on the war.

The Type 14 "milk cow" submarine was a resupply boat for other German submarines. It had no offensive weapons and was very slow when surfaced, having a top speed of less than fifteen knots, and an even slower submerged speed of slightly over six knots. Only ten of these boats were built and they were never mated with the V-1 cruise missile.

The Ship's Inertial Navigation System (SINS) used on the fictional German missile-launching submarines evolved from the work done by Wehrner von Braun on the V-2 ballistic missile guidance system. This system combined two gyroscopes and a lateral accelerometer with a simple analog computer to adjust the azimuth of the rocket in flight. Refinements of this system are currently in use for space flight and guidance for ballistic missile-launching submarines.

The American airdropped passive sonar homing torpedo, known as FIDO, was quite real, as a number of both German and Japanese submarines discovered. This weapon entered service in March 1943, and by the end of the war, 204 had been fired, resulting in the sinking of 37 submarines with a further 38 sustaining damage.

The fictional atomic bomb produced by the Germans in the book was much simpler to make than the bomb that resulted from the American-led Manhattan Project. The Y-12 electromagnetic separation uranium plant, the K-25 gaseous diffusion enrichment plant, and the S-50 thermal diffusion enrichment plant were just a few of the massive facilities constructed for this project by the Americans. The Germans, on the other hand, fictionally produced their fissionable material using the process of converting U^{238} into uranium hexafluoride, then passing it through a cascade of thousands of high-speed centrifuges, resulting in a gas of highly-enriched U^{235}. This very real process was used successfully in the Soviet nuclear program, and is currently in use by Pakistan to produce its nuclear weapons.

The fictional atomic weapons produced by Germany were based on the Mark 8 and Mark 11 nuclear bombs and the W9 nuclear artillery shell, all developed by the United States and deployed in the 1950s. The W9 nuclear weapon was a 280-millimeter artillery shell that weighed 550 pounds. It produced an explosion equivalent to fifteen thousand tons of high explosive, the same as the "Little Boy" nuclear bomb dropped on Hiroshima on August 6, 1945, which weighed 9,700 pounds.

Acknowledgements

This book would not have been possible without help from many people. I am particularly indebted to my brother, David, a professor of mathematics at Amherst College, for the story about David Hilbert and the Nazi minister of education. He credits this story to a quote from the book *Courant in Göttingen and New York* by Constance Reid. This quote omitted the name of the Nazi minister of education with whom David Hilbert had the conversation, but further research revealed that the German minister of education at that time was Bernhard Rust, who was appointed to this post in 1933. If this is an error, then it is entirely mine, as are any other errors in this book.

Most of the material for this book was researched online, and the list of the sites visited during its preparation is too long to be included here. Other sources of material for the book include the following:

Cross, Robin. *Hitler: An Illustrated Life.* London: Quercus Publishing, 2009.

Donald, David, ed. *Warplanes of the Luftwaffe.* New York: Barnes and Noble, Inc., 1994.

Eberle, Henrick and Uhl, Matthias, eds. *The Hitler Book: The Secret Dossier Prepared for Stalin from the Interrogations of Hitler's Personal Aides.* Cambridge, MA: Persius Books, 2005.

Hitler, Adolf: *Mein Kampf,* Manheim, Ralph, trans. New York: Houghton Mifflin Company, 1943.

Muir, Malcolm: *The Iowa Class Battleships: Iowa, New Jersey, Missouri and Wisconsin.* New York, Sterling Publishing Company, Inc., 1987.

Neufeld, Michael J. *Von Braun: Dreamer of Space, Engineer of War.* Toronto: Vintage Books, 2007.

Powers, Thomas. *Heisenberg's War.* Cambridge, MA: Da Capo Press, 1993.

Speer, Albert. *Inside the Third Reich.* New York: The McMillan Company, 1970.

Waite, Robert G. L. *The Psychotic God: Adolph Hitler.* Cambridge, MA: Da Capo Press, 1993.

Watson, Peter. *The German Genius.* New York: HarperCollins Publishers, 2010.

Zeigler, Mano. *Hitler's Jet Plane: The Me 262 Story.* London: Greenhill Books, 1994.

My wife Mary, my daughter Gillian, and I visited Berlin in November 2009 to participate in the twentieth anniversary celebration of the fall of the Berlin Wall. Gillian was there in 1989 when the wall came down, and for all of us, but particularly for her, it was a life-changing event. Her enthusiasm for this book, and her help in plotting the route taken by Lieutenant Johann Rinehart from the Old Reich Chancellery to the fictional Müeller's Funeral Home and Crematorium, and for determining its location at Unter den Linden and Friedrichstrasse, is gratefully acknowledged and appreciated.

Finally, my wife also contributed to this book, even though, as she has told me several times, "this is not the kind of book I read." She has patiently listened to me as I explained the plot of the book, and more than once, she pointed me in the right direction. Her patience was that of a saint, particularly when it came to the sharing of our one and only computer, which, as a newspaper editor, she relies on heavily for her living. Many thanks, my love.

John T. Cox
North Miami, Florida
Summer/Fall 2010